PARADOX

PARADOX

Nivar Woods

authorHOUSE®

AuthorHouse™
1663 Liberty Drive
Bloomington, IN 47403
www.authorhouse.com
Phone: 1-800-839-8640

First published by AuthorHouse   01/24/2012

ISBN: 978-1-4634-2264-6 (sc)
ISBN: 978-1-4634-2265-3 (hc)
ISBN: 978-1-4634-2266-0 (ebk)

Library of Congress Control Number: 2011962141

Printed in the United States of America

CONTENTS

A Shadow in the Midst

Walking on the sidewalk, the cool night air was carried by a slight breeze creating a very crisp and rejuvenating feel. Glancing up at the stars that shone ever so brightly, it became apparent that no clouds were in the sky while I turned around the corner of an old apartment building on the street. This led into an alley between two of the buildings.

My name is Aaron. Standing six feet, three inches tall I could look a little imposing. Physically in shape, my t-shirt showed off lean, but strong muscle. My family was off on vacation, and I took the opportunity to go out each night and look at the stars.

Home was around the old part of my town. You could easily judge how ancient some of the buildings were with their worn down bricks, and crumbling bits falling off various places. Still, it was home. It was about to get a little strange when compared to my usual nights out. Turning the corner of the apartment building the dark figure of a man loomed before me. He donned black clothing from head to toe, so he was very hard to pick out in the night.

A black hat covered his head. The rim of it turned downward in front, partially covering the black goggles he wore. The goggles were followed by a black scarf wrapped around his face and neck, effectively creating a mask. This item sat on top of a black duster coat, its sleeves ending in black gloves that emerged from the arms, and topped off by a black shirt underneath it which was tucked into black cargo pants. Black heavy boots adorned his feet, his pants falling over them finishing off the presence that he gave off.

In fact, if I hadn't been alert as I usually was, I'd have probably missed him.

I studied him as he lifted one arm to show that he was no threat, or to not be afraid. Still I kept my guard up while trying to discern his features, but his clothing completely hid everything. The darkness of night certainly didn't help. He lowered his arm and waited a moment, perhaps seeing what my reaction was going to be like, before suddenly speaking out. His voice was deep and heavy, with a bit of a rasp.

"You need not know who I am . . . but more so, who you are, what you do, what I do, and what you can be. As one of my fellow compatriots once said, 'Eventually, everyone has the opportunity to awaken and become who they've always wanted to be. Most people just hit the snooze button and go back to sleep.' . . . indeed, how true those words are. So now I'll leave you to ponder this on your own. Once you figure out who you are, I will find you to begin the next step. Until then, don't bother trying to seek me out. I'm found only when I wish to be found."

With those words, the man's figure seemed to move with the darkness. Spinning around and walking away, heavy boots thudding against the pavement he turned a corner and the sound died as the distance grew between us. It was tempting to go after him, but something told me that those words he spoke were true. This man would only be seen when he wished to be. Slowly turning in place to leave, my mind was busy trying to make sense of everything that had just happened. My thoughts jumbled together eventually, and my feet began moving me forward. Treading home under the little light that the stars provided gave the area an almost supernatural look.

Entering my home I sat down at my computer, where I'm typing this now. Placing my thoughts here and what had occurred during the night. This is where you choose to believe what you are about to read and wish to continue on. If you do not believe, I understand, and you may go on your way. Things happen in the world. Things that are unexplainable. Things like a simple shadow in the midst of the night.

Days moved on while studying my past, trying to learn everything about myself that I could. I changed, such as helping others quietly and without question. Giving comfort where it needed to be given, listening to the problems of those who asked me to listen, and even asking some if they would like to talk about their problems. Some things didn't change. I still pulled my own weight, going about the mostly sunny, bright days. For some reason the sun caused problems for me. It would eat into my skin, and damage my eyes. I was very sensitive to its light, always had been.

Then, one night, while sitting down to report that nothing new had happened recently. The very light itself appeared to dim down, being suppressed by another unseen force. Darkness began to pour in from the windows making me look from one window to another nervously. Then whispers started to speak in my head. Each of the whispers seemed to be the same but different.

Backing into a corner while listening, I tried to discern what they were saying. It was like they were speaking some unknown language and trying to give away a secret, never slowing their chant while I tried to make it out. The darkness began to converge near the center of the room, bringing the whispers with it. Then the same man a few nights before stepped out of the thick blackness that was now swirling like a vortex in the middle of the room, his body still dressed in the same clothing.

My mouth hung agape at this display of strange power, strange . . . yet incredible. The man took a step forward, some of the darkness moving with him, shielding him. The lights seemed to suppress it somewhat, but it almost appeared like this person could generate, or form, a sphere of darkness around him. I stood totally still, unsure what to do. Had this man known that I was alone at this time or had this planned? Had he been watching me until he deduced it was the right time to appear?

More than ever now I believed that his words were true, that I wouldn't have been able to find him unless he wanted me too. It was like he could near-perfectly blend in with the darkness that was around him, making him hard to discern, but still knowing he was there. He waited unmoving as the blackness continued swirling around him, pulsing with an almost life-like behavior. Partially stunned, I forced myself to take one step forward. When I did this the man raised his head in confirmation.

"Congratulations. You are willing to face your fears, and most likely any fears in general. You've passed the last test." He said in that same heavy, rasping voice.

After he spoke those words I went rigid, feeling as if the words had pierced me to the very soul. A chilling embrace, but it didn't feel harmful in any way. A soothing feel also accompanied it. I took another step forward, mesmerized by the feeling, almost as if it were pulling me towards the man. Drawing closer the dark blackness of the void reached out to me, beckoning me, trying to draw me closer so it could envelope me.

The man stood there while I moved closer, showing no emotion that was noticeable as I continued inching forward. Within grabbing distance, he reached upward with one arm. However it wasn't to grab me like I thought he was going to do. He just held it there, in a gesture showing that it was my choice to take hold of it. I watched his hand carefully, studying it to make sure there were no weapons. Who was I kidding? This thing or person could control darkness itself. I'm pretty sure that was his weapon.

Feeling compelled that there was no danger I slowly reached forward, taking hold of his hand and feeling that same chilling, but comforting stab when I touched it. The black vortex pulsed ever more violently now. Looking at it I realized there was probably no turning back. I got a distinct feeling that the man, whoever he was, was smiling behind that darkness and black scarf that he wore. Not a bad smile, but one of genuine care and happiness. He slowly reached up and placed his other hand on my shoulder, making one last simple statement, "It's time."

Training

"It's time," the last words that had reached my ears before I was engulfed in blackness. The very void that pulsed, collapsing down on me, pulling me in deeper and farther away from the world that I knew. Filled with that same cold yet warm sensation, and sent spiraling onwards into its thick nothingness. Slowly I began to lose focus. Not just focus on where I was, but also who I was, where I was from, and what had happened.

I grew fainter as time passed. Almost losing myself to the strange comfort that the void provided, and then feeling as if I was ripped from my place in that darkness by falling and hitting a cold concrete floor. Then I was being lifted upward into the cool air of this new place. I opened my eyes weakly, struggling to keep my eyelids up. They felt as if I hadn't used them for many years. Then I saw the man that had said those words which seemed so just as long ago.

He was reaching out towards me, but I wasn't being lifted by him, I realized. He had his arm outstretched before me, while that same black substance poured out from where his hand should have been, and was lifting me off the ground, setting me gently into some sort of bunk. Glancing around slightly I noticed we were in some dimly lit area with hardly any light. The only light emitted was from small candles, and one or two lights which appeared powered down. They hung from multiple sections of a concrete wall, its cold surface extending beyond my view.

Attempting to sit up, the muscles in my body refused to respond. The man spoke with his heavy, rasping voice. "Don't bother. That was your first trip into my realm . . . or power, if you prefer. Many would have died or succumbed to it. Yet, I had you prepared. Rest for now, and regain your strength. Soon we will begin your training." He said, his voice seeming to grow softer near the end.

"T-training?" I somehow managed to utter out. I heard him chuckle softly to himself, as my eyes grew even heavier. Closing them and listening to the slight chuckle, I began to slip away into sleep.

The last thing I heard was his soft chuckle ending, and the words, "I was right to choose you for this."

Once there was a man who pronounced that he had a dream. I also had a dream. I'm fairly certain that my dream was far different from his. My mind swam with images as I slept. I was sleeping, wasn't I? How else could I explain the images flashing before me?

They were marvelous, titanic battles. Thunderous crashes rang all around me. Lightning seemed to pierce the air. Fire flew from another direction, striking someone or something, that let out a roar. The sound of charging muddled with weapons blaring. It sounded like a war was taking place.

The images danced before me, showing the same man that had spoken to me. He winked in and out of the thunderous battle. Defeating one contender then warping on to the next. Wherever he moved the dark followed him, the strange and marvelous power always at his beck and call.

Suddenly I saw lights flash on, extremely large ones, spotlights perhaps? They converged on the dark being, and as they did so the light from the beams diminished while his dark powers also shrunk back from battling it. More lights, far more, turned on him, his mighty power shrinking back farther from it all. He tried to fight the best he could without it, but was soon overpowered by hordes of soldiers. At least that's what they appeared to be with their heavy combat boots thudding on the ground, and strange uniforms along with some kind of gasmasks covering their faces.

With a cry of despair the strange power collapsed in on its master, hiding from the light. The uniformed soldiers grew closer together on him, struggling with the man that they outnumbered greatly. With one last roar of determination the man threw his arms outwards. The dark-like mist exploding outwards from him, as he fought against the beams of light and engulfed the soldiers near him where their screams of terror rang outwards.

Eventually the dark was soon forced back by the bright beams of light, leaving empty uniforms where soldiers had been engulfed by the spheres thick substance. The soldiers that had retreated away from the sphere would only hesitate for a moment while eyeing the uniforms. Then they began surging towards him once more. The soldiers closed on the epicenter of the now rapidly shrinking sphere, treading over the empty uniform husks of their fallen comrades. I could make out the figure of the man that controlled the dark power inside.

He was lying totally still on the cold ground making no movement at all in his death-like posture. The soldiers drew in on him, multiple personnel reaching down and grabbing him, lifting him up. One individual stood out from the soldiers, his uniform slightly different from the others signifying he was an officer. His consisted of more red then gray and black, which were the soldier's main colors.

This officer reached up, removing his own mask to reveal the face of a man. His face quickly changing from a composed looking manner to a sneer, as he opened his mouth and began speaking. I strained to listen, but couldn't hear anything. He reached down and took something off of his uniform, sending a blow across the captured man's face with the item. Afterwards the officer reached up, grasping the black scarf and tugging it lightly as if taunting the captive.

I grew cold, a terrible feeling surrounding me. Making me think that whatever lied behind that scarf should stay there. I began to yell and scream, but nothing came out. No sound at all. I could feel my mouth open and close, my lungs wringing themselves out to produce even a whisper, but still the silence pressed on. Attempting to twist and turn, my body seemed to be frozen in place, with only my mouth able to move.

Then my eyes grew wide, as the officer turned his head, his sneering face turning into one of surprise, if only for a moment. He reached forward and pointed directly at me, as one by one the other heads slowly swiveled around, their strange masks staring straight at me. The officer without the mask began to speak barking orders out, and a small detachment of men started moving towards me.

I screamed and attempted to move once more, but my body held still. As the soldiers rushed towards me I began to submit to defeat, when I noticed the man who controlled darkness slowly raise his head, looking at me. I called out to him for help, struggling once again to free myself from the invisible bindings that held me. The soldiers grew near enough that I could see their eyes looking at me through the goggles of their masks, reaching out for me with their arms, trying to detain me. Using the last of my energy I made one more pathetic jerk to free myself . . . .

When I shot upwards in bed, making it about halfway up before my back muscles refused to go any farther. Letting out a groan of pain as I settled slowly back down, a cold sweat beaded my forehead. Struggling to move one of my arms to wipe the sweat off, all I could manage was a slight twitch. Letting out a sigh of relief I turned my head slowly, realizing I was back in the bunk where the man had placed me.

The cold concrete walls emitted a feeling of solid safety, as if no one could ever harm me here. Moving my eyes around, taking in all the detail I could, there was the faint dripping of . . . water? Suddenly realizing how thirsty I was I struggled to twist my head towards the dripping sound. It appeared to be coming from a dark hallway, the dim light ending at the door of the room I was in. Pitch blackness took over from there.

Shouting out in terror as the sweat was somehow wiped from my forehead I turned my head quickly around and saw the man standing next to my bunk. He held what looked like a piece of cloth, probably what he had used to wipe my forehead. Gazing past him at the concrete wall I shuddered realizing that the pitch black hallway was the only way in or out of the room, and he'd somehow gotten in without my knowing.

I attempted to lean up and speak, but he reached down and made me stay put. I had to tell him about my dream. Opening my mouth, I spoke in a dry whisper. "I . . . I had a dream. At least I think it was a dream. It started out like a battle and then-" He cut me off by raising his left hand, and producing a cup of water with his other. He placed the cup to my lips, motioning for me to drink.

He watched then spoke while I gulped down the liquid. "That was no dream, at least none that your mind would have produced on your own. I know what you saw, and what it all means. In fact, that was part of your training. It will all make sense in time, and only fully through time. There's only so much I can explain."

Sitting there and watching a brief moment, while wrapping my mind around this, I immediately shot into questions as soon as the cup was removed from my lips. "But how could you have seen inside my mind? How are you able to have powers like that? Why am I exactly here?" I demanded answers the best I could, my voice receiving some strength from the liquid.

He stood as still as a statue for a moment or so, before chuckling lightly once again. If he was hoping to make me frustrated and angry, he was succeeding.

"What's so funny about that?" I croaked out, trying to sound fierce but failing miserably.

"Nothing." He answered quietly then somehow made the cup disappear. "I'll answer all the questions you want when you've regained your strength. As for now, continue resting. I will let you know that you have passed a phase of training."

"Oh, that makes me feel so much better." I grumbled, as I watched him turn and walk into the blackness of the hallway.

"Don't worry." I heard his voice echo down the hall. "It's about to get a lot better . . . much, much better."

Attempting to figure out what this meant for me, as the last echoes of his voice reverberated off the cold concrete walls, I slowly closed my eyes.

Waking up from my now dreamless sleep and staring up at the concrete that seemed to float above me, I slowly tested out my limbs. Moving them bit by bit trying to figure out how much strength they had regained. They moved with little effort, and I soon found that all my muscles had fully recovered. How long I had been sleeping I don't know, and whether it was day or night didn't seem to matter, as the dimly lit room stayed at the level of light it was meant to be. Slowly sitting up in my bunk while gazing around, I noticed another glass of water set on top of a table that had not been there before.

Reaching for the glass and quickly downing the entire thing, it temporarily quenched the thirst that had been scorching my mouth. Standing up and stretching, my hands almost reached the roof of cement. I glanced at the dark hallway that led out of the room, and called down it.

"Hello? Are you there?" I called out, listening to my voice reverberating off the walls and coming back to me with silence, "Anyone?" I tried once more, with the same result. Walking forward and placing my hands on the sides of the narrow hallway I slowly moved down it.

The dark seemed to press in on me, attempting to smother me in its inky blackness while I walked through it. Reaching a turn that headed right, I moved to the right with it. Then there was something, a strange sound. Buzzing? Continuing along more dim light appeared from beneath what I discerned to be a door.

I knocked on it a few times, to no answer. Placing both of my hands on the cool metal of the door I pressed against it. The door swung lazily open to reveal another dimly lit room. The buzzing sound emanated from here I realized, turning in place in an attempt to locate the sound. Then the buzzing stopped.

Standing completely still the new silence rushed at me. I slowly turned my head, trying to figure out what was going on, or, what this room was for? A red light sprung to life in the middle of the room pulsing. Wincing at the sudden dose of brightness I studied the room, seeing multiple cages lining the walls. All of the cages were different sizes, from ones only half my size to others easily towering above me. Then I heard the snarls.

Snarls and shrieks from another world that was never meant to be seen by man. They grew louder from the multiple cages. Some of the cages shuddering from blows on the other side. I got the distinct feeling that whatever was on the other side wanted to harm me, or worse. Turning to leave and growing uneasy from the feeling that I had received, the door I'd entered swung shut.

Running to the door and pounding on its thick metal hull with both fists to open it back up didn't move it at all. It was like the cold metallic surface was smirking at me as I futilely tried to pull it open. A voice blared throughout the room, a computerized voice that mechanically announced that 'Training level one' was about to commence.

I spun around eyeing the cages as the shrieks grew to a roar, as if they knew what was going on. Looking frantically around for anything useful to help me get the door open, or another way out, was when my eyes landed on the door across the room. I took a step forward then stopped, stepping back in fear as the cage that was only half my size opened its metallic barrier slowly.

A horror slowly emerged from the cage, as the shrieking and roaring suddenly died down. Squinting with my eyes, I tried to make out what it was. It felt like it was eyeing me in return. Drawing a deep breath, whatever it was stopped for a moment continuing to gaze in my direction as if sizing up a challenge. Slowly it moved forward, cautiously making its way closer to the red light pulsing in the middle of the room.

Then it charged, straight towards me as I caught a glimpse of sharp teeth and scraggly fur. I dived to the side as it lunged right where my head had been seconds before. I winced as I could hear and feel the force of the creatures jaws clamping shut. Rolling away I stood up, not sure what to do as the grotesque thing turned back towards me.

It lumbered around like a gorilla, but was much smaller at only half my size, but eerie none-the-less. It had four inch long needle-like teeth, all arranged into jumbled rows. Its face was a contortion of flesh, as if its creator hadn't known what to do with it. One small eye was overhung by mounds of skin and bits of fur here and there. No nose was able to be seen on the creature as its small eye rolled around for a moment then sunk into the flesh, leaving a hole where it had been.

I fell back in terror as it began lumbering towards me slowly this time. Then the horrible thing reached up ripping some of its own excessive flesh off. The small eye was then revealed once more. Gagging I backed away from the creature, watching it devour the very chunk of skin that it had torn off. Using the wall to help myself stand up, the creature drew closer using its small eye to watch me before lunging forward once more.

Instinct took over as one of my legs flew from my side. My foot connected with its face in midair during the time it lunged for me. With a sticky wet ripping sound I watched my foot carve into its skin, ripping off more than a handful of the creature's sick figure. Rebounding along the wall to the left I watched the creature fly to the right, landing on its side from the blow.

It stood up then turned towards me as my mouth fell open and my stomach lurched. My foot had carved a jagged canyon down its face, tearing off the layers of skin and revealing multiple beady black eyes peering from the fleshy canyon at me. The creature turned from me to the glob of skin lying on the ground. With a snarl it rushed over to what had once been part of it and began gorging it down.

Watching in sick amazement as it did this, the hundreds of black eyes began to emit a liquid which ran down the gash that had been created by me, hardening into more skin and re-covering the eyes.

It regenerated its skin, I thought, as it turned back towards me. Now there was only one eye peering through the mountain of deformed flesh that was its face.

I glanced behind me for only a second to view the other door in the room, but that's all it had taken was only a second. The creature shrieked and belted towards me. My head only made it halfway back around before the creature had tackled me to the floor. I felt its rancid breath against my neck as I tried to hold its head back. Its mouth opened wide, ready to make the killing bite.

Struggling helplessly under the surprising strength of the sickening creature, I tried to keep its needle pointed teeth away from my neck. Its mouth forced its way slowly towards my skin as I began crying out for help, my own strength about to fail me. The creature's teeth began gnashing back and forth, its jaw moving its teeth with lightning speed and closing within mere millimeters away from my neck. Then the creature's small eye swiveled away from my neck to view something else in the room.

With a shrilling grunt the creature pulled its head away from my neck, its full attention now on something else in the room. I didn't dare take my eyes off the creature, but out of the corner of my eye I spotted someone striding towards me. The creature stood up to its full height. It was shrieking and clawing its hands through the air as if in an attempt to ward off a larger predator away from its meal. The person continued striding forward and I finally risked turning my attention to whoever it was. It was the man that had brought me here in the first place.

Opening my mouth I called out to him for help while losing myself to panic, "Hey! Help me, oh please! I don't know what this thing is . . . it's going to kill me!" I said as he stopped, peering at me through his black goggles then back at the creature.

The creature turned back towards me as I spoke, making a guttural sound and sending a fine sheet of sour smelling spittle over my face. It raised one distorted hand up into the air as claws emerged from the flesh, gleaming with an almost metallic sheen to them. I raised my arms as if to block the blow, closing my eyes and waiting for the claws to dig down into my skin, when I felt the creature turn once more.

Peeking open my eyes, I saw that the creature was now in a crouched position on top of me facing the man who now had his arm raised. Slowly a dark looking mist began to crawl up his arm and moving towards the palm of his hand. The inky looking substance began to gather itself in his palm and I could feel the creature shudder.

Whether it had shuddered through fear or a primal rage, I didn't have time to determine. I could feel the creature's legs tense up for a pounce. Opening my mouth to warn the man, I was only half-way to doing so when the creature lunged through the air straight for him. Almost instantaneously the dark substance that had gathered itself in his palm shot forward, taking a whip-like form and wrapping itself around the creature in midair before bringing it down to the floor.

Watching in a mixture of fascination, shock, horror, and wonder, the creature struggled with the dark that continued to be wrapped around itself. The creature's shrieks of rage turned to shrieks of fury, and then melted away to bloodcurdling cries of terror as the dark substance forced its way into the creature's mouth. It continued to cry out, growing louder and causing me to place my hands over my ears from the earsplitting sound.

Then it quit struggling. Its arms and legs fell limp as the whip-like dark matter finished entering the creature. Studying its unmoving body on the concrete floor and lowering my arms, the dark substance seemed to trickle outward from where the creature's eye had been moments before. As it trickled outward the dark vanished into the glow of the red light, blending in with the rest of the darkness whenever the lights pulse faded.

Stepping forward towards the creature slowly, unsure if the mist-like substance would harm me, I glanced at the man that stood like a statue. His arms were folded across his chest, and he was nodding towards me as if in confirmation that it was alright to get closer. I took a few more steps forward as the matter halted its trickling, finally dispersing itself. Reaching forward with one leg I tapped the creature on the head, and realized that it now felt much lighter.

Bending down and looking into where its eye had been I gasped. There was nothing inside, nothing at all. What lied before me was an empty husk and nothing more. Using my foot once more I tapped the top of what had once been a fierce creature. The top of it caved in on itself from the tapping and then, almost immediately, turned into what seemed like a fine powder. It was as if it had been decaying for the many years it had needed to do so, in just a matter of seconds.

'Training Level 1 Completed.' Announced the robotic voice as the red light pulsed its last before shutting off.

Turning back to the man who still stood perfectly still, I eyed him from head to toe, unsure of what to say. Finally I let my shoulders sag, and a sigh of relief emit from my chest. Suddenly feeling the urge to grin, and doing so I asked, "So . . . what's your name? Or am I going to have to refer to you as something else."

"You may call me Paradox." He stated, as if that explained everything.

"Paradox, huh," I said once more while still grinning, "Well, this certainly doesn't make sense."

At that statement we both burst into laughter, killing the twisted mood that had been hovering about for some time. We slowly quieted down, enjoying the moment, as Paradox motioned for me to follow him.

"I will admit," He stated, "that was not part of your training. No. Your training will be much simpler at the start then that was."

Walking up to him as we both moved casually to the door, I turned and watched as he put some sort of code in it. Thinking about what he'd said about that not being part of the training, I asked him, "Then what was that?"

He glanced back at me as I once more felt like he was smiling behind his black scarf.

"That . . ." He said, "is called being in the wrong place, at the wrong time."

I stood there dumbfounded, as if I could never have made a mistake in this new place. The door swung open and he stepped through it, waiting for me to come through to the other side. He let out a quiet laugh at my confused look saying, "Come on, do you really want to stay for 'Training Level 2'?"

At these words my eyes grew wide and I hastened through the large metallic door. It closed behind me, which engulfed the hallway in blackness as he snickered again and led me down the pitch black tunnel.

Stumbling a few times as I followed him, the cool air of the tunnel caressed my skin. Paradox seemed to move with ease through the darkness, turning and checking on me every once and awhile while I continued to lurch forward. This went on for what seemed only a minute or so, but even in that short amount of time I'd hardly made any headway in the dark.

With a sigh Paradox turned. I felt him place a hand on my shoulder then speak as he said, "Here, take a hold of my coat. Then just follow wherever it moves. It will be much quicker until you get used to the dark." His voice reverberated off the walls. It was now quiet and almost fragile sounding, but it still held great power. Nodding blindly at the blackness before me I felt his hand remove itself from my shoulder, then another placing the back of his coat in my outstretched hands.

Treading down the seemingly endless halls of concrete, the silence started to feel as if it was pressing in on me. I began to wonder how large this place was, when I realized I had forgotten to introduce myself this entire time. "Ah, um . . . oh, by the way . . . my name is-"

"Aaron. I know." He cut me off precisely as I continued walking behind him, my hands tightening around his coat. My mouth hung open and my brain ran frantically to figure out how he knew my name already. Shuddering slightly I was unsure of what to exactly say or do.

He almost seems to know as much about me as I know about myself, I thought.

Continuing to walk on I let the silence retake its lost ground. I soon bumped into Paradox, his body not budging as I did so.

Freezing in place I wasn't sure if I should apologize or not, but before I could answer he tugged his coat out of my hands then announced, "We're here."

Looking around I wasn't able to see anything but the same black darkness that had been strangling me since I'd arrived here.

"Where exactly is here?" I asked timidly, as I heard Paradox walk off silently away from me.

Standing still I was sure not to move at all. After the ordeal with the room that held those cages I didn't want to spring anymore surprises.

"Umm . . . what am I suppose to do? Where are you going?" I called out a little frantically, not wanting to be left alone again in this labyrinth.

Then the humming sound returned. It was the same sound I'd heard in the room of cages. My body went rigid, and my arms moved upwards automatically in a feeble defensive posture as I half expected another creature to come howling out of the darkness. Waiting while the humming sound grew louder, I turned towards the direction it was emanating from. Unsure of what it could be there was suddenly a loud bang. Dropping to the floor and covering my head I began to breathe heavily. The humming sound quieted to a low steady rhythm and lights slowly came to life above my head.

Glancing up to see a large room emerging out of the darkness before me, the lights took their time powering up. Focusing on the humming noise I started scolding myself after I realized what was creating the sound. A very large older looking generator rested near the concrete wall on one side of the room. I stood up slowly as Paradox emerged from behind it, his heavy duster coat sweeping behind him in the light. He stopped a moment, adjusting his black gloves and looking at me as if wondering why I had been on the floor.

"Hmm . . . funny, you can stand up to creatures that'd eat you, but not an old generator. I'd better make a mental note of that." He joked as I felt my face flush, no doubt going red.

This made him laugh and poke fun at me even farther, stating that he wouldn't have been able to see my face like this in the dark. I somehow believe he could've.

After calming down a bit I looked around the room, noticing various pieces of furniture. There were chairs that surrounded a rectangular table in the center of the room, and a very large television situated inside the concrete wall on the opposite side from the generator. Another smaller room was connected to this larger one, with the words 'Experimental Area' painted on its front door which was made of Plexiglas. Inside were multiple devices and gizmos on a visible shelf. I could only wonder and imagine what they were for or could do.

There were three halls leading out of the room. The one I'd entered from had a yellow arrow pointing down the hallway, which was now lit with luminescent lights on the roof. The arrow read 'Training Area'. The next hallway also had an arrow pointing down alongside it, this one labeled 'Living Quarters' and 'Communications Area'. The last one had something simple above its doorway, which I was glad to see, and this one said 'Exit'.

Taking this all in while Paradox moved about, he began adjusting one of the chairs there, and dusting something off here. I turned to him and opened my mouth to ask him a question about the lights when he spoke up.

"I've been having problems with the generator lately, so I apologize that you had so much trouble when you first woke up. The Training Rooms computer seems to . . . malfunction . . . at bad times also."

Closing my mouth, then opening it, then closing it again, I was totally shocked and confused on how he knew what I was going to ask. However I had another question strike my mind.

"So what was that thing, the creature? Would it have really killed me?" I asked, partially hoping that the second part would be a 'no' but doubting it.

"Those cages you have seen hold creatures not of this realm, but from a completely different realm. There are concentrated portals behind those cages that allow them through into the holding cells. The cages are just there to retain them. When they enter I use the creatures as training objects." Pausing for a brief moment to inspect something on his black sleeve he continued, "Ah, and yes, the creature would have killed you. That particular type you encountered are called Rethagins, nasty little beasts that can regenerate their living tissue on the outside for protection. What's really nasty is right beneath the skin, which I believe you caught a glimpse of. It's far more horrible then the outside. Luckily, they aren't that hard to take care of. But if it had been on training level two or higher . . . ."

Paradox trailed off, leaving the rest to my imagination as I sat down in one of the chairs trying to get the image of the snarling monster out of my mind.

"So how are those portals created?" I asked, as Paradox sat down across from me, his black goggles shielding his eyes as he answered.

"To tell you the truth, I'm not sure. But others are ripped in time and space every so often letting them out into the world, and I have to stop them."

Digesting this, I sat up straighter and looked at him directly. "So we've got to fight these creature things? That doesn't sound so hard!"

Paradox seemed to study me for a moment then leaned back in his chair, lifting his heavy black boots and setting them on the table.

"We?" He said. "No . . . I have to fight those creatures. You don't need to at the moment. Also, those creatures aren't even a drop in the bucket."

I frowned at this, feeling angry like a child who'd just been told no by a grown up.

"Why can't I fight them?" I burst out, "You know I can take care of myself."

Paradox tilted his head, perhaps amused at what I was saying.

He sighed a bit then said, "You wouldn't last five minutes *with* me, and even less by yourself. When I said those creatures weren't even a drop in the bucket, I was referring to the things that are much, much more dangerous."

I prepared to argue some more, when he held up his hands.

"But," He said, waiting for me to calm down, "if you are able to be taught by me, to train with me . . . your chances will increase exponentially. Then you will be a powerful weapon, even by yourself."

Sitting back, I imagined myself as some sort of hero, defending people from monsters and other beings. It certainly seemed like it would be worth the effort, and how hard could this training be after all? I grinned at the thought and looked towards Paradox, who was now resting his head on the back of his chair.

"I'm in." I said, sounding confident as Paradox raised his head once more, feeling his eyes pierce into mine through the goggles he wore.

"As was expected of you." He spoke matter-of-factly.

Pushing his chair back I watched as Paradox stood up and looked upwards towards the ceiling. He stared at it for some time as if seeing something there, while I looked up and saw nothing. I cleared my throat which caused him to look down at me.

"Take some time to yourself. Look around and get to know this place. You'll be living in here for some time. Just take care not to enter the experimental area or the training area while I'm gone taking care of business."

Paradox turned swiftly and walked away towards the hallway with the exit sign above it. I felt an urge to follow him, but decided to obey his orders.

After all, this could be part of my training, I thought.

Watching him for a moment I wondered why he didn't just teleport out of the room like he seemed to do so much. Laying my head back, I glanced up at the circular light glowing softly above me.

"Humph, business?" I said out loud to myself as soon as Paradox had left, and contenting myself by swiveling the chair around. "More like, 'you stay here while I go fight evil'."

Sighing I stood up, wondering what I should do until Paradox returned. I yawned, walking down the hallway which was labeled 'Living Quarters and Communications Area'. The hallway split into two different arches, one leading to the living quarters, and the other to the Communications Area. Choosing the living quarters, I walked towards another large metallic door that I was reluctant to open at first. After a moment's hesitation I shrugged, pushing on the door to no avail, and then realizing that there was a button to open it on the side.

Pressing the button to open the door it seemed to do nothing, and then the door smoothly rolled upward. As it rolled upward I was bathed in a blue sparkling light, unsure of what I was seeing I squinted my eyes which rushed to process the images before me. Slowly they grew wider into full circles, as the picture I was seeing was completed in my mind. Standing there, I was shocked and amazed at what I was seeing.

Sabotage

Tentatively I took a step forward into the large room. Beds lined the walls on either side, but that wasn't what had me in awe. It was the walls. They weren't the same concrete walls I'd been seeing. Each wall in the room was made of glass, except the wall that the door was set in which was the usual concrete. Each glass wall held something different in it, one displaying creatures of the ocean, the fish swimming around seemed to peer at me as I drew closer to it.

Pressing my hand against the glass, I realized that it was indeed a giant aquarium. I drew back as an entire whale glided by through the bright blue water, its massive tail making graceful strokes to move itself along. Taking a deep breath, it was like I could smell the salt emitting from the water. Somehow Paradox had an entire oceans ecosystem in this complex.

Turning from the gigantic tank and reeling at the thought of how big it truly was, I wondered how it worked exactly. The next glass segment between the two other walls held what seemed like a universe. Small lines moved about the tiny stars inside of it. At first I thought the lines showed trajectories. Then strange languages displayed outward from the lines. They were languages I'd never seen before. Walking towards one I touched the magnificent glass. No fingerprints were left on it, and as I touched it the galaxy grew larger as it zoomed in on the area I had disturbed.

"Whoa." I said aloud, "How much did this all cost? What's the purpose of it . . . ?"

Pondering this I turned towards the last wall. This wall glowed a sickly gray color, which gave a stark contrast to the cheery blue that was emitted from the ocean habitat. Stepping towards the dim glow, my hands began moving upwards to press it. With my hands making contact I felt a slight shock move throughout my body that wasn't painful. The screen lit up and directories began pouring over the screen.

The directories were labeled A-Z. I watched them line up along the glass surface, some of them too high to reach. Stepping a little closer and almost pressing against the glass with my body, a glass ladder materialized. The steps formed inward from the glass, and wherever I moved along the glass they would follow alongside me.

This is incredible, I thought, while climbing the ladder slowly and testing my hold to see if it would be easy to keep my grip.

Climbing a few rows upwards I pressed the letter S on the glass screen. The other directories disappeared and began to be replaced by new ones, bringing up everything from 'Security' to 'Sightings ". Rubbing my chin I debated which I should choose before reaching up and tapping the 'Security' directory.

Once more the directories vanished, but instead of being replaced by more directories video screens began appearing. I climbed back downwards, backing away to look at each of them. Each screen showed a different part of the complex. I spotted myself on one of the screens and glanced in the direction it was coming from. For the first time I noticed a small camera viewing me.

Waving at the camera I went and sat on one of the beds, slowly sinking downward into a laying position. Yawning I turned over onto my side, watching the giant aquarium and the whales floating along inside of it.

Why does Paradox have these here? I wonder while closing my eyes.

Feeling safe and secure in the room, I fell asleep to the sounds of the ocean.

It was a sunny, bright afternoon as I walked down the street not having a care in the world. I smiled happily to the passerby, and whistled a happy tune. I stretched as I continued strolling, slowing down as I noticed the bright sunlight slowly disappear. I looked upwards towards the sky, as dark clouds began to move in, blotting out the sun and blue sky.

Glancing around I saw everyone else continuing on as normal, not seeming to notice anything strange. I began walking across the street as a car suddenly loomed in front of me, blocking my path, I turned to the side to continue on as more cars appeared, boxing me in. Then they started beeping, all of them at once. An annoying persistent beeping in unison and a steady rhythm, causing me to clutch my head, feeling as if my mind was going to implode on itself . . . .

Turning I fell off the bed I'd been laying on. Glancing around quickly I was unable to get my bearings of where I was at until it slowly came back to me. The sounds of the oceans creatures called out gently trying to soothe my panic. But there was something else . . . a beeping sound? One that sounded like it belonged to the vehicles that had been in my dream.

Acting as casual as possible in case anyone was somehow watching me, I located the beeping sound which was quietly repeating on the screen that still had the Security Cameras displayed on them. Scratching my head lightly I glanced from one to another, finally resting on one that had a dim red glow emanating around it.

"What's this?" I asked the empty room, as if expecting an answer.

Studying the screen it appeared I was watching a large metallic door. After a few moments I began to turn away. The large door was over the entrance that had the exit sign above it. Otherwise nothing had happened that was interesting.

Just as my eyes were veering off the screen the metallic door exploded outward from where it had been positioned. Black smoke streamed outwards from the entrance while alarms suddenly blared out. Two objects were thrown from the black smoke, each emitting their own white smoke.

Continuing to watch this event I saw the figures of men move throughout the smoke carefully and precisely. The men were nothing more the gloomy blobs in the smoke which filled the large room. One of the blobs stopped in the center of the camera screen, making a motion which I guessed to be an arm. A few seconds passed and the figure hefted something upwards, pointing it directly at the camera just before its screen went dead.

Oh crap, oh crap . . . what should I do? I thought as my mind churned the images over and over again.

That room they'd entered was the only way in or out that I'd seen, and the only room near here besides this one was the communications room.

That's it! The communications room, I can call for help!

Sprinting for the metallic doorway, I lunged over a few of the beds, almost diving for the button to open the door. The door slid open with a slight whirring sound. Silently jogging down the hallway I carefully moved forward when the junction appeared. Pausing and unsure if I should dash across or not, I listened for any sound of advancement.

A few moments passed with only silence greeting me. Taking this chance to peek around the corner, only the empty hall met my gaze along with a few strands of smoke pouring down the hallway. Inching past the junction I began sprinting down the hallway towards the communications room, slowly rounding a corner then stopping dead in my tracks.

The door to the communications room was already open. Two soldiers that seemed identical to the ones that had appeared in my dream stood inside with their backs towards me. Stifling a gasp I tried to control my breathing and backed away slowly. Turning around to head back the way I'd come, I was suddenly jerked off my feet.

Screaming and alerting the two soldiers in the communications room, they spun around raising their weapons. Struggling to free myself from whoever was holding me was futile. They seemed far stronger then I was. Kicking backwards at my assaulter I watched the two soldiers lower their weapons slowly. My foot connected with a part of the person behind me. Hearing a grunt and muttering along with static I was thrown to the floor. Spinning around onto my back I was just in time to see a third soldier wearing a gas mask, helmet, and uniform lift their rifle and forcefully strike the butt of it to my face.

Blackness and pain slowly crept inwards towards my mind as I began to regain consciousness. Lightning bolts of crackling fire seared through my neck as I turned my head slightly from side to side, my eyes trying to focus on any thing. I was lying against the wall of the communications room, multiple lights from switches and dials flashing from the controls on one side of it.

Groggily lowering my head someone's thudding footsteps drew near me. One large black combat boot moved under my chin, lifting my head upwards until my eyes met with one of the masked soldiers.

"Heh, it looks like we have a little hero here guys." The soldier stated with a bit of sarcasm spilling through his masks radio. The other two soldiers burst into static laughter.

He lowered his boot, along with my chin as he placed the muzzle of his rifle on the top of my head.

"You're lucky I didn't kill you, boy. Especially when I was on edge patrolling for someone else." He said through his masks radio, accompanied with some crackling along with it.

He turned from me as I forced my head in their direction through the pain, trying to study the soldiers in more detail.

Watching them I felt a small amount of blood trickling from my nose. Wincing I was unsure if it was broken. Shrugging mentally I turned my attention back to the three soldiers. All of them were far more fit then I was, and taller too. They held rifles that I'd never seen before, strange red lines of light pulsing under the barrels of their weapons creating a sci-fi look. The one that had spoken to me stood ready in front of me, his back turned but alert. He seemed to be the one assigned to watch me. The other two stood near the communications control panel, adjusting dials and pressing buttons.

Whether the one in front of me was the one I managed to kick I couldn't tell, but that gave me little comfort. Watching as the two soldiers near the panel finished up with whatever they were doing, they placed their hands up towards their masks and began speaking. No doubt they were using better communication devices then the radios in their masks to contact others in the complex.

"S-01 to S-02 calling to see how things are going on your end, we're finished up here." Spoke the one farthest away from me.

They paused for a moment, listening then nodding along with his partner.

"Roger that S-02, rendezvous with S-03 as soon as you are done." With those last words they let their arms fall back to their weapons, nodding to the third soldier nearest to me who hadn't used his comm. device.

"They're almost done making the modifications. We've got to be ready to evacuate as soon as they're . . ." The soldier appeared to be interrupted by something and trailed off, as all three lifted their arms and pressed their comm. systems.

"What's going on? Say again? Stay calm. What the . . . it's hard enough to make out what you're saying as it is. What was that? Who's firing? Come in, I repeat, Come in!" The farthest soldier demanded as they held their arms up a few moments longer, then dropped them as a new sound came from the hallway.

Screams, shouts of pain and terror along with gunfire rang and echoed down the cold concrete hallway. The three soldiers listened for a moment then quickly moved about, cocking their weapons and preparing them for whatever was happening. The two soldiers that had been near the communications controls moved towards the door. They had rifles at the ready and pressed towards their shoulders. Slowly they threaded across the hallway back and forth.

"Charlie-01 . . . you stay with the boy, make sure he doesn't do anything stupid, we're going to go check out what's going on. Also try and raise HQ on this thing to see if we can't get back-up." Spoke the same soldier that seemed to do most the talking.

"Yes sir." Charlie-01 said with a quick salute then went back into his guarding posture. After a moment he went strolling towards the communications controls while the other two soldiers disappeared down the hallway. The screams were now dying down in volume along with what sounded like fewer gunshots.

"HQ, come in, this is Charlie-01 of S-01. Come in." Charlie-01 spoke, and I watched him while huddling in the corner, unsure of what was going on.

A few moments of static passed, and Charlie-01 was just about to try again when a voice sounding full of authority spoke back.

"This is HQ, Charlie-01, what's your status?" Charlie-01 adjusted a few dials and began speaking, sounding calm yet tense.

"We are under attack, I repeat, under attack by unknown life-forms, we require back-up, over."

The gunshots and screams had totally died away now. Listening carefully for any signs of life emanating from the now silent hallways the same voice began talking through the comm. systems.

"Have you completed your objectives Charlie-01?" Gunshots rang out from down the hallway. Radioed shouts and screams belonging to the two soldiers that had gone were heard. Charlie-01 quickly replied back into the radio.

"We have completed the objectives, over."

"Then you are no longer needed." The voice spoke through the radio casually, as if finishing business. A click was heard and the communication station went silent.

Charlie-01 turned around and re-checked his weapon before glancing at me, his eyes wide.

"Well kid, it looks like we both have bigger problems to worry about now." He said as he turned back towards the open door where the screams and gunshots were emanating from.

Invasion

S hriveling inward I watched Charlie-01 kneel down onto the floor. He pointed his rifle toward the open doorway which led into the hallway. The screams and gunfire had ceased from the two soldiers who had left only moments before. Charlie-01 didn't look too comfortable as he raised one hand from his rifle. Keeping one goggled eye looking down the scope he touched his comm. device.

"Alpha-01, this is Charlie-01 do you copy?" He spoke precisely and professionally into the masks radio, but still it quivered with a mixture of fear and adrenaline.

"Beta-01, this is Charlie-01, do you copy?" He tried. He shook his head slightly and tapped his comm. device once more then stated with a bit of hope and authority.

"If there are any members from the remaining squads alive, I'd like you to know that we were just expired by HQ. There are two survivors here in the comm. room including me. If you can make it here then perhaps we can mount some sort of defense. Only come if you are closer to this location. If you are near the exit, get out. Otherwise bunker down somewhere. Charlie-01 out."

Charlie-01 finished speaking. The static of his radio voice quieted down, and only his steady breathing emitted from the mask. I began to stand up slowly as he glanced at me sideways, nodding slightly to show that it was alright. Striding over to the communications controls I tried to figure out how they worked.

"What are you doing?" Charlie-01 asked in a controlled calm, his eyes never leaving the hallway.

Sounding as if I was about to break I replied, "I'm going to try and call for help."

Charlie-01 moved around towards me as if in slow motion, and just began to emit a static burst from his masks radio to offer advice when one of the two soldiers that had left came charging down the hall. Their front armor had a large slash across the front, but didn't seem to have been penetrated deeply enough to sustain injury. His eyes were wide with fear through his goggles as he raced towards the door. Another much larger figure came bounding up behind him from around the corner.

The soldier didn't look back as he ran on but was far slower than the hulking beast behind him. It had hands that were more like clubs with spikes jutting out of random fingers. Eyes and mouths were misplaced all over the tower of deformed flesh. Gagging at the site of it, I noticed a black combat boot hanging slightly out of one of the creature's mouths.

Charlie-01 reacted quickly as he snapped back around, rifle flying upward and unloading multiple rounds into the creature. The fleshy mass slowed down as if wounded, then suddenly split into several smaller pieces that turned out to be various other creatures which immediately gave chase.

The soldier that was running was only a few feet from the door, and the creatures were mere inches behind him. Charlie-01 stopped firing, eyes opening wider as he took a strange looking device from his belt. He pressed several buttons in rapid movement, faster than my eyes could follow. Without hesitation he rolled it through the doorway, before diving and smashing the doors close button.

A wail came from the soldier as the outside door crashed downward blocking him out of the room with the creatures. His cries of terror were muffled to a dull roar accompanied with a small thump against the door like a body smashing into it. Charlie-01 lowered his head as multiple thumps sounded on the other side of the door. The screaming rose to its highest pitch ever just before all the sound stopped at once. Then it was replaced by an eerie low-pitched sucking sound which rose higher, and then dropped along with a large rumble emanating from the area.

The rumble stopped as Charlie-01 lifted a gloved fist and pounded against the heavy metal door over and over, beginning to sob and break down. Watching him for a moment, I felt myself getting sick. Watching the hardened soldier crumble under losing his friends and fellow comrades wasn't helping. The soldier finally turned to me and ripped off his gasmask to expose his face. He was clean-shaven with brown hair styled into a crew-cut. His bright blue eyes peered at me as tears streaked down his cheeks.

"So . . . what's this help you're planning on calling in?" He choked out, wiping his bleary eyes to no avail.

Waiting a moment for him to regain some of his composure I opened my mouth to speak. I wasn't able to get anything out before a very large thud and creak emitted from the opposite side of the door. Charlie-01 removed his fist which had been placed on the door and raised his rifle a little. Laughing he lost all hope as he studied the door. Another large thud hit the door, causing it to creak with a little more intensity this time, as if protesting the pressure being forced on it.

"There are more of them . . ." Charlie-01 said as he backed away from the door, "I certainly hope that help of yours is ready to deal with an invasion." he said. As he shrank back against the wall opposite from the door he was cradling his rifle.

Another thud on the door, this time the creaking brought a small bend in the doors frame.

"We won't have much time anyhow." He whispered, almost sounding optimistic about it.

"Hey, at least it can't get worse than this." I said as I turned back towards the controls.

"Don't say that, it can always get worse." He immediately warned.

Looking at him with a smile on my face which betrayed my real feelings inside, I stated my next phrase as if waiting for an explanation. "Oh yeah? How so?"

As soon as I was done speaking I turned back to the controls and flipped the comm. button to hopefully contact Paradox, just as the power suddenly turned off.

"That's how." Charlie-01 snapped back miserably as I grimaced, now facing the black space where the comm. controls had been moments before.

Reaching out I felt for the buttons, tapping for them blindly in the dark and pressing a few with no reaction. Turning towards where Charlie-01 had been sitting I sighed and listened to the thudding on the opposite side of the door increase.

"Now what?" I asked, feeling as if I were all alone, but knowing I wasn't. A moment passed and Charlie-01's face lit up with two beams of light shining outwards from it.

Instinctively I stepped back, thinking that he had somehow changed his very face. The light brown crew-cut was now gone, and so were his eyes along with his mouth, until I realized he had put his mask back on. His mask had two lights attached to the sides of it. Two that I either hadn't noticed before, or had somehow come out of the mask.

Charlie-01 gave me a thumbs up sign, watching my expression as he stated, "Auto-lights. They automatically move from the inside of the masks helmet to the outside and power-up when it's dark. It can take awhile though."

Smiling at his change of mood I was grateful for the bit of comfort that the small lights gave. He turned his head towards the door, while I lied back against the comm. controls and watched. It was now bent considerably inward. Every thud moved it a little more towards us, as if the door itself was trying to come through into the room. Standing up I paced back and forth slightly when Charlie-01 turned towards me with a wry smile.

"Well, I guess this is the end of the road for both of us then." He stated with a bit of remorse in his voice. He was reluctant to give up without a fight.

Nodding I smiled back, feeling the urge to give it all I had before the end along with him. Looking around for anything I could use as a weapon, the small beam of light providing me with nothing to find. I shrugged, clenching and unclenching my fists while watching the door move a little further towards us.

"Hey kid, here take this." I heard Charlie-01 say as he reached to the side of his armor where a slot opened, revealing a sidearm.

He reached for the pistol and grabbed it. After checking its ammo and apparently satisfied, he turned to me with a slight toss causing the pistol to fly through the air and into my hands. Parts of the pistol glowed in the dark. Small pink strips pulsed along the pistols barrel, and a small circular button flashed on and off a little above the hilt. I looked up as I heard

Charlie-01 cock his weapon. After he'd done that the rifle resumed its red pulsing along the barrel.

"By the way, the flashing button above your hilt is the safety." Charlie-01 started walking towards one side of the door, as I pressed the button turning the safety off.

As I walked towards the opposite side of the door from Charlie-01 we both raised our weapons and pointed them towards the bent metallic frame that was preparing to give way. Charlie-01 smirked, letting his radio clear before saying, "My name's Justin. Want to see who can get the most kills?"

Grinning at this, I competitively said, "Well, it's kind of unfair, you have a rifle. You're still on though, and my names Aaron."

Suddenly I really felt glad that Justin was with me no matter what he'd done. To be alone through something like this. I would have lost my mind in this situation if he hadn't been there. Justin was a little tense, but kept his cool and made the bleak situation a bit lighter. He looked down the sight of his rifle, waiting for the moment to fire and catching me off guard with his next sentence.

"So . . . no hard feelings, right?"

Looking at him in confusion I attempted to figure out what he meant. Before I could say anything the door made a loud squealing sound, the top half of it coming inward, just enough to leave two inch cracks through to the opposite side. Justin adjusted his small beams of light towards the cracks, showing us an image of snarling teeth, skin, fur, and bodies attempting to force their way in once the creatures gleaming eyes had seen the opening.

Shocked at first, my hands quivered slightly as I watched the things in motion, trying to enter the room as the door bent downwards. Gunfire ripped out of Justin's rifle and began tearing into the creatures which snapping me out of my trance. Lowering my eyebrows I was determined to fight until the end. Taking aim I began pulling the trigger to open fire. The pistol lurched in my hand, fire spewing outwards from the barrel and sending what looked like a pink shard into the nearest monster.

The pink shard glowed as it sunk into the beast. Its howls of pain, agony, and anger filled the room and hallways outside along with the rest of the nightmarish chorus. Firing a few more times I noticed the same effect as I glanced over towards Justin, who was now firing short controlled bursts into the creatures. His bullets left a red glow wherever they struck flesh.

Observing this I realized that the creatures weren't bleeding, but the light from the projectiles seemed to have as much effect, or possibly even more, then the bullets themselves. The light emanating from the creatures caused them to shrivel inwards on themselves, disintegrating from the strange projectiles. As the shrieking creatures perished a black substance much like the what Paradox had manipulated to his will poured out of the creatures, cancelling the light out.

The damage that was done stopped the lighted projectiles, but too slowly. Beginning to cheer in victory I watched as the monsters began retreating down the hallway, with our bullets flying after them. We pressed our assault until the last of them had either been defeated, or had rounded the corner. Justin and I turned and clasped our right hands together, both letting out roars as we celebrated our victory.

Turning and looking at the door which had been forced open up to five inches now I looked through the opening, trying to look at some of the creatures shriveled bodies.

"Hey Justin, shine some light on those bodies will you?" I asked as he stepped over, his head peering out the door and the streams of light hitting the now motionless beings.

Just as I thought, most of them are Rethagins.

Justin shrugged, turning back towards me.

"What about them?" He asked as I looked towards him with an expressionless face.

"Nothing." I simply stated in return.

Then the nightmarish screech was heard. There was a bloodcurdling cry of indescribable rage. I turned towards the ruined door as the cries grew closer. Its torturous sound filling our ears and making both of us wince. Forcing our weapons upward we both pointed them towards the turn in the hallway as the shrieking seemed to make the very walls tremble.

"Are you sure what you wanted to tell me was nothing?" Justin asked. His eyes were wide and bloodshot.

My face darkened as I jumbled my words together quickly, not taking my eyes off the hallway while trying to steady my pistol as it quivered in my hand.

"It's just that those creatures we killed are called Rethagins. I guess I thought that's all there was, or maybe just what had gotten out of the portals."

Shifting my feet slightly I took a more comfortable stance as the shriek emanated down the hallway once again.

"Portals?" Justin asked me, his radio blurring the word slightly with static.

Looking at him, my eyebrows pulled upward in confusion as I shot him back a question in return.

"You really had no idea what you were doing here, did you?"

Justin didn't send a look back. Continuing to stare forward he answered, "We were told what to do, and how to do it. Not the reasons why. We don't question orders."

"Well that's real nice. Look where it got us now." I muttered turning back towards the hall as the ground trembled slightly.

Justin didn't say anything as the trembling grew more apparent. With a crash against the rounded wall a creature emerged that took up the entire space of the hallway, and without slowing it began charging down it towards the door.

Immediately we both opened fire as our bullets sprayed down into the creature. We were only able to see its vulgar body through the small light from our bullets, the muzzle flashes, and the light streaming outwards from Justin's mask. It had two "arm" appendages that swiveled around its body, ending in two jagged ends that resembled scythes. Its body twisted and turned whenever a bullet struck it only looking like it was causing damage. The rounds from the weapons were pulled in by the writhing flesh and disappeared from view. A mouth adorned the top of the monstrosities head resembling a large grotesque flytrap of some sort, while its eyes bubbled all over the body.

The creature drew closer very quickly, the bullets unable to slow its dreaded progress. Aiming for a few of the eyes I fired shards of the glowing metal into them. Slowly they closed, and when they'd disappear new eyes came up through the skin. The damaged ones were being replaced as the old ones were moved inside. Shouting over the gunfire I tried to tell Justin to take cover as the beast bent down and rammed the door with full force. Bending considerably more under the monster's strength, the door hung halfway open now.

Jumping back I fell to the floor. My pistol fell from my hand as Justin dashed to the side of the door. He kept cover and stayed against the wall to avoid the sickle arms that came through the door way, flying around in an attempt to impale anything alive. Frantically I looked at Justin hoping he had some idea to get us out of the situation we were in as the creature made an earsplitting shriek that caused me to go temporarily deaf.

Opening my mouth I spoke to Justin, not being able to hear myself. After a moment I'd try again, slowly hearing the words grow louder.

"Do you have any more of those things you tossed outside the door before you closed it?" I asked hopefully, not even knowing if it would do the trick.

Looking at me he shook his head, turning it just in time as part of the creatures arm passed mere inches from his turned cheek.

"You mean a Violight Grenade? I'm afraid not." He said loading another clip into his rifle.

Cocking it again then turning towards the damaged door he'd proceed to empty more rounds into the nightmare at point blank range. When his mask lights turned away from me it would leave me in darkness.

Turning I looked for my pistol that I'd lost. I saw the dim glow of its barrel lying in a corner of the room and crawled towards it, listening to the shrieks and wails mixed with gunfire.

Reaching for my weapon it suddenly disappeared into the darkness. The strip of light emitting from the pistol had seemed to evaporate. Reaching forward I placed my hand where it had been, but nothing was there. Frowning I stood up and turned towards Justin and the noise of battle. When a gloved hand moved over my mouth and an arm held me in place.

Separate Worlds

"*D*on't make any noise." The person behind me whispered into my ear. I recognized his voice, it was Paradox!

He released me as I turned around to see his dark figure. He was standing in-between me and Justin, who was kneeling on the ground just below the abominations appendages, reloading his weapon.

Opening my mouth to speak, Paradox clamped his hand over my face while whispering, "What did I just tell you? If you want to get out of here without any problems then don't make any noise."

Paradox removed his hand from my mouth a second time. Silently I stood in place. I watched him turn his head in the dark, looking towards the ongoing fight as the creature began slowly peeling the door away. Justin was now on his feet and firing right into the creatures snapping face while its arms were preoccupied. He was shouting something that I couldn't make out or understand, perhaps just a battle cry.

Paradox turned back towards me nodding, as he lifted both of his arms and held them outward away from his sides. He began to move them rapidly in different directions as one passed directly in front of me. I heard him begin to mutter while his hands passed in front of my face one after another. Then when one of them had passed before me during the rotations, the dark room vanished and I was standing under the bright moonlight of a beach.

My mind reeled in confusion as Paradox stood before me just as it had before when he had been in the room. His arms now rested at his sides while I spun around taking in the strange trees behind me, and the darkness of the sea. Relaxing I'd noticed the sounds of the battle had died away and that Paradox had somehow brought us somewhere else. Then I realized that Justin wasn't here!

"Where's Justin?" I blurted out, looking at Paradox for any confirmation that Justin was also safe.

Paradox tilted his head slightly, as he asked, "Who's Justin?"

My mouth dropped open in disbelief, images playing through my mind of Justin still battling that gigantic creature, or worse. Raising my fists in anger at Paradox I was pleased when he actually took a small step back, hands rising upward.

"Do you mean the Twilight Soldier? He could've posed more problems for us then the Urthigeon that was busting through the door." Paradox stated calmly then seemed to think a moment as I took a step towards him fists still raised.

"Go back . . ." I said as tears welled up in my eyes, "enough people have died today. Please, go back and get him."

Paradox's shoulders sagged in a sign of defeat then muttered, "Alright."

He proceeded to bring his arms up and crossed both of them in front of himself. Without a word he then vanished in a globe of black mist which slowly dissipated. Pacing back and forth I finally plopped down on the ground while waiting. Time felt like it was moving slowly as I listened to the waves breaking upon the beach.

"Hey. Wake up." I stirred from sleep hearing Paradox's voice call out to me.

Opening my eyes wearily I sat up looking for Justin. There was no sign of him and I turned towards Paradox, opening my mouth to ask him where Justin was when he interrupted me.

"I couldn't find him. When I arrived the door was in pieces, and neither the creature nor Justin was to be found. Anyways, it looks like he put up a nice fight."

Lying back on the sand and looking up at the stars which were slowly growing dimmer Paradox sat beside me. Too tired to cry, or even be angry, I thought about how different the situation would have been if Paradox had taken them both from that place.

How could it have been worse? I thought as the stars shimmered above me.

Justin had turned out to be a soldier who followed orders. Not some crazy person like so many people make villains sound like. In the end he was just someone else who struggled to survive alongside me.

My thoughts flashed briefly to the moment where he had thrown the grenade outside of the door, closing it on his comrade.

I'm sure he only closed it because those creatures would have gotten inside with us if he had waited. I sighed out loud letting the air inside my chest slowly release.

Paradox had said Justin was a Twilight Soldier. Hmm . . . no clue what that was, I thought.

Paradox looked out towards the sea as the sun began to rise over its waves. At least I thought it was the sun, but I must have been wrong. Sitting up I looked at the image that rose above the sea. It was purple, bathing the landscape with an eerie light. Looking down at the sand my eyes narrowed at its color. Its color was green, a light green, almost like grass. Turning my head I watched the trees which rose up towering above the beach.

All of the trees weren't really trees. No, they looked more like appendages. They rose up ending in claw like fashions, eyes dotting some of them and creating a land of flesh. Some of them moved every now and then, a single one striking down with powerful force in the distance. The land rose upwards at an angle that must have been a mountain. I looked towards Paradox.

"What is this place?" I asked him, feeling like he already knew what my question was.

"This is another planet, aside from our own. The entire planet is one giant organism. We are guests here, and I advise that you do not upset it." Paradox said, looking towards me and chuckling at my grossed out expression.

"So . . ." I stated with a bit of disgust, "We're like germs then."

"Precisely," Paradox announced to the surrounding area. "It also looks like we will have to stay for some time here, and we don't want to upset our generous hosts bodily defenses."

I raised an eyebrow while looking at Paradox.

"What do you mean? Can't we just teleport out of here like the way we came?" I inquired of him, as he shook his head no while replying.

"Not during the daytime. Ah, also . . . when I say some time here, it means one of this planets days. They could be longer, or shorter, then our own. You see, I can only teleport wherever the darkness connects. The brighter the light is, the weaker my powers are. I can only create a small sphere of darkness around me in sunlight, which is obviously the strongest type of light."

"Well that's just great." I muttered. "What about my family? Did you think about that?"

Paradox shifted uneasily then spoke, "I did."

By his shifting I could easily tell that this was a delicate subject with him, one that he would rather not speak about.

"What about my family? Well? Tell me what's wrong!" I said fiercely as Paradox bowed his head under pressure.

"The truth is." Paradox answered slowly, "Is that you probably won't ever see your family again."

My mind reeled backwards at this, taking in the thought of 'never again.' Feeling my face go red with anger, I bolted upwards onto my feet turning towards Paradox and shouting right into his masked face. My arms waved frantically in an attempt to do anything aside from striking out at him.

"What do you mean I won't see my family again? What gives you the right to just take me from my home!? Why are you . . . even doing this!?!"

Paradox sat quietly in the sand, not saying anything. I tried to discern his expression behind his mask, one of anger? No. His posture told a different story. As he sat there it became evident that he was filled with-

Sadness, I thought.

My anger melted away as I watched this person, this man. He had great power, but was also carrying a heavy burden upon himself. One that he had kept hidden deep within himself, something that Paradox hadn't thought about in years.

"Family . . . ." Paradox spoke softly and slowly, his voice dragging out the word slightly.

He looked directly towards me as he continued to speak in a calm, controlled manner.

"I didn't force you to come here, if you recall. It was your choice since the very beginning. A choice that you, Aaron, only you could make, a choice like the one that I made so long ago, so very long ago."

Paradox lowered his head and I felt chill run throughout me. I recalled the meeting in the alley, and the swirling vortex in my home. I'd walked forward while Paradox had stood there with arm outstretched to receive me. It had indeed been my choice. My legs wobbled causing me to stumble downwards into the sand.

"Sorry." I whispered as I felt a tremor run along the beach.

Raising his head Paradox stood up, almost immediately after feeling the tremor.

"We've got to move now." He said quietly then began walking towards the fleshy forest.

Forcing myself to stand, my thoughts turned on what he had said about making the same choices I had long ago. Jogging to catch up I fell in place behind him, walking in rhythm to keep my pace the same as his.

As we entered the strange canopy I couldn't help but feel like every eye on the strange arm-like trees were turning to follow us. Shuddering I kept turning my head to look at them, watching as the gruesome eyes stayed totally still. They had sentience and an intellect sparkling in them. Turning to watch one side I felt like the eyes behind me moved, then stood still once I jerked my head around and the process repeated.

"Be sure not to cause any irritation." Paradox said as he continued striding onwards. "It's best overall if you ignore them."

Pondering on what he'd said for a moment I replied, "Irritation?"

He shrugged saying, "You know. Like an itch."

Scratching my head for a moment and wondering what he meant, I stopped and brought my hand to the front of my face and looked at my fingers. My eyes moved up towards the clawed figures with jagged ends pointing every which way, looking as if they could tear through any amount of steel. Now I wasn't just nervous, but scared.

We continued walking, while looking straight ahead for the most part. It took time but I became aware of the environment apart from the eyes and claw figures. The ground was soft under my feet, sinking inward slightly as I trod over it. The air was warm along with plenty of humidity and a smell. Taking a quick whiff of the air I tried to determine what the smell was and frowned. It was a familiar, unpleasant smell. Looking up at the sky I grimaced, noticing that the purple sun hadn't moved much at all.

"Paradox," I said as I walked on behind him, "Have you been here before? It almost seems like you have, you sure know a lot about this place if you haven't."

Paradox turned his head slightly, one goggled eye focusing on me from the side. I thought I saw his scarf vibrate slightly from his answer, "I've been here a few times."

My eyes narrowed in on him as my face turned into a look that suggested he was crazy, "Why would you come here? I can't see a reason."

"There's always a reason for me." He stated before turning his head away from me.

My crazy facial expression turned to one of confusion as I said, "Quit being so cryptic about things."

He trudged on a little more then stopped momentarily. Turning his head to the left then the right, it looked like he was trying to decide which way to go. "You could say that I have an old friend that lives here. He just doesn't necessarily know we are here yet, and we are going to meet him."

Who in their right minds would want to live here, I thought, my mind reeling with disgust. Then I felt as if Paradox was smiling once more behind his scarf. I guess I'll find out soon enough.

Paradox finally shrugged and settled on a direction. Turning right he began to walk. Yawning I looked up again at the sky and frowned at the non-moving purple sun.

This sucks, I thought, who knows how long we could be here? It could be days in earth time, maybe even weeks. Once I get out of here I . . .

My thought process was interrupted as I noticed a change in scenery. Everything was the same, with one small exception. There were holes, and not just any, but holes that were big enough to swallow a small vehicle. Paradox seemed unconcerned about this, striding on as usual without a care. I thought about asking Paradox what the holes were when he held up one hand. He stopped, and in turn, stopped me.

"It seems we have some uninvited guests." Paradox spoke in his 'I'm right' way.

Looking around I wasn't seeing anything and asked, "What do you mean?"

He shook his head pointing to his ear signaling to listen. Quieting down and letting silence take command I heard what must have been what he also heard. There was a scraping sound like scratching or digging, and it was coming from ahead. Stepping around Paradox to get a better look I noticed that there was another hole where the sound was emanating from.

"What is it?" I questioned again.

Paradox shook his head saying, "You can never be sure about what lives here naturally, and what comes from somewhere else."

Nodding I watched the hole. The scraping sound grew louder as something began to emerge from the pit. In it's own simplistic way it was very ugly.

It had tiny eyes that peered at us while its overly large round body barely fit into the hole it climbed up from. Rising up the rest of the way out of the hole, four large legs emerged with it moving about and supporting the bulk of its body. Lumbering slightly away from the hole, its legs pushed it forward, tiny hairs protruding from the legs moved back and forth along them. When it breathed, the bulky mass would inflate, and then deflate, while its eyes never left us. Lowering its front end and growling at us it showed an impressive row of sharp teeth. Two tubes emerged from the sides of its mouth where the cheeks would have been, and they ended in sharp points which made a sucking noise.

"So you have no idea what that thing is?" I asked Paradox, believing he knew the answer as he folded his arms and stated, "You know as well as I do."

The creature bellowed, causing the appendage—like trees to quiver. Moving its back legs it rapidly began to dig into the ground. The ground quivered slightly at this, and before I knew what had happened the creature was gone. Its powerful legs had propelled it high into the air the moment one of the appendage-trees smashed down, where, it had been only a second before.

Landing on one of the appendage-trees the creature peered down at us from a sideways angle. It would then focus its attention somewhere else, turning its head to watch the other appendage-tree that had struck where it'd been moments before. Slowly the tree curled back upwards. Paradox rubbed his clothed chin, examined the creature which was now chittering, and moving down the appendage tree it was occupying.

"Interesting," Paradox said as he continued to watch it. "It's like a parasite. Like a flea occupying a host."

Reaching, the creature once more dug its powerful legs into the ground. Bringing its teeth forward, it would clamp down on the ground. The tubes would proceed to pierce the planets flesh and draw up blood.

The creature's eyes didn't leave us while it did this. I didn't know if it was deciding if we were a threat or something else. In a lightning fast blur another appendage-tree shot downward, but still not fast enough. Like an automatic response, the creature's powerful legs caused it to lunge out of the way.

"I might as well help my friend." Paradox stated as he began to move his hands rapidly about him, making strange symbols and a sphere of darkness moving outwards from him.

Grunting at this, Paradox forced it to struggle against the light that was produced from the purple sun. The creature landed with a loud thud and turned towards Paradox as if sensing aggression. It snapped its powerful jaws a few times then dug its feet in the ground once more preparing to lunge straight at him!

"That thing is your friend?" I asked Paradox, as he continued moving his arms quickly.

"No. Not that creature, my friend that lives here. I'm going to help him."

Like a bullet the creature shot forward, just as Paradox threw his hands outwards. The darkness created a barrier of darkness in front of Paradox, catching and absorbing the creature.

It screamed in rage, and I thought about what he had done to the Rethagin. Instead of doing the same thing he had done to his last opponent that I'd witnessed, he lowered this creature to the ground and held it there. It clawed all around itself trying to escape. The ground began to shudder again in response. This time the creature was unable to leap away from the large appendage-tree that fired downwards, impaling it.

Paradox looked satisfied as he released the creature, allowing the large appendage-tree to lift it up into the air. The creature cried out, still not quite dead as I watched in amazement. The flesh of the appendage-tree moved on its own accorded. Stretching upwards past the scythe-like part it enveloped the creature, shutting out its last cries.

"That," Paradox said, "Is why we don't irritate my friend."

Continuing to watch with my mouth agape, Paradox simply nodded and began walking in the same direction we had been moving since the beach. Walking quickly to catch up to him, I whispered quietly as if the tree-like things could hear me.

"What's it doing to that thing?"

"Digesting it and providing nutrients to the surrounding area." Paradox responded swiftly as he kept his swift pace.

Gulping I digested the information then stated, "So it's like a Venus Flytrap, or a carnivorous plant?"

Paradox took a moment to think, then nodded and replied, "Yes and no."

Shaking my head I began to think that I wouldn't ever understand any of this, when I was struck with the words Paradox had said about the scythe-like tree being his friend.

"Um Paradox, that tree or whatever it was, is your friend?"

He glanced back slightly at me as he reached up and tightened his scarf.

"No." He answered while I let out a sigh of relief, thinking that I had indeed gone crazy, when he finished speaking, "That was just part of my friend."

My eyes grew wide as I caught the gasp in my mouth then replied, "Do you mean that this Planet is . . . . ?"

He nodded as he moved into a wide clearing.

"It will all make sense very soon."

Keeping my mouth shut I knew he would just lead me in circles until I learned what it was really all about by myself. I looked out over the clearing which was dotted with numerous holes. Some were larger than others, and these ones were different from the one the creature had emerged from. Walking over to the nearest one I put my hand over it, and then pulled it back quickly as I began to sweat.

Air was coming out of the hole, in a steady movement. It was hot, and the air had a slightly rancid smell.

Like Breath, I thought, the Planet is breathing.

"Don't fall in." Paradox whispered in my ear right behind me. This startled me almost causing me to fall in.

Laughing to himself, he walked over to one of the larger holes and looked all around. Glaring after him I moved away from the hole that ended in blackness before sitting down on a patch of clear ground.

Paradox continued moving around the area, going from hole to hole and peering in. Beginning to doze off, I heard him suddenly shout, "Speculatio Unus, it is I, Paradox!"

Now I thought he had lost his mind, somewhat, when the ground suddenly started trembling. Watching in amazement the clearing began to split in half. I noticed that while it split apart, the ground had just been a thin shell. Continuing to rumble some of the holes filled up with what looked like water. I knew I wasn't going to find out what it really was as I held onto where I was for dear life.

The ground shuddered a little more as the crack finished forming. Now the majority of the holes were filled with liquid. Standing up I felt the shudder change to a quivering then stop. Turning to Paradox I began running towards him. It was too late. He was on the other side of the now massive crag! Peering over the edge of the canyon all I could see was an endless depth of blackness. The ground was still moving slightly around the edges. Looking up just in time, I watched Paradox fold his arms like nothing was wrong.

"Para-" I began to shout when a massive gale of wind hit me in the face from the jagged line in the ground. It had almost enough force to rip my head off, and it sounded like a roar.

Jumping back my arms moved up instinctively to defend myself as the ground moved towards each-other to meet then fly back apart. This let loose another gush of wind that almost blew me off my feet, but this time there was something different.

"Paaaraaadooox," The Planet boomed out with gusts of wind, the bass of the sound making the air vibrate, **"Do you know how rude it is to wake someone from their sleep?"**

—— ∞ ——

Twilights Setting

"It's nice to see you again too." Paradox shouted with a mixture of joy and sarcasm.

"**It hasn't been too long.**" The planet roared out, "**Of course I live much, much longer than any of *your* kind.**"

"Please, you sound like an old man." Paradox retorted.

"**Bah, you never change. I guess that's a good thing.**" The Planet stated with a hint of satisfaction.

Watching on, I was too dumb-founded at what was happening to speak. This entire time I had been with Paradox I had been seeing strange incomprehensible things, but, nothing as strange as a planet speaking. Taking a step forward towards the moving "mouth" of the planet I quivered with excitement and adrenaline. As I took a step, one of the scythe-like trees erupted from the ground. It grabbed me quickly, but carefully, as it positioned me over one of the pools of liquid.

"**And who might this be, Paradox? Can I eat him, or is he valuable to you?**" Shuddering at the thought of being dropped down into an endless gorge to be devoured by a planet, I looked at Paradox who spoke up in reply.

"No, he's with me. He's had enough hard times already."

"**Hmph, I've never known you to be the caring type Paradox. Perhaps you have changed.**" The planet grumbled.

"He's my apprentice." Paradox answered almost immediately. "That's all."

I frowned a little at this, which was hard to do being positioned over a pool of liquid that looked like it was studying me.

"Very well, I won't eat him. Still, it would be nice for a proper introduction." The planet boomed out.

"Of course, being so polite and regal, after wanting to eat him . . . ," Paradox said bluntly. "You certainly don't change."

The pool of water seemed to flash at the last comment made.

The scythe-like appendage moved me over the open gorge as I began squirming and stuttering, "I-I-I'm Aaron." I managed to squeak out.

"Aaron, eh? Well, well, well, it's about time you speak, even if I can barely hear you. Yet unlike *some* ruffians I will allow Paradox to introduce me."

Paradox sighed as he waved his hand over the planet and calmly said, "Aaron, meet my friend, Speculatio Unus . . . the Observant One."

"N-nice to meet you Specu—what was it again?" I stammered out, my eyes continuing to watch the crevice below.

The crag in the ground slowly formed into a frown. It opened wider and the scythe-like tree loosened its hold on me. Beginning to slip I struggled to hold on. The blackness grew closer towards me. Looking over at Paradox I began shouting incoherent shouts of terror while He just shook his head.

"Don't tease him, Speculatio. You remember how much trouble I had with your name when *we* first met." Paradox spoke politely like nothing was wrong and I wasn't dangling over an open maw in the planet.

"Bah, if you insist. I just haven't had any fun in a long while, as you would know." The Planet bellowed out as it flicked me towards Paradox.

Bracing for impact, I opened my eyes only after I didn't hit the ground. The same feeling came over me that I always felt when embraced by the darkness that Paradox controlled. It held me gently in the air and brought me to his side. One of Paradox's arms lowered as he released his grasp on me.

"Thanks." I muttered, as I stood up slowly brushing myself off. Just an apprentice, I thought with a little vehemence.

Speculatio Unus trembled violently. Struggling to stay standing I heard a loud explosion in the distance. With a roar the watery liquid in a few holes drained away. After a few moments they returned and sparkled with what almost appeared to be fear.

"**Paradox, we are all in danger.**" The Planet spoke calmly and professionally now, as Paradox raised his head in question.

"What is it? What could be the cause of your distress Speculatio?" Paradox asked with a serious and caring tone.

"**It's the Twilight Soldiers.**" The Planet spoke out softly like he was trying to whisper, but still quite loud to us.

"What? Here? But how!" Paradox's voice boomed out this time, just as I was about to ask the same question.

"**I do not know. The only way that I know of, that they could travel here, is through you Paradox. Yet I highly doubt that you knowingly brought them here, much less that they co-operate with you.**" Speculatio Unus stated with a twinge of pain in his voice.

"Is something wrong?" I asked. The planet grumbled a little then shuddered slightly again.

"**They are drilling towards my core.**" He answered as one of the liquid eyes fell on Paradox. "**Whatever they are doing, it cannot be good.**"

Nodding Paradox turned towards the direction of the explosion saying, "I can't just stand by and watch. I'm going to stop them."

"I'm coming to!" I announced.

Paradox started thinking about this and was about to object, when the planet muttered through pain with a bit of humor in its voice, "**He is your apprentice, Paradox.**"

"What will he use as a weapon though?" Paradox countered as he looked at me.

"I'll use my fists if I have to!" I raged out, holding them up and clenching them.

"**You won't need to.**" The planet said calmly. "**I know what Paradox is hiding.**"

Paradox sighed as he reached into his coat and removed the pistol that Justin had given me. "Always the Observant One you are, Speculatio." He said under his breath.

"**I heard that.**" The Planet coughed out and making another shudder. "**Eventually, he won't need that.**"

Immediately I began to wonder what he meant by not needing the pistol. Perhaps it had something to do with being an apprentice. When

Paradox handed me the pistol he also found a few clips for it from deep within his coat. While I loaded the pistol he said, "We've got to hurry. If there is one thing I know, it's the Twilight Soldiers speed and efficiency at carrying out their objectives."

We began heading off at a jog in the direction of the explosion. I listened to the last thing that the Planet boomed out. **"Remember Paradox to beware of my immunity, I have no control over that."**

Swallowing hard I focused on the anger burning within me. The scythe-trees flew past us as we moved among them. Somehow we were moving faster then what normal jogging could achieve. Looking down I realized that the ground was propelling us forward, and the eyes on the limbs were following our movement.

The ground began rumbling again, this time more violently. We stopped a moment to get our footing, but failed as the ground still propelled us forward through the commotion. Moments passed while we moved onward with the ground helping us. Eventually we stopped behind a small mound. We could hear noise over the obstacle, and I strained to listen to it. There was the sound of machinery, and voices. Paradox crouched low as he motioned for me to follow him up the mound.

We climbed upwards and peeked over the edge. Paradox let out a sigh that wasn't one of relief, but one of disgust and disappointment. Before us sprawled outward what looked like a camp. A few tents pitched here and there around what looked like a hastily constructed tower that rose into the air. All around the area the scythe-trees laid strewn about the ground uprooted and cut down while a large mechanical vehicle with two automatic saws drove about, making quick work of more scythe-trees and underbrush around the area.

Men patrolled between the tents. Their masks and uniforms gleamed in the strange sunlight. They wore the same uniforms that the Soldiers had been wearing when they had invaded Paradox's home. One of the soldiers was operating another vehicle which had a larger drill that moved down a makeshift road away from the camp.

"Twilight Soldiers," Paradox grunted while we watched them move around the area. "How they got here is a good question, and what they are doing here is an even better one. It can't be good at all."

"Do you have any idea why they might be here?" I asked hopefully, watching the drill disappear over a ridge.

"None at all, but, that explains the grounds shuddering." Paradox turned and stated, nodding to the drills engine sound that began dying down due to the distance. "They've been digging, and inside a living organism no less. I'm sure it hurts. That raises the question of what they are drilling for."

"It's got to be something they want pretty badly to bring all this." I said, motioning to all the equipment, and watching a column of troops march to attention.

Paradox watched the soldiers for a moment as he said, "This is just part of Alpha force, and not even the main unit. Don't underestimate them though, these guys are sent to get whatever their job is, done quickly and quietly."

"Then what type of force was sent in to sabotage your home?" I asked thoughtfully while Paradox began climbing back down the mound.

"That was just a crack team. Sent for very small missions, and are expendable. It all contributes to their larger, twisted picture." Paradox commented on reaching the bottom of the slope. "Are you ready for this?" He asked.

I nodded back to him while checking the clip in my pistol and moving down silently towards him.

Creeping through the scarce brush towards the camp Paradox melded in wherever he went. He wasn't using any of his powers so this had to be coming from pure experience. Following his tracks I stayed as close to the trail provided by him as I could.

We reached the final line of scythe-trees that remained standing around the camp. Whispering I made a quick prayer of thanks because the large saw-vehicle was working on the other side of the camp. Making a quick sweep of the area Paradox headed for the nearest makeshift tent. Following quickly after him, I also looked and listened as someone's voice grew louder while traveling towards the tent.

It sounds like that voice is coming from the direction of those troops I'd watched, I thought, straining to listen.

I couldn't make out anything they were saying yet. The large saw-vehicle began working on another tree, its blades continuously roaring throughout the area and blocking out the words spoken. Leaning forward Paradox also tried to listen in, but then looked towards me and shook his head, signaling that he also couldn't understand anything.

Moving towards me he quietly spoke, "Wait here, I'm going to see if I can't stop that saw-machine, then we can mo-"

The ground started violently quaking, cutting off Paradox's sentence as he tried to maintain his footing. Another large explosion was heard off in the distance, but much closer then the first ones we'd heard while speaking to Speculatio.

The sound of the explosion began to die down when a high pitched squealing sound issued from the direction of the saw-blade machine. It rose to the point that I had to cover my ears. Paradox and I then watched the machine. One of the scythe-trees had entered combat with the machine, both of them interlocked in a deadly duel of gleaming blades.

The machine moved back a little and the scythe-tree swung at it, the razor sharp end of the tree missing by inches. The machine took a swing of its own, connecting with the trees metallic looking tip. Sparks flew through the air and the machine pressed closer, attempting to move towards the vulnerable part of the tree. As the machine closed in on it, the scythe-tree reared back and swung downwards once more toward the threat.

One of the saw-blades managed to move up in time to counter the blow, while the second blade began chewing into the base of the scythe-tree, a sickly colored yellow liquid began spurting from the wound. We heard laughs and cheers from among the tents from the soldiers that must have been watching the display. Those laughs and cheers quickly turned into angry shouts as a second scythe-tree near the first one swung down, smashing into the saw-machine and cracking through its armor.

The machine sputtered a few moments, and looked as if it was about to press on when the scythe-tree that was in the process of being cut reacted once more. In its dying state the tree raced down and cut into the machine. The sound of grinding gears rang out through the camp as the mechanical unit came to a grinding halt. This seemed to spark the other scythe-trees, and they showed no mercy beginning to tear into it farther. A squad of Twilight Soldiers rushed forward towards the machine, a few of them sporting heavy packs on their backs with multiple lights activating upon their backs.

The first of the soldiers got near the trees that had wrecked the machine, making sure to place themselves at a safe distance. The soldiers carrying the packs then approached. The last soldiers that carried a standard rifle stopped and glanced over the flashing lights on the packs. One by one they patted the pack carrying soldiers on the arm, and gave them a thumbs up.

Nodding at this signal the soldiers lifted their arms upwards. Two tubes moved outward from their shoulders, extending beyond their arms length. A second passed, and then a blinding white flash engulfed my vision. Covering my eyes with my arm I wasn't sure what I had just seen. My vision slowly came back to me, recovering from the flash.

Feeling like my eyes had readjusted I opened them. My mouth locked into a grim frown as I looked at the scene before me. The scythe-trees were now ablaze with a white fire. At least it looked like a white fire. The trees quickly began to melt. The skin on their base turning into goop, the metal tip itself eventually disintegrated with the rest of it.

"What are those packs they have?" I asked Paradox while I still watched in trepidation and awe.

"Plasma packs." He answered while studying the soldiers, "and those aren't even their full suits. Our job's a lot easier since they aren't fully combat ready."

"Of course, our job would be much easier if they didn't have those at all." I said with a bit of sarcasm.

"That's why you never underestimate the enemy. Always expect the worst." Paradox stated, then said, "There's four plasma troopers and four standard Twilight Soldiers. I can't hear anymore talking, so if we want to act, now is the time."

"Alright, I'm with you!" I said, readying my pistol which now seemed insignificant compared to what the enemy wielded.

"No, you wait here. Provide me with backup." Paradox commanded.

Standing up he began charging the enemy in broad daylight, or whatever daylight you could say this planet had.

"You're crazy!" I whispered to myself, and stood up ready to run after him. Catching what I felt was a stern look through his mask I dropped to the ground, and exhaled.

This is going to be interesting, I thought, as alarms and shouts began to blare throughout the camp.

Paradox charged towards the group of men as they turned towards him, their eyes behind their masks wide in surprise. The four plasma soldiers formed into a single line facing Paradox and knelt down on one knee. The other soldiers immediately patted them on the back and gave them a thumbs up, proceeded by drawing out their rifles and standing in another line behind the plasma carriers with their weapons pointed towards their aggressor.

Watching his oncoming rush the lead soldier judged his distance, while the other soldiers patiently waited for his command. He held his hand up to signal the rifle men to prepare to open fire, as sweat began to run down his face. He was thankful for the mask hiding it. He'd heard the stories about this man, this thing, called Paradox. Paradox was unstoppable for any force he'd yet faced.

"Your orders, sir?" One of his troops calmly asked.

He couldn't tell which one it was, his mind was too focused on the enemy in front of them to think clearly. He shook his head and narrowed his eyes as he thought, who am I kidding? This is just a man, and he hasn't tasted Alpha Forces power yet!

The lead soldier nodded. Paradox had gotten close enough to be an easy target with their rifles.

Grinning he let his combat training and experience take over, dropping his hand as he roared, "Rifle men open fire, fire at will!"

The rifles roared to life as the soldiers took aim and squeezed their triggers. Bright flashes emanated from the muzzles of their rifles as their brightly lit bullets flashed forward towards Paradox, who also grinned behind his mask as this started. Jumping into the air he began to spin around as some of the brightly lit bullets zipped past him by mere inches.

Time stretched on as Paradox continued spinning and darkness bloomed out from around him. Hundreds of bullets pierced into the darkness and emerged from the other side, making the soldiers unsure if they had hit their target. Still they kept firing on command, and would do so, until they were sure he was dead. The dark mass took off and began flying towards the soldiers as they continued firing, reloading their clips, and firing once again.

The lead soldiers eyes widened in terror at the large bulk of blackness that now rushed at them through the air and threatened to envelope them. He looked at his men who now seemed unsure of what to do as they continued firing at the approaching mass.

The squad leader thought, how can he be dodging all of the bullets. No man could do that, he's a monster!

Raising his hand once more he now prepared the plasma carriers to open fire. He hoped that this would finally stop Paradox in his advancement as the dark blackness moved upwards into the air looming directly over them.

"PC-Assault troops, fire, fire, FIRE!" the lead soldier started shouting in a panic as he threw down his arm.

The PC-Assault troops aimed upwards with their arms outstretched as they pressed downwards on the triggers. Each hand allowed the tubes on each shoulder to spray outwards.

Watching from the tent I was hiding behind I was in complete amazement. How Paradox had managed to dodge all those bullets and fly in the darkness he'd made, I'd have to ask him. Beginning to stand and shout out in triumphant support I caught plasma carriers issuing forth another blinding flash. Blinking a few times while the white cleared from my eyes, I looked at the burning white plasma churning out of the nozzles in a torrent against Paradox's darkness.

The two forces struggled with each other. The burning white pressed firmly against the blackness that fought against it. Somewhere in my gut I felt like Paradox was losing now, the feeling confirmed when the brilliant white flames began to press the darkness back and enter into it.

I have to do something, I thought, as I carefully took aim with my pistol.

It was a very long shot, but if I could even injure just one of those men, or perhaps draw their attention. It didn't matter. Whether I liked it or not I had to take action. Letting out what sounded like a strangled battle cry I pulled the trigger. I aimed at one of the riflemen and hoped that it would hit him and draw them to me, even if for a split second.

The bullet issued forth from the pistol, its kick feeling familiar in my hands from when I had used it alongside Justin. The round burned brilliantly and flew in the right direction I had aimed it, crossing the distance quickly and striking something metallic that now spurted out white flame everywhere.

Crap, crap, crap, I thought as my eyes registered what I had hit, it was one of the plasma tanks!

Pretty sure about what was going to happen now. I closed my eyes and ducked behind the tent.

The lead soldier roared in victory as he watched the white plasma flames begin inching their way into the black cloud above them. Patting one of his riflemen on the back he turned in time to watch one of the plasma tanks suddenly rupture. White plasma spewed out of its back and enveloped one of his men behind it. The soldier didn't even have time to yell before his skin was seared from his bones, and then turned to powder.

The plasma tank quickly cracked around the sides, causing more plasma vents to open up on it and spew out their deadly contents. The lead soldier knew that he didn't have enough time to warn his men, much less think. The plasma tank formed one last crack before the world turned white. The last thought the lead soldier had wasn't whether or not the blast had destroyed Paradox, but was of his blocked memory that now shattered open of his wife and children that he was forced to leave.

Hearing the large explosion and seeing through my closed eyelids a white flash I knew the tank had exploded. After a moment I raised my head and looked to where the battle had been taking place. The entire area was engulfed in a white aura, which had enveloped Paradox's black shield too. Shivering inside I thought of the people I had just killed, perhaps even Paradox himself!

Slowly the white aura dissipated and I stood, jogging towards it not knowing what to hope for. I could see that there was nothing left of the soldiers that had been there, and the ground was so hot that I could feel it through my shoes. Drawing closer I realized that a small condensed spot of darkness still hung in the air dissipating. Paradox hung in the air for a moment before falling roughly to the ground on his stomach.

"Paradox!" I shouted as I ran towards him.

Laying on his stomach a moment, he then rolled over onto his back saying, "It's hot, what did you do?"

"I-I killed them." I said as the words rolled off my tongue.

"Don't worry about it. You had to do, what you had to do." Paradox said as he sighed. "You see. I try to not kill them. Some of these people joined the Twilight Soldiers voluntarily, while others were forced to join. The ones that were forced to join either had the majority of their memory wiped, or blocked."

"So I could have killed someone that was actually innocent." I muttered and sat down on the ground, which was cooling down rapidly.

"I said don't worry about it, it's not your fault." Paradox said as he sat up and began coughing heavily into a closed fist.

"Are you alright?" I asked, as he slowly stopped coughing.

"Yeah, just not what I used to be." He said, and pointed towards the camp. "Anyhow, we have more to worry about with our current situation."

Turning I tried to not look surprised when I saw about one hundred soldiers with their weapons all poised at us. Great, I thought, this wouldn't have happened if Paradox had been stealthier about his approach.

Seeming to pick up what I was thinking he looked at me with a slight shrug of his shoulders.

"At ease men!" One of the soldiers said then moved forward and stopped while all the other soldiers lowered their weapons. His uniform was decorated differently from the rest, much like the one I'd seen from my dream but not as grand. He had bright red trim displayed about the grey uniform. He was larger and spoke loudly with authority.

It must have been the soldier that was speaking to the rest of the troops before the trees had attacked the machine. But there hadn't been this many troops when we had first scouted out the camp. They must have come from inside the tents and tower that lay behind them.

"Paradox," The larger soldier proclaimed, "as third in command of the Alpha Force regiment of the Twilight Core Branch, and in absence of the Commander, I have been ordered to exterminate you on sight. As for those who accompany you, they will either be integrated into our ranks, or also exterminated."

"Any ideas?" I whispered to Paradox as the soldier stepped back into the ranks and gave the order for his men to take aim.

"None," Paradox said almost jokingly as the command was given to prepare to fire, "and I'm just about too tired to stand."

"Fire!" The soldier commanded. As the rifles issued forth their deadly munitions, the ground suddenly drew itself upwards creating a shield between the soldiers and us. Stumbling backwards as the ground lurched again, it tossed Paradox and I away from each other.

Landing on my back I quivered as the giant mound that had risen up split open, revealing a jagged opening full of needle-point teeth. It lurched forward and fell upon the soldiers that were now firing upon it, consuming a good chunk of them while the others scrambled in different directions. The large opening that now seemed to be a mobile mouth let out a massive roar. Pieces of tattered bloody uniforms hung from the opening of it. Shifting, the massive maw lurched forward again.

Most of the soldiers had now given up on fighting the new monstrosity before them and were scrambling past their tents into the forest of scythe-trees. The trees began springing to life, swinging downwards, not sparing any that got near them. The gigantic mouth surged ahead towards the makeshift tower where a few soldiers had retreated, consuming everything that got in its way.

Just as the mouth was about to fall upon the tower it stopped. A few holes appeared on the sides of the mound as it waited next to the tower that stood before it. Managing to stand, I was terrified and fascinated at the creature that fought on our side.

It must be Speculatio Unus . . . but why didn't he help before? I thought.

Looking in the distance I watched Paradox standing and brushing himself off, when I felt something pressed to the back of my head.

"Don't move." I heard a voice say that was covered in static. It was obviously one of the soldiers.

Dropping my pistol and holding my hands up the soldier moved me forward towards Paradox. The soldier made sure that Paradox could see that I had a gun pointed to my head. Holding his hands up slowly Paradox waited, as the soldier began to breathe heavily and shake. I could tell he was scared, I guess I would be too if I had to face someone like Paradox.

"You, Paradox . . . or whatever your name is! You tell that thing over there to stop attacking the other soldiers or I'll blow this kids head off!" The soldier shouted angrily, the gun rattling in his hand as he pressed the muzzle of his pistol closer to my head.

"You think it'll listen to me?" Paradox said, nodding towards the large mound that was still sitting quietly by the tower.

The soldier looked from Paradox to the giant mound and shuddered as he stated, "It appeared to protect you, now tell it!"

"Speculatio . . ." Paradox sighed, as he turned towards the mound, "Please stop, I can't lose my apprentice."

The mound made a guttural sound as it disappeared back into the rest of the planet. The mouth closed and looked as if it had never been there. The soldier was only somewhat satisfied as he trembled in place. His hand quavered as he tried to think about what to do next. Paradox turned slowly back towards him as the soldier pressed the guns muzzle as hard as he could against my temple.

"Don't move!" He yelled through his masks communicator, watching Paradox, "I won't hesitate to kill him!"

Just standing there, Paradox would wait to see what the soldier would do next. Calculating he noticed the man pull back the pistols hammer. The soldier grinned at Paradox, a look of pure insanity on his face as he laughed, while his finger slowly began pulling the trigger. Closing my eyes shut, I knew that any moment my end would come. All I could do was wait for it.

It didn't come. I felt the soldiers hand loosen its grip as a gunshot was heard from far away. He was dead before he had heard the shot. Scrambling away from my would-be killer, I turned to look at him. He still stood there, a look of surprise now on his face as blood could be seen through his mask dribbling downwards from his forehead. His eyes began to also bleed slowly as the soldier tried to make half an attempt to turn around but instead fell over, now dead from whatever had struck him.

"Are you alright?" Paradox asked while running up to me.

"Yeah, but what happened to him?" I asked, still looking at the figure lying on the ground.

Paradox turned the soldier over, examining the back of the head. It looked like something had punctured into the back of his helmet, and now a strange liquid was pouring out of it.

"I don't know what did this, but I'm sure you heard that gunshot. It was definitely a projectile, but one I've never seen before."

"So whoever shot him was aiming for him and not me . . . right?" I asked as I gazed around the surrounding hills that were covered by scythe-trees.

"It appears so. Otherwise you probably wouldn't be standing right now." Paradox said as he too examined the surrounding area, then turned towards the tower.

The tower still loomed above what was left of the camp as the door to it opened. The Twilight Soldiers that had taken refuge there began to pour out of it, their weapons ready. The tower itself coming alive, as parts of it slid around and large turrets appeared. The turrets turned slowly in our direction, the barrels glowing bright neon green inside. The soldiers took up defensive positions right around the towers base to try and repel any advancement on the tower.

"Watch out!" Paradox shouted as he grabbed me and forced a bubble of darkness to appear right as a thunderous blast flew from one of the turrets towards us.

I didn't have time to react as Paradox teleported us. We appeared a little ways off from where the large glowing projectile had struck. Whatever had been fired left a sizable crater where we had just been standing. Coughing forcibly as the darkness around us dispersed, Paradox looked up. The turrets started turning our way once more.

This didn't seem right, every time Paradox used his powers heavily he'd have a large coughing fit, I thought.

Continuing to cough he fell onto his hands and knees, noticing the turret was almost in position and motioning for me to run. Looking upwards I didn't know what to do. I didn't want to just leave him there to die. The turrets finished taking aim, and the inside of their barrels started to glow once more. I could feel their power charging, and I turned to run when the ground started to rumble again.

Losing my footing I fell to the ground, wondering why it had to end like this. Why of all things a slight tremor would be our undoing. Turning to stare death in the face, I was surprised to see that it wasn't staring back. The tower slightly tilted, the ground erupting upwards from under it and enveloping the entire thing. I watched as the last of the turrets disappeared under the rush of teeth and power that trumped its own, and fell back almost laughing with relief.

"I apologize for being late again." I heard the planet, or rather Speculatio Unus rumble, **"But I cannot create eyes anywhere I please."**

"About that," I heard Paradox gasp out, "How exactly did you see us?"

"I had someone else be my eyes." Speculatio Unus stated, sounding rather pleased with himself, **"Of course, that was after I had interrogated and threatened to eat him. It took awhile for him to convince me he would help you."**

"He who?" I asked and watched the mound contort itself into what I would guess was a smile.

"That would be me, Aaron," Pronounced a voice that I recognized immediately, "Like I said, no hard feelings right?"

Turning towards the voice that I knew could only belong to one person, one that owed me a little explanation, I saw Justin standing there on a small mound. A big grin under his piercing blue eyes adorned his face, and his uniform was badly damaged. A large pack was on his back, and in one of his hands rested a very long, sleek silver looking weapon with the barrel resting on his shoulder.

"Justin! You're alive!" I shouted and ran towards him as we grabbed each-others hands in a friendly welcoming handshake.

"The question is . . ." I heard Paradox say quietly behind me, "Is how you are alive, and how did you get here?"

"AND," I added with a lot of emphasis, "What do you mean by no hard feelings?"

Justin laughed a little at my question, "As for your question, Aaron, I'm the one that rifle butted you in the head. I realize now that it wasn't right and that I was following orders from a lunatic!"

Paradox snorted at this and stated, "The Twilight Soldiers leader may be a lunatic, but a very smart one at that."

"Well," I said, pretending to think it over, "apology accepted. No hard feelings."

"As for your questions Paradox, "Justin stated a little more seriously, "That will take a bit to explain, you see I-"

"Pardon me for interrupting," Speculatio boomed outwards, **"but we have a very big problem, Paradox."**

Justin went silent immediately, as Paradox asked, "What is it, Unus?"

"While I was attacking the soldiers and approached the tower they had constructed I caught them communicating. I was able to listen in on the communications and discern what they are here for. It appears the remaining Twilight Soldiers are heading for my heart. I can feel them drawing close, and more importantly the item that my heart contains." Speculatio spoke softly, his tone serious and of the utmost importance.

"You don't mean?" Paradox said, not finishing the question and leaving Justin and I in the dark.

"Yes, I'm afraid so." Speculatio solemnly said.

Justin and I looked at each-other in confusion as Paradox grew very silent. He stood there, looking at the ground while we didn't say anything, not wanting to interrupt whatever he was doing or thinking. Finally Paradox's back straightened and turned to us. I could feel his cold gaze wash over us as he looked upon us.

"We have no choice, "Paradox said. "We have to go stop them, now. You can explain things that happened on your end on the way. Justin? Wasn't that your name? Let's go."

Justin nodded and adjusted the rifle on his shoulder, "I'm with you, and perhaps when I explain things it will clear up some holes."

Paradox just nodded as he walked away towards the road that the drill machine had driven down. Starting to walk after him I stopped momentarily and headed over to where my pistol had dropped to the ground. Grabbing it I frowned, feeling as if something very bad was going to happen in the short future.

Into the Heart

*A*fter catching up with Paradox and Justin I pressed the bad feeling out of the way. I had the same questions that Paradox did for Justin. I had some for Paradox as well. Taking the lead, Paradox walked a little ways in front of Justin who was quietly moving along with his head hung downwards. Walking slightly behind Justin I wondered what he was thinking about.

"So Justin," I said, watching him carefully and being cautious about what I said to him while he was deep in thought. "You were one of those Twilight Soldiers? Paradox mentioned that you were one, back when he got me out of the communications room during the fight with that creature."

Stirring a little Justin looked towards me. His eyes were questioning, and I couldn't hold for gaze for long before looking away. Staring at the road that stretched into the distance, it wound up and over another hill then disappeared from view. Turning back to watch Justin out of the corner of my eye, he slowly smiled and stated, "So that's how you got out of there."

"Paradox teleported me out, then I sent him back after you when I realized he hadn't brought you with us. After returning for you he came back and said you were gone." I said a little defensively, not wanting him to think that I'd left him to die.

Justin nodded showing that he understood, "I was gone. It's going to be kind of strange to explain, but it will help both of you understand."

"So begin explaining." Paradox said coldly, continuing to march on in front of us without turning around.

"Let me think about where to start." Justin said thoughtfully. He didn't seem to notice the cold tone in Paradox's voice.

"While you think about that, I want to ask you something Paradox." I said, moving a little faster to walk next to him.

Shrugging at what I said, Paradox kept on walking. I couldn't tell if he didn't care, or if he did mind my questions. He was certainly being grouchy. Glancing at Justin, it looked like he was also waiting for my question. Turning back to Paradox I realized it was because of Justin that he was acting so different, probably because he was a Twilight Soldier.

"When you were fighting with that squad of soldiers, it looked like you could fly." I said while thinking of the black moving mass that had went through the air above the soldiers. "I know you can teleport wherever darkness connects and touches, but can you fly too?"

Shaking his head no, Paradox made another small cough. Finally looking at me after he'd finished coughing he said, "It wasn't flying." Holding up one hand he opened it. A small sphere of darkness appeared within his palm and rested around his fingers.

"You see," He spoke softly, and moved his hand around with the darkness following it. "I wasn't exactly flying. I was teleporting at such extreme speeds that it only appeared that I was flying. Whenever I teleport to the edge of the darkness I generate, it will follow me. This way I can stay in the air because I can teleport fast enough to stay suspended in one place."

Nodding I wondered why I hadn't thought of that, and for a split second thought about asking him about the coughing attack he had experienced before it was pressed out of my mind. It was interesting, his power. I could imagine during the night he would be unstoppable, but during the day he was much more vulnerable, but still no pushover. If you had to fight him on his turf, then the chances are you wouldn't even know what had hit you. Grinning, I thought of all the stuff I still needed to learn as his "apprentice".

"Is that the only question you had?" Paradox asked, watching me a moment more.

"Yeah that's all." I said, imagining what it would be like to have powers like him.

"Alright. Then it's time for him to explain things." Paradox demanded.

It grew very quiet as we approached the hill that the road went up. Curious myself as to how Justin had escaped that nightmare, I waited for him to begin explaining while I looked at the scythe-trees. It looked like they were all trembling in place. I was about to speak up and point this out to the others when Paradox explained why they were trembling.

"They are all agitated. I wouldn't go near them even though Speculatio and I are good friends. It must be due to the fact that the Twilight Soldiers have been operating nearby. Imagine how you would react if a small needle dug into your skin." Paradox spoke almost like an educational video.

Looking over at Justin who was frowning and looked like he was waiting for us to finish, I nodded. Holding one hand up, Paradox showed us that he was done speaking, and then motioned for him to begin when he was ready. Opening his mouth he was about to start explaining when my stomach let out a large growl. Grabbing it I realized how hungry I was. It had been a long time since I'd eaten.

Laughing a bit, Justin was about to start once more when Paradox interrupted and said, "Let's rest here a moment. Perhaps I could find something to eat and-" He stopped speaking. My mind conjured up all the sick and exotic things on this planet.

What would he eat here? I thought.

Although clearly exasperated at being cut off so many times, Justin managed to grin as he took off his pack and began to rummage through it.

"Never mind looking for food, I have some right here in my pack." Justin said as he brought out what looked like a couple of military styled M.R.E.'s. As much as I wanted normal food, this was as close as I was going to get. Making a polite thank you to Justin as he handed me one, Paradox waved the one offered to him away while judging the rest of the distance up the hill.

"Don't you have to eat?" I asked, realizing I hadn't seen Paradox eat or drink once since I'd met him.

"Not anymore." He replied rather flatly.

With no intention of probing any farther than that, I opened my M.R.E. It was supposed to be spaghetti. Slowly tasting it, I decided that it wasn't too bad and ate quietly. It was nice enjoying the time I had, able to sit down and relax without having to worry about much else for the moment. Sitting back down Justin closed his pack back up before looking at the surrounding area.

"So you want to know how I survived." He said, his eyes looking at something away in the distance. "Well, where to truly start at. The Twilight Core Branch is just part of a much larger organization. I was one of the many who joined this conglomerate voluntarily."

Scratching his head he continued, "I'm sure you know a lot about this conglomerate Paradox, perhaps more then I."

Standing there a moment more, Paradox watched the edges of the road that met with the fleshy ground, "In all truth, I don't know much about them. The most I know is of the Twilight Core Branch. I also still believe that what I know of the Core is very little. Some of their troop types, their equipment, combat styles. That's it. They are very good at keeping things secret."

"Then I'll explain what I can." Justin almost whispered. "The Twilight Core is the military branch of this conglomerate. They have other branches. Business, science and technology, research and development, production and manufacturing, you name it they've got it. No one really knows who brought all of these together and formed the corporations under one flag, but just for the fact they were able to suggest they are pretty powerful." Pausing for a moment he kicked a small piece of dirt away, and watched as one of the scythe-trees struck out at something unseen.

Waiting for him to continue, Paradox didn't move a muscle as he stood like a statue, towering over Justin who sat there explaining everything. Having some questions of my own arise I held them in check because I didn't want to interrupt, and I believed that Paradox wouldn't like it if I interrupted either.

"I don't know much about the other branches, but I was a part of Alpha Force. The Twilight Core is set into forces, from Alpha to Omega. All deal in combat, but each force also deals in something a little more specialized. For example, Alpha Force is usually sent in to do quick jobs. I know that Omega Force is the elite combatants, those who are better at fighting than anyone else. As for the others forces? Who knows? They only tell you about the force you are placed in, and I've only learned about the Omega Force because of their brutality and the way they treat everyone else." Justin said sighing.

Listening to this, the wind picked up slightly. It blew quietly around while I thought about everything he was saying.

It'd looked like that group of Alpha Squadron soldiers would have beaten Paradox. So if they aren't even the hardcore combatants then Omega Force must be—The thought of it made me shudder.

"From the first time you are introduced into your Force, they feed you information which I now know is misleading. Like you, Paradox. They showed a lot of things about you, but they made you look like you were a villain. Totally corrupt, while they made our fellow soldiers look like heroes. We would be sent in to rescue people every once and awhile, which would spread rumors about our reputation and us being good. This was all according to plan. Not that it matters much. Most people don't even know we exist." Justin stopped and looked like he was searching for something then said, "In fact that's about all I know, besides the harsh training and bad food."

Smiling at this I felt Paradox stiffen. He obviously wasn't in a humorous mood, and didn't like that Justin and I were. Snapping my mouth shut I tried to make a straight face while waiting for Justin to continue on about how he'd escaped. With a clap of his hands Paradox started moving up the hill as Justin and I fell in place behind him.

"So during the fight with that creature," Justin began now, starting where I'd been taken by Paradox, away from the nightmare. "I just about lost all hope. It wasn't giving in, and when I'd turned around to see where you'd gone you had just disappeared. The creature began tearing the rest of the door away," Justin said quivering throughout his body. "I'll never forget those eyes that were staring at me."

"Right when hope seemed lost, one of my new proto-type instruments picked something up." Justin stated, reaching to his side and removing a very small device about half the size of a grown mans fist. "This device Paradox, allows us to trace your power signature as long as you were nearby and teleported. Once you do that, we are able to teleport wherever you have, although it's a one way ticket."

Paradox had stopped walking, and was now studying the device as he muttered looking over it. The device looked like a metallic cylinder, with a couple buttons on the side and a light on top. After a moment he looked at Justin saying, "If it's a one way trip then how are the rest of the Alpha Force members going to get back to Earth?"

"That's the thing." Justin said as he placed the device back onto his belt. "This device sends the recorded signature of you back to home base, where they have a much larger version of these. Once the recording is saved they can open a portal to anywhere you have been, and allow people to come and go through that portal."

"So that's how they got here." Paradox said sounding very saddened. "I'm the one that led them here, and may be even the cause of my friend's death."

"No." I said, placing a hand on Paradox's shoulder. "We can still stop them!"

"He's right, Paradox." Justin said, supporting my support with some enthusiasm. "We can both back you up. You aren't alone!"

Saying this Justin patted the sleek silver rifle resting on his shoulder. It seemed to shimmer a moment then stopped, returning to look like plain old silver. A strange weapon that even Paradox was interested in it during the time that it had shimmered.

"What weapon is that?" Paradox asked Justin. He was holding it in both hands for a better look at it.

"This is one of the Twilight Cores Proto-Weapons. I don't know much about it yet, but it was designed to combat creatures from the alternate realm." Justin patted it and placed it back on his shoulder. "It doesn't have anywhere to place ammo, and shimmers every once and awhile. It's also as useful against other living things as it is against those creatures."

"Interesting weapon, one I've never seen before." Paradox turned and began jogging up the rest of the hill, "So when you say alternate realm you mean the realm of darkness, correct?"

"Yeah," Justin said sounding pleased with himself. "Managed to take it from the armory without anyone noticing, I just had to bypass the security using one of the egghead's identification. Otherwise it would have been near impossible to get, even for a high ranking officer. I thought I would take a little 'retirement pay' for serving the Twilight Core those few years."

Actually letting out a small laugh at this, Paradox fell quiet again as we neared the top of the hill. Realizing that it had been Justin who had saved me from being shot in the head, I thanked him silently even though he hadn't mentioned it. When we reached the top we all halted, a little amazed at what we were seeing. Before us was a gigantic hole with one small metallic walkway extending towards the middle of it. Looking down the side of the hole I peered inside. It was pretty dark, except for lights that had been planted on the sides of it.

Noticing teeth all along the sides of the hole, I wondered if this was one of the mouths that Speculatio Unus had made.

If so, then why didn't he close it? I thought, looking around the area.

The fleshy ground was a different color from the usual brownish-red that had covered the land. Now it looked like it was a pale grey. Stepping on a piece of it, it crumbled away turning into a powder.

"The area is dead, or dying around here." Paradox said as he too examined what was happening. "They must have chosen this mouth to start heading downwards. After all, why dig longer when you can move down fairly deep from one point."

"But why didn't Speculatio close it up before this area died?" I asked.

Paradox reached up and scratched the back of his scarf. "Perhaps he didn't even know they were there before it was too late. It could be like bacteria in your mouth, or a cavity."

Nodding I walked out towards the small metallic walkway. Slowly I stepped on it, unsure of how strong it. It held my weight, Paradox following after me, and then Justin. Once we reached the end of the walkway I looked downward into the deep mouth, the small lights dotting the way into the abyss. Reaching over, Paradox tapped on a control panel that didn't respond. Waiting a moment we were about to pull back, when something slowly began rising upwards from the mouth next to the platform.

Noticing two people standing on what now appeared to be some sort of elevator platform that rose upwards. I figured that the two men were Twilight Soldiers. They didn't look up, and were instead looking at each other. As they ascended upwards on the elevator platform I could hear one of them speaking through static. Listening in as they rose closer I leaned forward, Paradox and Justin doing the same.

"-creeps me out. That's all I'm saying." One of the soldiers said causing the other one to snort.

"What, are you afraid?" The other one replied after he had finished snorting.

"Man, don't pull that one. Just think about it! We are working inside a living organism, who knows what could happen? And after we lost contact with the surface outpost . . . ." The first speaker said as they neared the top of the mouth.

"You know how faulty that shacks radio is up top. It's probably nothing but a little glitch, and when we get up there you'll—hey!" He shouted as they finished rising out of the mouth and saw us.

He raised his weapon, but was far too slow. Justin swung his own weapon outwards and managed to make a full on blow with his opponents. The rifle flew from the soldiers hand and fell downwards into the mouth as the first soldier raised his rifle while going for his radio. Before he could speak, much less do anything else, he was knocked out cold by a second blow to the head by Justin's rifle.

Applauding this, Paradox held his hand up creating a sphere of darkness around the two men. The one that was conscious began to scream inside the dark cocoon of energy, and soon his screaming abruptly ended. As the energy dissipated there was nothing left of them. Turning towards Paradox questioningly, I watched him step onto the elevator platform.

"They're alive." Paradox said as I got on alongside him. "They are someplace where it will be determined whether they have any blocked or wiped memories. If they don't, then they will be dealt with accordingly by the law."

"How can you prove to the law if they are evil?" I asked.

"You can't always. You just have to hope for the best."

Knowing what he meant, I made some more room for Justin, but made sure that I was nowhere near the edge of the platform. Reaching out Paradox pressed something on the control console to head downwards, but nothing happened. Frowning, Justin reached forward where he placed his thumb on the down button and the lift began moving.

"Well, I guess I'm not officially a traitor yet." Justin smirked, nodding to his thumbprint that had shown up on the down key.

The wide open mouth slowly began to close inwards as we moved farther down, the area ending in a small cylinder shape that barely let the lift through. Crammed together we watched as the teeth got smaller all the way to the point of disappearing.

This must be a throat, I thought while looking at the velvety reddish and orange that padded the walls on all sides.

The cylinder eventually opened up into an area that didn't head downwards, instead it moved straight ahead as the lift touched down with a soft squishing noise. It was very humid down here, and the only light that showed were the multiple lights lining the moist walls which led deeper into the living planet. Stepping off the lift I scrunched up my face in disgust, feeling my foot sink a little into the warm tissue that lined the area.

Paradox and Justin didn't seem to mind this as they began walking down the tunnel, aside from being a bit more cautious now. It felt oppressive, and none of us dared to speak while we pressed onwards. The difference from being on the surface was quite a switch. Now I knew why that one soldier had been scared. It was like you were being watched. You were an invader and weren't supposed to be there.

Noticing small holes about the size of basketballs all over the walls, roof, and even floor, I approached one. They looked like little tunnels that led off somewhere else, but were far too small for any of us to fit through. We continued on as I watched for the holes in the ground, knowing it would be an unpleasant surprise to have a leg fall into one.

The tissue moved ever so slightly with our presence as we began moving around a bend in the tunnel. It made me feel sick, and Justin was a little more cautious because of this. The walls even caused Paradox to be wary, and I doubted that he had been here before.

The most he probably knows about this place is through what he's been told about. Even then, that would be like me explaining the inside of my body to someone, I thought as we continued on. Then came the voices ahead of us.

It wasn't loud at first, but the noise rose in volume the closer we continued forward. Obviously there was a lot of shouting going on, and most of the noise sounded like commands being given. Whoever it was apparently didn't care about the place they were in, and the quiet demand it pressed on you for silence. The person was barking orders loudly all the same, the radioed voice now booming throughout the tunnel.

Venturing to speak quietly as we crept closer around the bend in the tunnel, more lights appeared up ahead. We had to be getting very close to the person shouting.

"Justin, is that the commanding officer of Alpha Force?" I whispered while wondering who had the guts, or stupidity, to be making noise like that in a place like this.

"I have no idea, to tell you the truth. I never met them . . . not even once. He only called whoever he trusted for assignments, or if you did something very prestigious, whether good or bad." Justin whispered back.

Stopping and taking off his pack, Justin set it down. Taking the sleek rifle and positioning it for combat, he took aim. Its sleek barrel was too long for that of a normal rifle, and would be more at home on that of a sniper rifle.

Noticing me eyeing the rifle, Justin looked like he was thinking the same thing. The next event caused us both to gasp in surprise. Turning around to see what had startled us Paradox leaned forward in interest to see what was happening.

The sleek silver had begun to shimmer brilliantly, and was now reforming itself into a different style. Becoming shorter and thicker, the long barrel split into two pieces. The pieces formed half cylinders with the flat sides pointing towards each other. This resulted in two barrels which provided dual firepower from a single weapon.

All three of us watching it change had different reactions. I was confused because I didn't know what the hell was going on. Justin seemed almost afraid of the weapon that he was holding. Paradox just seemed interested on how it was changing shape. Its single trigger slid into the glimmering silver and was replaced by a larger one in the same area. Between the two barrels a large opening had appeared, and a much larger barrel moved outwards. To finish off the new look, a handgrip appeared underneath the massive barrel which could slide back from its position much like a shotgun.

After this last change the shining weapon returned to its usual normal silver. His hands shaking, Justin fell to his knees looking rather tired. Still confused I examined the object. It had to be the same weapon, but it was different. It didn't have the same shape it used to. Out of all of us Paradox just kept looking in its direction. After taking his time he then made a simple statement, "I'd like to get that weapon to my lab." He said.

"It sapped my energy." Justin gasped out, taking deep breaths like he'd just run a marathon. "I could feel it . . . absorb my energy."

"Interesting, very interesting . . . ." Paradox muttered to himself more than anyone. "Could it be that it used your energy to transform itself? Hmm, an interesting question that I think you cannot answer. It will have to wait. Are you still able to fight?"

Taking a few more breaths Justin nodded as he stood up, holding the transformed weapon in his hands. Confusion had finally turned into amazement. My brain was spinning in circles like a laundry machine on spin cycle. The images of it transforming replaying in my head, and I felt like it wasn't quite right. There was something more to it.

Shaking my head to clear my thoughts, I knew this wasn't the time to be thinking about the weapon Justin had. The shouts had grown closer and I tensed, wondering if they had heard anything. It didn't seem like it. Perhaps the people had just moved in our direction for something, and now I was able to make out what was being said.

"You know what our mission is, and you know where our priorities lay." A radioed voice shouted with harshness brimming through the static. "You will follow my orders, and it's to acquire whatever object we were sent to get. The objective is located at these coordinates, which are the right coordinates, and we're almost there."

"But sir," Another voice said mildly, afraid to stand up to whoever was speaking, "What about the lost radio connection to the surface base? We also don't want the drill to damage the object, right?"

"I don't care if we lost contact with the main headquarters itself. If I have to I'll make you all form a human ladder back to Earth, for all I care! I also don't care if the drill damages the object. We don't even know what the object is! We have orders to drill straight towards it, and if you don't start drilling there are going to be consequences that aren't on my head." The harsh voice roared back, it sounded like he was about to rip out whoever's throat had just spoke to him. "So start drilling!"

"Yes sir!" The other person said quickly and professionally.

"Idiots, all of them are." The harsh voice crackled out moving away from us, not seeming to care if he said that whether he was in earshot of others or not.

We looked at each other, waiting to see if there was going to be anything else said when we heard the heavy drill machinery fire up. It drowned out any other noise in the tunnel, and I wondered how they had managed to fit that large vehicle down into the small throats tunnel in the first place. Maybe it had swollen up after they had gotten the large machinery through, I thought.

The ground began rumbling as the drill connected with the wall in front of it. We could feel the tissue jerk itself around in pain from the tearing caused by the gigantic machine. Paradox nodded to Justin and then to me, as we started moving around the twisting tunnel. Finally the bend ended. Peeking around it the three of us scouted out the enemies forces.

There appeared to be two squads of soldiers. One of the squads carried all sorts of mining equipment. The other squad consisted of what appeared to be six standard soldiers and two plasma carriers. These plasma troopers looked like the ones that had fought against Paradox. According to him they weren't fully combat ready. Lucky for us, I thought. I couldn't tell which one was the commander, or if he was even present in the group.

Most of the soldiers sat behind the drill as it chewed its way through the tissue. We could see pieces ripped off of the wall, and a strange greenish substance oozing outwards from the cavity. I guessed that was the planets blood. The drill didn't slow down at all. It began to speed up as the tissue recoiled from the onslaught. Breaking through the walls tissue, the drill went flying forwards into the newly opened hole which led into a cavernous room.

The soldiers with mining equipment all stood up and headed forwards, filing into the new opening as the others with weapons held back and faced away from the opening to guard the entrance.

All of them look relaxed, that's a good thing. Not one of them thinks anyone is here but them, I thought. The plasma carriers shifted their packs, and each one walked to opposite ends of the tunnel.

Looking around a moment, the riflemen seemed to get bored. One of the troops looked like he was talking as they all sat down in a circle and the speaker produced a deck of cards from one of his pockets. We heard the others cheer. One of the men even patted him on the back as he pulled the cards out and shuffled them before dealing.

"This is too easy." I whispered to Justin as he shook his head no.

"It's not too easy. Just think about it. If you were in their position and you thought you were all alone here, and away from the big boss, what would you do?" Justin quietly said then muttered, "They always cheated though."

"You must continue to never underestimate your enemy." Paradox breathed out as he watched them.

"He's right. We've also yet to see the commander." Justin spoke softly, as he readied the weapon he held in his hands.

"You mean none of those were the commander?" I muffled while glancing at each of the men.

"No. You'll know 'em when you see 'em, that's what everyone's always said and been told." Justin whispered, "They are chosen to lead the forces because of their combat abilities. I've heard that once in that position they get special goodies provided by the eggheads."

Nodding at this Paradox said, "I've never seen one myself, but I've heard the rumors too. Justin, you take care of these guys. I need to save my energy for the leader."

Justin looked as if he wanted to debate with Paradox's demand. He didn't have any powers. The only thing he had was a strange energy draining, shape shifting weapon. Grimacing, he looked at it. He wasn't even sure if its original form was the one it had been previously. Taking another look at the soldiers then looking back to Paradox, he frowned.

"You want me to kill them?" Justin asked quietly, while Paradox tilted his head to one side.

"Unfortunately . . . yes." Paradox answered in reply, "If I fight them all, I'll be too drained to combat the leader. Especially after the battle with the troops that were topside."

Justin's shoulders sagged slightly at this, signaling his defeat. Standing up he made no noise as he moved around the cover into the soldiers view. At first none of the soldiers noticed, because all of them had congregated on a card game which they were now focused on. Justin raised his weapon as some of the soldiers finally took notice his presence. Jumping up from their game of cards they made excited and surprised gargles of radio spatter.

Closing his eyes only for a split second Justin heard his name called out by one of the soldiers, and opening them when he heard the uncertain priming of weapons. He probably knew most of the guys in front of him, but only in name. He also knew that once they figured everything out they wouldn't hesitate to cut him down.

"Justin?" One of the soldiers shouted his weapon half raised, "We heard you were dead! What's that weapon . . . ." The soldier trailed off as his eyes widened, realizing that even an officer would have a hard time obtaining such an object.

"Sorry guys," Justin said, his weapon still pointing at the group that now began to finish raising their weapons. "But all of my friends were killed by the Core already."

Justin pulled the large trigger on his weapon just as the soldiers pulled down on their own. Nothing seemed to happen for Justin at first. The soldiers own rounds sprayed outward from their rifles, the brightly lit bullets flying towards whatever their target might be. He steeled himself for the onslaught of bullets. Knowing that any moment he would feel their piercing points move into his flesh, his weapon began to shake and rumble.

The weapons twin barrels began to emit a visible heat that rose into the air as a barrage of rippling small blasts issued forth that were barely discernible. Justin couldn't tell how many there were, but it looked like enough to make a complete wall in front of him that spread outwards in a cone shape towards the soldiers. As the weapons projectiles collided with those of the glowing bullets that flew forward they seemed to liquefy in place, leaving nothing but small droplets that fell harmlessly to the floor.

The soldiers attempted to react in time, but the cone of strange blasts enveloped all of them. They stood there a moment, and even seemed to look around inside the volley as it passed through them. One of the soldiers made a gurgling noise then dropped his weapon. Falling to the ground the others followed one by one after him. From a distance it looked like their clothes deflated, and were left there on the ground as Paradox and I stepped up behind Justin.

"What did it do?" I asked. Still standing there Justin kept the weapon pointed forward. Sweating he carefully slid his finger off the trigger. Letting the weapon point downwards he shook his head and began breathing heavily again.

"It, feels like it used my energy again." He said shakily, "But not as much this time."

"Hmm," Paradox said as he once again looked at the weapon. "Maybe it used your energy to perform the attack? Let's go find out."

Justin shuddered as Paradox and I led the way, with him following slightly behind. We approached the clothes slowly and looked downward at the liquid which was seeping out from the clothes. The fabric and armor itself seemed to be between a solid and a liquid. Paradox nodded while he looked at this, as if realizing what the weapon had done and turned towards Justin.

"It liquefied them." Paradox stated. He turned around and bent his knees so he could place one gloved finger in the liquid that was now spreading outwards. He brought it towards his eye and said, "Almost instantaneously it looks like. I wonder why it liquefied the bullets and their bodies . . . but not the clothes, interesting."

Gagging a little I looked towards Justin who was now leaning against the opening that the drill had created, looking a little pale. I didn't know what to say to him. He had just liquefied eight people and had felt his own energy forced out of him to do it. It's probably something that not even Paradox has experienced, I thought.

"No matter how we feel, we must move on." Paradox said, turning towards the open cavity and starting to head inside.

"Easy for him to say, he didn't just liquefy eight people." I said quietly to Justin.

Not saying anything, Justin just nodded towards Paradox showing that he was moving on ahead too as I followed along. As we entered through the cavity a very dull thumping noise caused us to look upwards, it was a cavernous area. Lights had already been strewn through the entire place, the drill machine was lying at the bottom. Up above, suspended by what looked like giant veins in the center of the cavern, was a gigantic heart pulsing as it made the small thumping sounds.

"That's Speculatio's heart?" I asked in awe, as it continued thumping, noticing whenever it pumped a dim glow would appear within it. "What do they want with his heart, Paradox?"

"They don't want his heart; they want what's inside it." He said while checking to see if his gloves were on tight.

"But then they would have to . . . kill him." I said, gulping a little at the thought as I watched a small figure of a man with a rope descend from the other side of the heart.

The man stopped in the air and surveyed the area below, then stopped and pointed at us. We couldn't hear what he said over the thumping as more men appeared, rappelling from the heart then down into the bottom of the cavern near the drilling machine. It could only mean one thing.

"Trouble." I said out loud. Paradox nodded his head in agreement. Justin sat down where he was standing, still looking rather drained, not talkative as he watched the men touch down on the floor and rush towards the drilling machine. They stopped and appeared to be speaking. Paradox began walking towards them. Following I watched the men grow in detail as I approached them.

It was the eight that had been carrying mining supplies, and not one of them held a weapon as they huddled around the machine. Their conversation was starting to grow louder and more apparent the closer we got. Some of the soldiers were pointing at us and shouting, while others sounded like they were pleading. Soon I could make out what they were saying. Once we drew a little closer we stopped and waited as Paradox folded his arms.

"It's Paradox!" One of the soldiers shouted as he made a sweeping motion towards us.

"Please, sir! Help us we can't fight him, not with our bare hands!" One of them pleaded while facing the drill machine as they all grew quiet, and a radioed voice broke outward from each of them.

"You all really are worthless . . . I'll help you, but once we get back to base I'm going to have to make a full report of your incompetence." The same harsh voice we'd heard earlier in the tunnel said, blaring out of all the troops' radios and making them shudder. The soldiers almost seemed more scared about the report back at base then Paradox.

The drill machine's top opened up as a large man in a very sophisticated, and threatening combat suit emerged. His helmet concealed his face with what appeared to be a black Plexiglas visor, while the rest of it was gold with red stripes heading diagonally around the sides. The bulky suit of armor he wore made the other soldiers look less then half his size. He stood on top of the machine and folded his arms displaying his suit which was decorated brilliantly with gold, red, and black, while looking at Paradox. Then the behemoth began chuckling rather loudly.

"So, you are the Paradox I've heard so much about." The Alpha Force commander proclaimed in a heavy radioed voice, which was clear of static.

"I've heard a bit about the Force commanders myself." Paradox said as he studied the suit, then smirked himself saying, "Fancy suit you have there, a gift from your scientists no doubt. Is it one of the benefits you get for being a Force commander?"

"One of many." The Alpha Force commander replied as he jumped off the drill machine and landed on the cavernous tissue with a very large thud. The drill machine rocked back and forth, showing how heavy the suit was, and when he stood upwards he towered over his troops by a few feet.

That suit must be nine, maybe ten feet tall, I thought as I watched the Alpha Force commander look at his troops who stood rigid in his presence. Paradox took a few more steps forward to get a better look at the suit for himself, then spoke quietly to me.

"He's powerful." Paradox said quietly, acting like he was just examining the commander and his troops. "This is going to be hard, I can feel it. This is an opponent that could very well defeat me."

Gulping down my nervousness while Paradox said this I looked back at the suit. To me it just looked like a heavy suit, but Paradox wasn't one for underestimating the enemy. Now when I thought about how he never underestimated them, I got a sick feeling in my gut. Watching the Force commander take one step forward and stop I stood in place.

"Who's that with you? A new recruit for us . . . you shouldn't have, Paradox." The commander joked as he eyed me. Suddenly I felt queasy that this man wasn't in the least bit frightened by Paradox. It's like he had something up his sleeve, an ace that he was waiting to use. I was about to speak to Paradox when the commander spoke up once more cutting me off, "I must ask that you to let my men leave here unharmed, Paradox."

Paradox shifted slightly, looking over the men as he said, "Why?"

"So that they don't get in the way while we initiate business." The Alpha Force commander replied to his question, smashing one large armored fist into the palm of the other.

"Very well, enough have died today." Paradox said after thinking a moment.

The commander motioned for his troops to move out. They moved forward without hesitation, running past Paradox. Wondering if there was anything I could do, I turned towards Justin who sat by while they moved through the cavity that led to the tunnel. After the troops left, the commander turned around to face the drill machine with his back now to Paradox.

"Before we begin, let me introduce myself." The Alpha Force commander said while standing still and facing the drill machine. "My real name is Walsh Loderman, commander of Alpha Force of the Twilight Core . . . others refer to me as me Gear-Crusher. I must admit, it is an honor to be the first commander to meet you."

Paradox tilted his head slightly as he said, "I can't say the same. It seems you are as stained as everyone else who has joined your little group. Commander or not, I'm going to beat you."

"Oh, but that is where you are wrong." Gear-Crusher said. Walking over to the drill machine he placed both of his armored hands on the side of it. "I will be the first to destroy you, and as a commander I will be elevated above the others and recognized for my greatness."

"As corrupted by power as ever, just like the others I'm sure." Paradox said tensing up and watching Gear-Crusher, unsure of when he was going to attack.

"Enough talk." Gear-Crusher began laughing, pressing against the drill machine with his armored hands and smashing into it, grabbing hold of the twisting metal beneath his fingers. Watching, I now saw the power that Paradox had spoken of as Gear-Crusher lifted the entire machine off the ground in one swift motion and tossed it through the air in our direction.

I jumped to the side and barely made it as I rolled over and watched the machine fall over Paradox with a resounding crash. I couldn't believe my eyes, as Gear-Crusher let out a battle roar, not noticing Paradox had appeared behind him in the air as he performed a side kick heel first towards Gear-Crushers head.

Paradox's boot heel connected with the helmet which didn't budge an inch, Ineffective even to the weakest looking part, Paradox thought, as Gear-Crusher spun around in place, his heavy armored hand flying towards him. Just as the punch, which could probably shatter steel, seemed to connect with Paradox he vanished, leaving what looked like an after image that melted away into darkness. Gear-Crusher's suit fired up, blasting into the air as fire roared outwards from his back and he slammed into Paradox just as he appeared.

"I can track your every movement!" Gear-Crusher yelled as he continued flying upwards, grabbing Paradox with both of his hands then spinning in place, finally releasing him and sending him flying towards the nearest wall. I watched, not sure what to do, as darkness crept outwards from Paradox, and he evaporated into the air just before hitting the wall. Gear-Crusher grunted, immediately turning as a weapon appeared out of the top of his left arms armor.

The weapon made an earsplitting boom as a large fireball erupted from it, streaming downwards towards an area on the ground where Paradox reappeared. Paradox countered by shooting his right arm forward, a stream of dark matter issuing forth from his arm, connecting with the ball of flame and forcing it back towards Gear-Crusher. Gear-Crusher didn't have time to move as the ball of fire rushed back at him, smashing into his armor and creating a very large eruption of flames in the air.

Paradox took this moment and started running forward as Gear-Crusher flew out of the explosion towards him at a speed that was almost too hard to follow. Paradox held his right arm up calmly once more, this time making his hand close slowly as Gear-Crusher was enveloped in darkness which formed into a hand that grasped at him. Paradox closed his hand tighter, and looked like he was beginning to struggle keeping his hand closed as Gear-Crusher burst from the dark hand that was restraining him, another weapon now on the top of his right arm.

Paradox quickly held up his left hand, forming what looked like a high five as a flat wall of darkness appeared directly in front of Gear-Crusher who smashed into it, his armor sounding like he struck some sort of metal as he backed away slightly. Gear-Crusher attempted to move around the wall of darkness now in front of him, and was irritated to find that it moved wherever Paradox moved his hand.

"Do you think this will stop me?" Gear-Crusher said as the weapon on his right arm fired off a swarm of bright electricity that struck against the black wall in a current. The wall slowly began to disintegrate as Paradox moved his right hand in a circular motion, creating a spiral of darkness as it moved over the area. The dark wall shattered and Gear-Crusher charged forward once more. Paradox watched his approach, keeping the dark spiral growing until it was as large as the area his arm could move around.

Finally Paradox pulled his right hand back, and shoved it forward towards the center of the spiral which caused it to fire towards Gear-Crusher in a spiraling drill-like mass. Gear-Crusher attempted to change trajectories, and dodged it at the last second as he continued on towards Paradox, who was now standing there with his hands connecting and fingers forming a point which he moved.

Gear-Crusher grinned as he fired both of his weapons at Paradox. Then pulled back and stopped, watching the visors tracking to see if he would dodge his attack once again. This time he didn't, and Gear-Crusher frowned as a shield of darkness sprang outwards from Paradox, slowing the blasts down and cloaking what Paradox was doing to the naked eye. He activated his thermal scanning and was surprised to see that Paradox had no heat whatsoever.

Interesting, He thought as he watched the blasts become enveloped by the shield. Gear-Crusher started wondering what he was doing, as he suddenly had an idea strike him. I'll lure him out by attacking his little comrade. Gear-Crusher thought, as he turned around to face me. My eyes widened as he raised his weapons and took aim, the barrels beginning to glow with energy as the spiral of darkness he dodged came up behind him!

It struck his back with terrible force, forcing him forward as he heard the darkness screeching against his armor, trying to force its way in. He slammed into the cavernous wall, the tissue of it padded him only slightly as he placed both of his armored hands on the wall and pressed against it to no avail. Thinking quickly he activated his flight systems to full power as the bright flames blew outwards from his back, licking against the black spiral that melted away from the light.

"Damage Analysis." Gear-Crusher said, checking to see if there was any breach in his armor, which promptly reported that there was none. "You fool, Paradox . . . no one has ever been able to damage my armor!"

Paradox let his shield of darkness fall, and watched Gear-Crusher a moment. He lowered his head and then spoke loud enough for us all to hear, "Indeed, your armor is quite powerful. That attack I used on you is able to pierce titanium like it's nothing. It's obvious your suit's made out of something other then that."

"It's too bad you'll never be able to find out what." Gear-Crusher said, while two rocket pods popped up from each shoulder and began firing off multiple salvos towards Paradox.

Paradox frowned as the incoming rockets fired towards him. He knew he was now in over his head. The stories about the commanders were true, and to think that this commander was the lowest ranked. He was probably going to die here, but if he did he would take the enemy with him. Paradox prepared himself to use an ability that would kill him, but also the enemy . . . he hoped. He placed both of his hands forward then slowly moved them back as the rockets just about reached their mark when they were intercepted by an almost invisible force detonating them in the air, startling him.

He turned to see Justin, the strange silver weapon in his hands gleaming as he let off another volley of the strange projectiles towards Gear-Crusher, who turned just in time as they pounded his armor. His armor began dripping . . . like an icicle dripping in the sunlight as Gear-Crusher rushed away from the weapon.

"Systems damaged." A mechanical voice stated as Gear-Crusher scanned over his visor. The strange projectiles he was hit with had begun melting his suit, but how was that possible? Nothing could break his suit . . . nothing! He turned towards the man who held the weapon that threatened him, quickly scanning his face which was automatically linked to one of his soldier's files.

"Traitor!" Gear-Crusher roared outward as he pointed an accusing hand at Justin before saying, "You have no idea what that weapon is capable of, you'll most likely destroy all of us if you use it!"

"That's a chance I may have to take." Justin said, now looking a deathly pale as he pulled the handgrip down. He tried to move it back up, but it wouldn't budge as he frowned, he looked up and cried out as Gear-Crusher began charging him. He pulled the trigger, as the two half-cylinder barrels began spinning in place and the large center barrel erupted with a visible wave of energy that seemed to affect the very air.

Gear-Crusher saw this, his eyes growing wide as he flew to one side just as the wave passed him. He turned watching it connect with the cavernous tissue, making it shrivel and die as it melted away. Turning back to Justin he watched him fall to the ground unmoving, as his visor started making a small beeping noise.

"Hmm . . . I'd love to stay and finish this Paradox, but it looks like time has run out. I must take care of my objectives before you . . . and next time you won't be so lucky." Gear-Crusher said, as he jetted towards Justin at full speed.

Paradox watched as he rushed towards Justin and began forming his dark shield around himself in an attempt to teleport to Justin before Gear-Crusher reached him. The black sphere made it about half-way before it collapsed on itself, throwing Paradox into another large coughing fit as dark matter seemed to emerge through his scarf every time he'd cough.

I didn't hesitate as I ran towards Justin and placed myself between the approaching commander and Justin's limp body. Raising the pistol I opened fire, the bright little bullets bouncing off the screaming mass of armor that was bearing down on me. I stood defiantly as Gear-Crusher slowed down, landing on the ground heavily and making it shiver.

"Out of my way." He said as he reached out and picked me up with one of his armored hands, simply tossing me to one side. I turned towards where Justin was lying, not knowing what to do and how I could help him, thinking the end had come for Justin when the commander reached down and procured the strange silver weapon from Justin's grasp and placed it inside a chest component that opened.

"This shall be returned to its rightful place." The armored behemoth stated as he looked upwards towards the heart. He watched it a moment and I turned to look for what he was looking at when I gasped. The heart had multiple red blinking lights on it, the lights emanating from small black dots that seemed to be placed strategically around it. Bombs . . . I thought. He's going to kill Speculatio!

"I'll have to be quick about this. Once the heart is destroyed who knows what will happen? I just have to get whatever is inside it." Gear-Crusher muttered to himself, not thinking about whom else might be listening in.

I watched, gawking and waiting for the inevitable as the lights stopped blinking, ending with one final long red glow before a thunderous flash was seen and heard above us. As soon as the bombs exploded engulfing the heart in fiery destruction it felt like the entire planet shook. The tissue began churning about, writhing as if in pain as a large moaning sound was heard throughout the area.

Gear-Crusher tried to maintain his balance as he took back to the air, watching as the heart fell apart and looking for the item he was supposed to retrieve. Green liquid began falling downwards in a torrent while something that pulsed slightly was swept with it. I stood, not thinking as I charged for it and heard the roar of Gear-Crusher in pursuit over the waterfall of Speculatio's blood. The item drifted towards me as the liquid continued to rise in level. I reached down, grasping for it while staying out of the blood, just as Gear-Crusher smashed downwards into the liquid where the item had been.

He missed it. I thought as I watched the item fly away from the splash created by Gear-Crusher and onto dry land. I ran towards it, picking it up and wincing at the purplish blood that burned my hand to the touch. Shoving whatever it was in my pocket, and frowning at the slight burning sensation it gave. I ran towards Paradox, who was still coughing lightly but motioning for me to come on. I'll get a good look at it later, I thought. Behind me I heard Gear-Crusher erupt from the liquid, roaring threats and running towards me.

"Come back here, boy . . . I'll tear out your spine when I catch you, I must have that item!" Gear-Crusher shouted out as he primed his two main weapons while chasing after me. He took aim, wanting to kill me and retrieve the item without any more complications as the entire room lurched. The top of the cavernous tissue collapsed inward as another long moan was heard throughout everywhere, the entire planet quaking as the falling tissue cut off Gear-Crusher from his target.

Forget this, Gear-Crusher thought, at least I retrieved the Proto-Weapon. Not a total loss. Gear-Crusher wasn't totally comforted by these thoughts, as the liquid began sloshing around his armored legs. He looked around, no clear exit in sight as his armors flight system sputtered.

"Bah." Gear-Crusher said, as he turned around and shoved his hands into the tissue and climbed upwards. The liquid continued to pour in, and he wouldn't have long until it filled up what was left of the collapsing room. "HQ, this is Walsh Loderman, commander of Alpha Force. I have retrieved a proto-weapon that the enemy had acquired. Requesting immediate portal opened up in my location."

"Walsh, this is HQ." A calm and controlled voice spoke, their professionalism showing as they continued, "Portal will open in t-minus five seconds around your designated area."

Gear-Crusher finished climbing upwards, scanning the area with his visor and locating the energy disturbance that was the portal opening directly below him. He smiled as he let go of the wall and dropped straight for the wormhole. We will meet again, Paradox, I can feel it, He thought as he fell into the portal and it quickly closed behind him.

The Seed

I heard the large wall of tissue crash down between Gear-Crusher and me. Thankful that it had happened before he was able to do anything to my friends or me any longer, but we still had to get out of here. Paradox looked as if he could barely stand, but managed to move by himself as we approached Justin. He had regained his natural skin color, and was breathing easily while I shook him.

"Wake up!" I shouted over the loud moaning that was echoing throughout the entire planet. Justin stirred slightly as Paradox walked up to him and booted him in the ribs, which caused him to shout in pain and sit up quickly.

"What's going on . . . where's my weapon?" Justin said as he looked at everything in motion around him.

"Gear-Crusher took your weapon . . . and they killed Speculatio." I answered, as I helped him up then said, "We've got to move out of here, now!"

"He's right, we don't just need to move out of here, but we've got to get off this planet altogether. Speculatio Unus is tearing himself apart. "Paradox said sadly, as he began running towards the cavity that was now slowly closing.

All three of us rushed forward, clearing the hole before it closed, and almost managing to lose Justin's leg in the process. We were in the tunnel now, and I realized that not only was the tunnel slightly filled up with the greenish blood that could burn you, but the soldier's weapons that had been left here were gone. Justin stopped for a split second and grabbed his pack, ignoring our protests as he charged forward with it now on his back. Those other soldiers must have taken the weapons, I thought as we began running down the tunnel, gunshots and screams becoming more apparent while we moved on.

We started rounding the bend when we came upon the first of the soldiers; they didn't notice us because of the things they were already busy combating. The small basketball sized holes seemed to pulse now while small little globules rushed out from them towards the screaming men who were firing upon them. They were doing a good job, but there were far too many as the men were engulfed under the assault.

Their screams died down as the globules made a type of slurping sound, and one of the soldier's arms disappeared into the mass, like it was sucked in and digested. Farther down the line we could hear the other soldiers fighting on frantically with the small blobs that seemed to sense their presence.

"Antibodies," Paradox said, "That's what they are. It's better to make a run for it and avoid them then try to fight them off, there would be far too many to deal with. For every one you harm, hundreds more will respond. They must have reacted due to the heart being attacked."

Justin and I nodded while we started running once more. Paradox led the way, zipping past the globules that followed us and gave chase. The farther we went along, the more that appeared. It must have been because of the soldiers that were fighting against them. They were designated as a bacteria or virus, I thought.

Up ahead we could see where the lift would come down, but were horrified to see it wasn't already in position. There's no way that we could fight off all the antibodies giving chase, it felt like we'd be enveloped and digested like the soldiers before us. Paradox slammed on the control panel, and then shouted frantically at Justin.

"Justin! Your thumbprint, use it, hurry!" Paradox shouted out, for the first time sounding frantic, the wave of antibodies pressing closer. Justin ran over, pressing his thumb down on the control as the lift slowly began its crawl downward. There was no way it could reach us in time before the antibodies did. I turned and raised my pistol, knowing that it was useless when the wall tissue made another jerk and tore open between us and the antibodies.

The green liquid gushed out from the tear, and I thought it would hit us before the small globules, but instead hindered them as the liquid rushed the opposite direction away from us and crashed into the antibodies, forcing them away from us while I looked upwards, and saw the lift gradually descending. It must have been slightly downhill, I thought, thankful once again for getting out of such a situation. The lift touched down while we clambered onto it and Justin once again embedded his thumbprint to move us upwards, when the green liquid finally began filling up the tunnel and the antibodies were coming with it.

A moment passed, and then ever so slowly we started ascending upwards towards the twilight that was lingering above us. The planet rumbled again, swaying the lift from side to side and forcing us to grab onto it while I glanced downwards. We were outrunning the antibodies, and as we passed through the throat area they stopped, seemingly unable to move any farther.

Paradox was able to tell that I began to relax, and shook his head as the Planet lurched once more, another moan moving throughout it but much weaker now. The mouth area twisted about, the teeth swinging near us as it ripped parts of itself into pieces. Paradox was right, it was finishing itself off. Justin grabbed one of the cables that suspended us and puked, finally letting the situation get to him as he looked upwards and sighed when the purplish light bathed over him.

The lift finished its course, stopping at the small platform that was swaying rather badly. Quickly we moved across it and I cringed at the sight before my eyes. As far as I could see the scythe-tees swung at each-other, some just flinging madly about as large holes opened up and the greenish liquid spurted into the air like great geysers. I looked to Paradox, whose head was bowed down unable to look at what was happening.

"Speculatio Unus!" Paradox shouted out with all his might, the ground reduced in shaking as he shouted his friend's name. Slowly a small mouth appeared in the ground, along with a smaller hole that served as an ear, not much larger then a fully grown man.

"**Paradox,**" It said, still louder then any of us shouting, but filled with pain. "**Did you fail?**"

Paradox fell to his knees as he began sobbing, something that I couldn't fully understand. He had been friends with this living being for who knows how long, and now he was losing him. The mouth of Speculatio

Unus cringed in pain as another moan roared over the planet, now dying down in volume from when it had first started.

"I failed." Paradox said, sobbing it out as he did so, "T-they got it. I wasn't able to stop them."

"No . . . ." I whispered, as I looked towards my pocket. "You didn't fail, Paradox. You did it . . . we did it! I got whatever they were after right here in my pocket!"

Paradox looked up, as both he and Speculatio became very quiet. The planet rumbled harder then ever as I reached down into my pocket and frowned, whatever was in there had grown some kind of roots that were now embedded into my pants. I pulled at it until it finally came loose then raised my hand for them all to see.

I frowned as I looked down at what was in my hand . . . it was a seed, it looked like a normal seed, except that it pulsed and glowed very dimly whenever it did so. Paradox stood up quickly as he reached his hand outward, and I gently set it into his hand. He studied it then began to laugh as he placed it into his pocket.

"You did it! We did it!" Paradox shouted as he sat down next to the mouth and stated, "He did, he got the seed!"

"Wait . . . so, what exactly did we risk our lives for?" Justin asked, then stood up watching as the planet began to break totally apart in the distance.

"The seed," Speculatio weakly said, **"Is what created me from the start. It has the ability to transform near anything into something more; I used to be a normal planet. The seed arrived from space, it's unknown where it came from, but it embedded itself into my core, and created the living, and now dying, being that you see."**

Paradox placed one hand near the mouth gently as he watched it begin to grow smaller. Justin shook his head and took a step back, watching the growing devastation drawing closer to us. Pieces of the planet were now moving away into space, the gravitational pull slowly losing its power as the planet crumbled inward and tore itself apart.

"But . . . we could save you now, couldn't we?" I said, thinking that since it had been created by the seed, it could be saved by it.

"You cannot." The now almost gone mouth said, sounding as if it was far away and growing fainter. **"If the seed was replanted, it would be too late to restore me. Even if I was restored, I would not be the same being that you knew. My heart is gone, and if somehow it were to be**

healed, I would still die slowly without the seed residing there. Simply put, my time has come."

Paradox nodded understandingly, as the mouth disappeared. The ears stayed, but they too slowly began to close in on themselves. Paradox watched onward as he bowed down slowly to one of the ears and quietly said, "Old friend, I will always miss you . . . but I have one more favor to ask of you, so that our time does not end here. I need you to face away from the light, so that I may be rejuvenated."

The remaining piece of the planet we stood on shuddered, as the ears disappeared from view and the alien sun began moving at a high speed across the sky. Quickly it fell on the other side of the planet, and darkness encompassed us. I felt the cold, but friendly feeling of Paradox's power wash over me as the ground cracked beneath our feet.

Then nothing but the now warm embrace of the darkness that sped us away from the planet that was once the one called Speculatio Unus, or the Observant One.

It felt longer, but couldn't have been long at all, as I seemed to blink and we were sitting in a dark area of a park. I looked upwards and was met with the leaves of a tree blocking out most of the twinkling stars in the familiar overhead sky. *We had come from up there,* I thought as I watched them. Paradox sat next to me quietly, looking at the strange seed that continued to pulse and glow ever so lightly in his gloved hand, while Justin was asleep . . . snoring rather loudly next to the tree.

"We're home." I whispered silently.

Paradox didn't move at all, as he continued to look at the seed in his hand. It was all that he had left of his old friend, and something that could never replicate what it had done before exactly. I yawned as I felt about lying down and taking a nap also, Justin seemed to have the right idea. As I stretched and prepared to take a nap a bright headlight beamed across the park and hit me in the face. I squinted to see the two uniformed officers that approached us, both of them waving their batons around while taking their leisurely time to approach us.

"Alright people, you know the parks closed during night." One of the officers said, as they walked up to us, the second nodding to Justin and adding. "We're just going to give you a warning this time, but next time choose to sleep somewhere else." Both of the officers had familiar accents.

"Thank you." Paradox said, as he placed the seed inside one of his duster's pockets and then stood up. The officers looked him up and down then frowned in distaste.

"Just remember that there's a mask law around here." The first officer said, "Keep away from any groups that wear masks, otherwise we'll have to question you."

"Again, thank you." Paradox said, as he turned and woke Justin up.

"Excuse me." I asked, as I glanced at Paradox who was busy waking Justin. "Where are we?"

"Come on, don't play dumb with us kid . . . this is Central Park. It's not like you stumble in here and don't know where you are." The second officer said then added, "Look, you got to get moving, we have to finish our patrol."

I nodded then didn't ask anymore questions, due to the fact that perhaps they suspected we were on drugs. I watched Justin stand, still bleary eyed while Paradox partially supported him and looked to see if I was ready. I nodded to him showing that I was then followed him. I wasn't sure where we were heading, but apparently Paradox knew. I listened to the patrol car slowly drive off then glanced back to where we had arrived.

"Paradox, why did you choose to appear here?" I asked while Justin finally seemed to be able to walk on his own.

"When I felt the planet began to shatter beneath us, I just instinctively grabbed out at a location for us to move to." Paradox said. He glanced back at me and seemed to think a moment before adding, "This is the exact location where I completed my training with my mentor."

"So you were taught by someone, just like your teaching me?" I asked curiously as he placed his hand onto his hat and nodded.

"Of course, his training methods were different then mine I think they all are . . . to each his own." Paradox finished while we continued to walk, this time leaving the open area and into multiple trees and underbrush.

Justin looked at each of us, then grinned slightly as he said, "Aren't either of you tired after what we just did?"

"I am." I replied then leaned towards him, as if sharing a secret. "But I don't think Paradox is, I've never seen him sleep, and he says he doesn't need to."

"Just like he doesn't need to eat anything either." Justin almost mouthed back to me, because it was so quiet.

We entered a small clearing that was full of underbrush but totally blocked from view by trees that were touching limb to limb. Paradox moved about, parting some of the bushes to look past them as Justin and I looked for a place to sit down. We moved over to what looked like a fine place to sit. Justin plopped down and I followed after him then cried out in slight pain as something struck part of my lower back. I shot up, and Justin moved over to see what it was that had made me cry out.

Placed in the ground, and concealed by the underbrush was a small metallic hatchway. Paradox marched over and knelt down as he grasped a small box on the hatchway and pulled it open. Inside was a number pad, where he put in a code. The hatchway hummed to life as it swung open, with very little light coming out of it. Paradox backed away, waiting for Justin and me to climb down in before he did.

After we were all inside there was a short walkway with another heavy blast door. Paradox also opened this one up then allowed everyone to enter. Lights automatically flickered on as I blinked, adjusting my eyes and noticed that this was Paradox's base. Alongside one of the concrete walls of the large room sat the old generator as I walked over and looked at all the signs that marked which hall led to where.

My legs felt weak, so I quickly moved to one of the chairs that were positioned around the table and took advantage of it. For the first time in awhile I felt safe, like there wasn't going to be some soldier that came up behind me with weapon in hand. Justin on the other hand had tensed up, and was quietly moving to each hallway and looking down the corridors, while Paradox was heading for the Experimental Area.

"Paradox," Justin said, still eyeing the furniture and hallways. "Don't we need to worry about the creatures loose here . . . and what about the soldiers?"

Paradox waved him off as he started pressing buttons on another control pad, having the Experimental Area door slide open while he said, "This isn't the same facility. This was my mentor's. All of them are created the exact same way. Don't ask me how, I've never seen it done . . . but there are many positioned throughout the world."

Justin didn't ask anything more before he turned towards the Living Quarters and Communications Room's hallway then started down it. I thought about following him, after all I was dead tired, but my curiosity was also working on me as I turned towards the Experimental Area that

Paradox had disappeared into. Standing up I forced my legs to move through the air, feeling like they had weights tired to every part of them.

As I drew closer to the door I peeked into it. Before me was a room that was much larger then I had first believed, but it was still smaller then the main area. Strange tools, weapons, and items of all kinds were filed along not just one shelf, which I had seen before, but six shelves that lined parallel to the door. The first was labeled A-D then preceded with each shelf all the way to W-Z. Paradox was no-where to be seen, so I took the liberty of stepping into the room.

I walked between the two shelves labeled I-L and M-P, looking at the filed items and wondering what they did. Most of them didn't even look like they were from this planet, and pretty much every name was unrecognizable. *Gerthiu Ilicom,* I read as I looked at one of the files. I reached out and pulled it open, getting a better look at whatever was inside. Whatever it was looked like an ordinary quartz crystal.

It reflected the light slightly as I reached towards it, my hand opening up to grasp it. Without even knowing he was behind me, Paradox shot his gloved hand forward and grabbed mine, stopping it mere inches away from the crystal. He pulled my arm back, as I stuttered, trying to think of what to say as he let go.

"Curiosity would've killed that cat." Paradox said as he took what looked like a piece of meat with his other hand, and waved it in front of my face. "Pretend that this was your hand." Paradox stated it like we were playing a game, then moved the piece of meat over the crystal and dropped it so that it landed on top. As soon as the two connected the crystal suddenly exploded into action, as multiple sharp points that look like smaller versions of the crystal grew outward from it, piercing the meat and continuing to grow. When these had grown to a certain size, more small points began spearing outwards from the others that had formed until the meat was totally encompassed.

"W-what is that thing?" I asked, now holding my hand and wincing as the crystal finished its small growth spurt once the meat was covered.

"I'm not totally sure." Paradox said, as he too watched it, then closed the filing case with it inside. "But I do know that once you would have touched it, it would probably have been the end for you. It grows absorbing organic matter of any type, until it's gone. Kind of like the seed that created Speculatio . . . but far different."

"So it's not sentient, or actually alive?" I asked, and started following Paradox as he walked away down the shelves towards the back of the room.

"Not that I'm aware of, it's just a crystal that . . . does that." He finished, as we reached the back of the room and looked left then right.

I looked around the room, and saw a table sitting in the left corner as Paradox began moving that way. He opened up a drawer that was positioned beneath the table and brought out a small metal box. Setting the box on the table with a clang, he reached into his pocket and retrieved the seed, gently setting it inside and shutting it as he looked at me.

"This box is the only thing that can hold the seed without being transformed." Paradox said, taking the box and starting to head to the shelf that held the S section.

I glanced down at my pocket, and remembered feeling the little roots that had been embedded there in such a short time. Reaching in I could still feel them, but they were brittle now. I pulled my pocket out of my pants, examining the small roots, which looked more like small veins now. I shuddered, wondering what would have happened if I'd kept the seed in my pants, but didn't want to think about it.

"I'm . . . going to lie down now." I said, keeping my eyes on the box that Paradox was holding.

He didn't say, or do anything, continuing on down the shelf and placing the box in one of the files. Probably under a file labeled as 'Seed', I thought, chuckling to myself. After I left the Experimental Area I started down the hallway that had the Living Quarters down it. I couldn't wait to sleep in one of those beds. It felt like it had been ages since I slept; it was only one day . . . but not an earth day, who knew how long it was?

I approached the split in the hallway, between the Communications Room and the Living Quarters. Grinning, I expected to hear Justin snoring any minute, but was surprised to see him walking down the hallway from the Communications Room. He stopped when he saw me, and looked back behind him before facing me once again.

"What were you doing in there?" I asked him. He looked down at the floor, perhaps thinking about what he was going to tell me, before he started walking again.

"Nothing." He said, walking past me towards the Living Quarters.

I eyed him a moment longer, then shrugged. He wouldn't betray us, I thought. Taking one last look down the hallway I turned towards the

Living Quarters and walked in, smiling at Justin who was already sleeping on the nearest bunk, his pack lying next to him. I moved over and chose one of the beds near the wall that held the gigantic aquarium, before I put my head back and fell asleep to the sound of the whales.

Friend or Foe

Once again I was walking down that same street, the very street that had me boxed in by cars, but now they were empty, and I pushed by them. I looked up and down the street, hoping to see a human face, but was only left with emptiness. I walked on, passing into another area, this time noticing something running away, away from me and the dark clouds that were forming overhead. I ran after them, feeling like I knew whoever it was.

The street didn't seem to end, but I was catching up to whoever was ahead of me. I passed by makeshift bunkers, sandbags torn and shredded about them by claw marks as I continued running. I noticed a worn down flag waving in the slight breeze, the symbol on it that of a strange sun either rising, or setting on the horizon. I had a feeling that I knew who that flag belonged too.

Why was the only other person that I could see running away from me? Were they scared? So many questions appeared in my mind as I looked about, at all the discarded military vehicles that were strewn about. Some of them had been torn open forcibly, by what I was unsure. Bullet casings lined the streets, as did blood . . . but not that of humans.

The figure was detailed now, and I felt glad that I finally recognized him. It was Justin, but why was he running from me? I called out to him and my voice rang loudly throughout the empty streets. If he heard me, he seemed to speed up. This was strange, and I sped up as well. I didn't seem to grow tired as I ran onwards, and was moving faster and faster.

Soon I'd be up close to him, but before I could reach him he swerved into an alleyway, forcing me to turn also. It was a dead end, the back of it ending in a black darkness that was different from Paradox's. I watched Justin run into it, disappearing from view. Stepping closer I called out to him again, then heard him weeping, as if in pain.

A photo drifted out of the darkness towards me, and I grabbed it while it flew by. Looking at it I could see a picture of a smiling lady with black hair and dazzling blue eyes, with two small children holding each of her hands. On the right was a little boy, the left a little girl. I was about to flip the picture over when I heard the sounds Justin were making stop, and lowered the picture to be met by a luminescent eye peering out of the darkness at me.

My eyes opened and I stared up at the roof for some time while I laid there and thought about what I'd just dreamed about. It had to be another nightmare, but it was so real, I thought. I sat up and looked for Justin, who was nowhere in sight. Sitting up in bed I stretched outwards, then fell to the ground and did a few push-ups to wake me up quicker. I then noticed how bad I was beginning to smell, and wondered if this place had a shower, and a change of clothes available.

I walked out of the room, heading for the main area. When I arrived I saw Justin sitting across the table from Paradox, with a steaming plate of eggs and bacon in hand. A second plate was on the table, and my stomach growled when I sat down in front of it. I looked at Paradox, who had the newspaper and nodded to me, showing that it was mine to eat. Justin was already halfway through his, wolfing the food down almost faster then a normal person would seem capable of.

I picked at my food for a moment then shoved a forkful of scrambled eggs into my mouth. "So, Paradox, I was wondering if you have a shower around here, and maybe some clothes I could use." I said in-between the scrambled eggs that I was chewing up.

"Did anyone tell you that it's bad manners to speak with food in your mouth?" Paradox said, his face hidden behind the newspaper, flipping through the pages slowly.

"My mother did all the time." I said, then chuckled adding, "Of course, you don't have to worry about speaking with food in your mouth."

Paradox violently slammed the newspaper onto the table, and I almost choked on the eggs as he stood up looking at me. He turned then looked over his shoulder at me and waited until I was done coughing up the eggs that had gone down the wrong tube before saying, "It looks like we're going shopping today."

Paradox walked out of the room without another word, heading outside through the heavy blast door, the gleaming exit sign above it. I looked at Justin, who was looking at me. I turned back towards my food and finished before standing and looking for a place to put my plate.

"Don't worry about it." Justin said, "He told me not to when I looked for a sink."

"Ah, alright." I said then turned to go outside where Paradox was waiting for me.

"Don't take it personally, but I think it's been a very long time since he's eaten." Justin said while I walked away. I gave him the thumbs up sign without looking back, taking my time to think about the best way to approach Paradox if he was angry.

As I climbed through the heavy doors I turned my head and said, "Take care of the base, Justin." He gave me a professional salute then headed off towards the communications hallway.

As I stepped outside Paradox beckoned to me. He waited until I was clear of the hatchway and looked all around making sure no one else was near. He closed the hatch then set a couple of the shrubs over it to block it from view in case someone ventured along here. I could tell something other then my comment was aggravating him, so I waited until he was done with the business around the facilities hatch.

"Do you really think we should trust him?" Paradox said putting a couple more of the shrubs around it, so that it would look like it was hard to walk through.

"Do you mean Justin?" I asked, pulling a leaf off the tree and examining it before letting it fall to the ground, "Yeah . . . why not?"

Paradox motioned for me to follow, both of us departing out from the trees. No one seemed to notice us emerge from them, and continued walking along a paved path towards one of the parks exits. "I've checked a few of the security recordings." Paradox said lowly, glancing behind his back once again.

"What about the security recordings?" I said while walking alongside him. I could tell he was nervous, or just alert. I think he was just being overly cautious about whatever it was, until he looked at me square in the face with seriousness brimming through the mask.

"He's been to the communications room twice already, and each time has contacted someone. He doesn't think he's being watched, but I've been keeping an eye on him. This is too big to ignore, what if he's contacting the Twilight Core?"

"But why would he do that? After everything else he's done, he's even stole one of their Proto-Weapons!" I said looking down at the pavement that soon ended ahead.

"Think about it, Aaron. What if it was all a setup? What if they gave him that Proto-Weapon, and teleported him away from the creatures to spy on us, in return for his life? If there's one thing I know in this world, it's that the Twilight Core doesn't care about its soldiers, and most of the time not even the Commanders know what the head being, whoever . . . or whatever they are, are planning!"

"Look Paradox, I know you've had a bad history for who knows how long with these Twilight Soldiers, but Justin isn't a bad guy. I mean, if he was a bad guy he could have easily used that weapon against us, especially when you were fighting against Gear-Crusher."

Paradox placed both of his hands on the back of his head as we exited the park. He looked up at the blue sky that hovered over us, the sun hanging there and its rays that burrowed into my skin, and started making his way towards a store that was across the street. We entered through the door, and he stopped a moment then turned to me.

"I guess your right." He said, "I'll give him the benefit of the doubt, so for now let's focus on some new clothes for you."

"Hey, Paradox . . . I do have a question, or concern, whatever you wanna call it." I said, browsing through the clothes in the store and frowning at the sizes and prices.

"What's up?" Paradox sounded almost like a normal person for once.

I smiled at the thought, and once again wondered what his face looked like under that mask. I turned from the clothes and leaned against the rack they were on as I asked, "Well, it's kind of two things, but . . . I've noticed whenever you use your powers extensively; you begin coughing, like you're sick. That's worried me awhile now. I also feel rather useless in the fights we've encountered, any tips on that scenario?"

Paradox continued rummaging through the black section of clothes, turning them this way and that like a specimen under the microscope. He turned towards me and placed one elbow up on a cupboard that held stacks of jeans, as relaxed as he'd ever looked before he talked a little brokenly, as if trying to figure out how to tell me something.

"Aaron . . . you see, I . . . hmm. It's hard for me to explain, I'll tell you that for now you shouldn't worry about it. I'm not sick as in a cold, but I'm sick in a different way. It's more like a long standing wound." Paradox said as he rubbed his scarf-covered chin with his free arm. "As for your other concern or question . . . I remember being like that myself under my mentor."

"So you had a mentor? Does that mean I'll have powers like you someday?" I asked excitedly.

"Perhaps." Paradox said, turning back to the clothes and going through them again. Inside he felt cold, and saddened by the thoughts that raced through his mind. He whispered sadly to himself, so that I would not overhear him, "But at a price."

I finished choosing some jeans and shirts for myself as I looked at the price tags again and whistled. It was a hefty amount of money, and I didn't have any with me. Paradox took them and looked at the price tags, then at the clothes themselves and simply said, "Not my style, but nice choice."

He wandered about the store a little longer then arrived at the cash register where he promptly paid for my clothes. I was about to protest against him when he moved his fingers in a zipper line across his mouth. He still wasn't in the best of moods it looked like, so I allowed him to do whatever he wanted with his cash. After all, I hadn't seen him buy anything else.

Paradox then offered to take me to a restaurant but I refused to eat at one unless he ate also, which resulted in him taking back the offer. He took me to a motel, and rented an entire room just for me to use the shower. Once done we headed back, and I asked him if he would let Justin use the shower there since it was checked out to us for the entire day.

"Certainly." Paradox replied as we made our way back into the park. I was happy the day was turning out good, and that nothing bad had happened as we entered the trees and found the hatch. Paradox knelt down and grabbed the box to the hatch, then stopped. He waited a moment before doing anything then started inputting the code.

"Everything alright?" I asked as him, watching the fingers dance over the control pad.

"Yeah," Paradox replied, his tone slightly worried. "I just thought the hatch felt unusually warm."

I frowned, then knelt down and touched the metal, it indeed felt warm, and much warmer then it should be naturally. Paradox finished entering the code as the hatch cracked open and slid upwards like it had the night previously, but now black smoke and heat streamed upwards into the air. I coughed as I inhaled some of it and tried to peer down into the hatch, my heart racing while I covered my mouth and found that I couldn't see a thing inside.

"Wait here." Paradox said, jumping straight down into the smoke that billowed out of the hatch. A few minutes passed, and I heard fire truck sirens and people heading this way. I turned, watching as the first person appeared through the trees, he was overweight and short, cell phone against his red face as they chattered away with the authorities no doubt.

They made their way over to me as a police officer emerged from the opposite direction, and started shouting at us to get back. The short man pointed at me with his cell phone and exclaimed that I was here when he had arrived, and the officer hastily moved in my direction. This is no good, I thought as the officer drew closer. I knew I would be interrogated about the hatch and what had happened . . . and I decided I'd rather not go through that.

I plunged into the hatch, followed by the abysmal roars of the police officer and excited speed-talking of the ruddy faced man. Coughing I crouched low, and headed in the direction of the blast door as the heat intensified. I entered the main area, watching for Paradox or Justin in the orange glow that came from the Experimental Area along with the crackling of flames. I headed over towards the Experimental Areas door, and reached up to close it when Paradox emerged from inside, his boots thudding against the floor while he walked upright in the smoke.

"Paradox, what's going on?" I shouted out then coughed some more from the smoke.

Paradox's boots turned in my direction, the door to the Experimental Area sliding shut as they did so and cut off the smoke and flames. "Wait here, and this time listen to me." He said, as he walked towards the blast doors to outside and closed them, his boots finally disappearing down the hallway towards the Living Quarters.

Soon vents opened up in the roof, sucking in the smoke that still plagued the main area and clearing most of it out. A clanging noise sounded on the other side of the blast door, most likely the firemen trying to force their way inside. I stood up as Paradox charged back into the main area, his fists clenched in a rage as he spun around to look at me.

"He's gone, along with the seed! The communications room is trashed, but the last known signal was sent to a blocked location." Paradox raged as he pounded his fist against the table. "I knew we shouldn't have trusted him!"

I couldn't believe this, Justin betrayed us? He couldn't have, perhaps he was forced to? No . . . that didn't sound right. My thoughts raced as I rushed to the communications room; there just wasn't something right about this. I arrived to see the door open, and the controls strewn about in pieces. Frowning I ran to the Living Quarters, everything of his was gone, like he cleared out, I thought now losing hope.

I moved over to the bed he used, and ripped the covers off, looking for anything that could serve as proof of his innocence, but there was nothing at all. I turned around, my temper rising as I turned in place and batted the pillow as hard as I could. It flew off of its resting place, where something was lying that caught my eye. I bent down and picked it up, my eyes widening at what it was. The photo from my dreams was now in my hand, the smiling black haired lady, her blue eyes that seemed to jump out of the picture.

The children were also there, each one grasping one of her hands as I swallowed at the déjà vu experience. Slowly I flipped over the picture, and stared at the back of it, revealing a residential phone number. This is it, I thought, this can show he was innocent. I turned to go, only to be met face to face with Paradox as he ripped the photo from my hands. I didn't speak as he looked it over then walked towards the wall that held all the directories.

He tapped on the directory labeled C, and then went on to tap the one that said communications. He pressed a few more control options and switched back to the ten most recent signals. The first seven were dated back by over fifty years, but the four others near the bottom were as recent as yesterday. The most recent did indeed show a blocked source, but the three before it were all the same number that was shown on the back of the Photo.

"He may be indeed innocent." Paradox said, the screen flickering to a different channel that I'd never seen before. "But we're going to have to find him to find out. I think it's time to bring the fight to the Twilight Core."

"But how are we going to do that?" I asked seriously, "Not only is there probably a mob outside waiting to see what's going on in here, but you don't know where their headquarters are!"

"To answer the first question . . ." Paradox said as he activated something on the screen that made the alarms begin to blare. "It's daytime, and because of that there's only one way out of here without delaying everything greatly, and that's through the dark realm."

I suddenly thought I'd rather get caught then go into the ferocious creature's realm, when a countdown beginning at two minutes started ringing out with the alarms.

"As for your second comment, we now have someone who can point us in the right direction." Paradox finished, holding up the photo of the lady as he shut down the screen and turned to go.

I followed after him, both of us running now while the countdown continued. I knew what would happen after the countdown ended and I hoped that everyone was smart enough to get outside before that commenced. We turned in the main area, heading for the training facility as the countdown reached one minute and thirty seconds. Barreling into the room I watched Paradox reach outwards with his hands, grabbing one of the cage doors and ripping it off forcibly with his power.

Before us was a swirling vortex that looked like it would tear you apart if you entered it. One minute left, and Paradox shoved me inside. I didn't know if I screamed or not, this dark portal was far different from teleporting with Paradox's power. It tore at me, feeling as if I had chunks of my body dismembered and fed through a small funnel. This lasted for what seemed like ages, and eventually I felt the vortex quake with me inside of it, a distant orange glow flying after Paradox who had entered after me and seemed disfigured.

Shooting out into cool air I landed on some kind of rough ground, feeling like I'd been sent through a grinder. I checked to make sure I was all there, never wanting to go through that again. I stood up, the portal glowing orange in the center as Paradox shot out of it overhead. Landing on the ground he grabbed my legs and jerked them out from under me. I fell with a thump to my head, wondering why he did it, when the portal exploded outwards, flames firing from its dark mass over my head just as Paradox had before them. Slowly it closed in on itself, one of the vortexes to our world was no more.

The Realm of Darkness

"Thanks." I said standing back up from the quick pull down that Paradox had performed and finally getting a good look at the surrounding area. At first it looked like the world dropped off farther out around us, but I soon realized that it was actually a plateau that we had emerged on top of through the portal. The ground was made of a brittle but hard substance that grabbed at my clothes, breaking off easily when I had stood up, but a layer of it holding onto my pants all the same.

I lifted my shoe, the ground cracking while I looked at the thin layer of the reddish-brown crust still grasping on the bottom of it. Paradox stood up, brushing himself off and looking towards the sky that held six different suns in it. Each one gave off a different kind of light, mixing in with each other that created a dream-like rainbow effect over the horizon, but wasn't cheery at all.

"Good for us." Paradox said, still looking at the suns and then turning towards the nearest edge of the plateau.

"How's that good for us?" I asked bluntly, watching him tighten his scarf which had loosened slightly, but not enough to reveal his face. "Your powers are stronger at night, and there are six suns in the sky giving off strange light that hinder your powers considerably for sure. So how is that exactly good for us?"

"Use the head you were given, we are in the realm of darkness. The brighter it is the better. We have a few advantages given to us, and that's one of them."

"What are the other advantages?"

"Another is the ground; the material it's made out of provides us with camouflage, both through physical appearance and masking us as a part of this world."

I raised an eyebrow in speculation as I thought about it a little. Paradox had obviously been here before, that's how he knew about these things, but the last part didn't quite make sense.

"What do you mean by, 'masking us as a part of the world'?" I tried to clarify, trudging after Paradox who had begun moving towards the edge he had faced.

"This world was much like ours; in a sense you could say it's an alternate reality. The creatures that reside here weren't native to this place. They arrived and wiped out every living thing in a matter of months. I'd tried to help, in a sense . . . but was unable to stop the inevitable outcome." Paradox bent down and grasped some of the reddish ground in his hand, grinding it a moment then dropping it and proceeded to move onward. "The creatures could locate anything living easily, we don't know how but it was like a sixth sense, then over time this ground started appearing, and we learned that it covered the beast's bodies and effectively blocked that sixth sense, but it was too little, too late."

Paradox approached the drop-off of the plateau, looking out over the land that was truly barren and dead. Far off in the distance I could see the crumbling remains of a city, the shattered skyscrapers reaching for the rainbow sky. A wind started to pick up, causing Paradox's duster coat to flare out behind him. He waved his hand over the dead horizon, while I watched the wind carry with it a dark gray cloud that hovered slightly in the distance.

"All that you see . . . is what's left of a world that was once as beautiful as our own. The only remaining traces of its beauty are the suns that give the planet their rainbow filled light. Yet even their beauty has become tainted and lackluster over time." Paradox said reverently, lowering his hand and turning to me. "This is what I fight against in our own world, and what the Twilight Core and its associates could very well cause . . . the end of all life."

I returned Paradox's gaze, wondering how often he had come to this realm before the disaster to fully appreciate what it'd once been. Turning away from me, Paradox climbed downward over the ledge, beginning his descent. I squinted once more over the horizon, noticing a pack of dots moving across the dead plains towards the ruined city, and the grayish cloud move towards the dots.

Hastily I hurried down after Paradox, knowing that the dots were hostile and if I could see them, they could see me. I certainly hope that Paradox is right about this stuff, I thought looking at the wall before me I was climbing down, its particles clinging to the front of my clothes. Halfway down the mesa I frowned, remembering that Paradox had brushed all the particle bits off of himself.

"Hey Paradox, why did you brush yourself off if those keep us from being spotted by the creatures here, like you said?" I asked, wondering what his answer could be to one of my questions this time.

"Not my style." I heard him say below me, forcing me to grin.

Just like him, I thought remembering him at the clothes store going through all of the black clothing they had available in men's. I wonder how he keeps his clothes and himself so clean, I noted for later, when we hit the bottom of the mesa. Paradox immediately started moving in the direction of the ruins, myself turning around to look upwards what we had climbed down from. It wasn't a very large mesa, but I was still slightly out of breath.

Paradox stopped a ways off; waiting to make sure I caught up to him. Turning to go and head for the city I heard some rocks fall behind me down from the top of the mesa. Nothing, as I glanced back and up it. It must have just been a loose rock blown out by the wind, I thought turning back to move on. Paradox had his arms folded, tapping one boot against the grounds crust that made a cracking sound every time he did so, looking very impatient.

"Alright, alright, I'm coming." I said, running forward and past him towards the city ruins across the plain. "So how do you know where to go?"

"I can feel the dark energy created by the portals. It's what draws the creatures towards them, to another world that hasn't yet been scourged." Paradox said, walking briskly in the direction that I had reverted to jogging slowly towards.

"Alright, so it's like a beacon to you. It probably leads to one of your bases too, right?" I said, now entering a walk because of the musty air that seemed to clog my lungs.

"Most likely," Paradox stated, "But if not, once we are through I can close it."

"Say . . . why don't we just use your old teleport and fly through the air trick to get there?" I said, sounding like I'd just discovered the greatest find in history.

Paradox looked at me seriously waving a finger back and forth in the 'no' direction. "If I did that then I would become a beacon that would call out to every Rethagin, Urthigeon, and who knows what else that's living on this planet. We can't have that happen if it is a portal that doesn't lead to one of my sanctuaries, because they would swarm into it."

"So you can't use your powers at all here." I said in dismay, checking my pockets and sighing. "Great . . . and I left my pistol back in the base, or facility, or sanctuary . . . whatever it is that probably doesn't exist anymore."

"If you mean the sanctuary that I had imploded so that nothing dangerous would fall into inexperienced hands? Then yes, it was probably there." Paradox said gruffly, closing off the talk for awhile as we moved across the plain.

I looked out as far as I could see, thankful that the area was relatively flat. This way I can see if we have anything incoming, I thought, looking at the ruins growing closer and seeming to rise ever higher. I felt strange whenever I looked at them directly, making me queasy. Perhaps it was just the idea that an entire planet had passed away here, and that I was going to go waltzing into the ruins of where who knows how many people had died.

Paradox moved on, quietly passing me as he watched what looked like one of the gray clouds blowing about the city, which was strange because the wind was moving only one direction. It swerved back and forth, but Paradox didn't seem too worried about it, so I didn't pay it a second thought. I yawned, stretching my arms upwards and decided to look back and check the distance we had made. As my head swiveled back my eyes squinted against the small musty particles drifting through the air with the wind. Then my heart started pounding, an icy shawl wrapping itself around my insides when I saw the things in the distance bounding stealthily towards us.

They weren't Rethagins, but their twisted shapes confirmed that they were out for anything's blood that was alive. Their twisted maws were placed vertically on the front of a wretched body where no eyes were seen, supported by four muscular legs. The muscles rippled as they propelled the snapping mouths forward, drool seeping outwards from the open crevices. The feet ended in a club-like fashion, small spikes protruding from them and a large curved claw made for swiping, these it dug into the ground for extra grip to maintain balance.

I turned from the bodies that expanded and contracted as they breathed inward, almost retching at the veins protruding from the bodies when they pulsed. I breathed in and out slowly, knowing that if I tried to speak now I'd just puke. I stared ahead at Paradox who seemed to grow farther away, not noticing what was going in. Finally I stood straight up, and roared out his name.

"Paradox!" I called out, as the creatures gave a shriek that made my ears ring for a moment.

Paradox seemed to turn in slow motion, his head finally looking in the direction of the creatures as I heard him say one word, "Run!"

I churned my legs, moving as fast as I could but feeling like I was moving nowhere. I rushed after Paradox while risking the chance of looking back, and wished I hadn't. The creatures were no longer trying to be stealthy, charging at full speed ahead as their bodies seemed to grow a bulge, much like a tail on the back end. Soon the bulge erupted open, spewing forth some black gunk that was flung around the ground and tentacles emerged. The ends of these formed into a bonelike spear point, making it flexible and dangerous, as if it hadn't been already.

"Don't look back." Paradox yelled back to me. Too late, I thought as he continued, "Follow my path exactly if you don't want to die."

"Not much of a choice." I said beginning to follow in his footsteps as the creatures gave another shriek, sounding much closer this time. "So what's your plan?"

"Since I can't use my powers, we have to use the terrain to our advantage." Said Paradox sounding totally confident in himself.

I didn't see what we could use to our advantage, but I didn't waste time asking more questions. Paradox had a plan, and if he told me to follow him exactly I'd better well do it, I thought. We were now swerving through the crust filled plain, and I wondered what exactly he was doing as the creatures bounded closer, their strange shrieks announcing their approach. Behind me I heard a large thump, like a rocket firing out of the ground.

I wanted to look back as the area behind me was filled with what sounded like a hundred bullets smashing into the ground. The creature's shrieks turned into ones of rage then pain as more thumps sounded behind me. Paradox stopped and turned around, while I did the same just in time to see one of the creatures lying dead, and two strange devices flying upward from the sandy crust. The creatures had activated them, whatever they were, and the devices now unloaded volleys of superheated shrapnel from the air that pelted the surrounding area.

Shuddering under the volley of shrapnel the creatures didn't give up, taking a few more steps as the shards of metal melted into their skin. These last steps would prove fatal to them, activating several more of the little devices that immediately rocketed into the air and rained down more shrapnel. Quivering from the many wounds they had sustained, they fell lifeless to the ground.

I gulped, noticing how many hits it had taken to kill just one of them as I looked over the holes that peppered the body. Normal munitions didn't work well against these creatures, unlike the Twilight Cores bullets which seemed to make short work of it. Perhaps that's why this planet was wiped out, I thought, they didn't have the right things to kill these easily. Paradox seemed somewhat satisfied with himself as he surveyed the carnage that was caused by the strange devices. The city was closer now, and all the running had certainly closed a lot of the distance from it.

"Those devices are Hopper-mines that were used to defend the cities from the creatures during the Crisis Days." Paradox said, pointing to the devices before I even had a chance to ask him about it. "It's too bad they didn't work as well as the worlds leaders had hoped."

"So these are just leftovers from when people still lived here?" I asked, unmoving because I didn't want to set any off.

"Yes, the creatures learned to avoid them, and make small gaps to get to the cities. Only reason why it worked on these ones is because they were after us." Paradox said, watching one of the bodies twitch in the process. "We'd better keep moving now."

"So how could they see us? I didn't notice any eyes on them, and I'm covered in this stuff." I said, following Paradox who was now zigzagging through the minefield. "And how do you know where the mines are?"

"As for the creatures seeing us, who knows? Maybe they could smell us. After all they were downwind from our location." Paradox speculated, continuing his jagged movement and stopping every once and awhile before moving on again. "The mines on the other hand, it's complicated. They were set up so that if you walked in a certain pattern, they could detect that and wouldn't activate. This way when they placed them in the ground, so they could come back and check up on the perimeters."

"So if I were to start walking straight." I said, watching Paradox who had stopped once again, surveying the area around us.

"Then you would set them off." Paradox finished, he then reached down and picked up two rocks, ripping them out from the crust. He threw one then the other, which landed a little after the first. "That's where this field ends. We'll take a break once we reach it."

I forced myself to cough a bit, trying to force the musty particles caught in my throat outwards. I finished following Paradox's trail, and was surprised to see him sitting down and watching the grey cloud. It still moved back and forth around the city, but now it looked like the cloud was made up of multiple objects flying together in a swarm. He reached up and wiped his goggles off, his gloved hand smearing more of the dust-like material in its place.

"We'll rest here for now." Paradox said, still eyeing the objects swarming around the city then saying to himself, "I have no idea why those would still be active."

"What would 'those' be?" I asked, sitting on the ground next to him and wishing that we could get out of this place right now.

"Recon Hunters." Said Paradox, as if I would figure out what they were from the name itself. He looked towards me, seeing me sigh because the way he spoke. I could tell he was smiling under there, when he continued on like a teacher giving a history lesson.

"During the Crisis Days, that's what they called the days when the population of the world was only about twenty percent of what it was, they released armed machines called Recon Hunters. These machines would fly about the world, and try to locate any survivors that had survived the brutal onslaught of attacks when these creatures arrived. Once a survivor was located, the Recon Hunter would activate a beacon that sent a signal to the others that were activated. These would swarm in around the survivor and protect them with their weaponry while they tried to get to a safer area."

"So what happened?" I asked, thinking it sounded like a good plan, "What went wrong?"

"A few things . . . there just weren't as many Recon Hunters as there were creatures. Not only that, but one person had the ability to attract more then enough Recon Hunters then was needed. This resulted in other survivors perishing because someone else had too many busy elsewhere to find them. The creatures also learned how to get past them too, just like the mines. If there were ten Recon Hunters protecting someone, then all the creatures had to do was ambush the person and kill them quickly. This resulted in the Recon Hunters to scan for any other life that they were designed to protect in the area, and if there was none they would just shut down to conserve energy and await pickup."

"I see." I said, watching the metallic mass continue to patrol about the city, circling it like vultures over prey. "So the ones that are activated have detected life, could it be us?"

"No not us." Paradox analyzed, his arms folded where he was sitting and looking down at his legs which were crossed in front of him. "If it was us, they would have moved over to protect us the moment we'd arrived. It's someone else, but that's impossible. There hasn't been anything alive here, except the creatures, for over two hundred years. The last few survivors had been wiped out long ago, yet before my eyes I see the largest congregation of Recon Hunters that I've ever seen before."

There had to be thousands of them, I thought. I could now see the suns light glinting off the little objects, and I wondered why we were waiting here. If these things are meant to protect us then why should we wait and rest? I thought, looking at Paradox who looked a little uncomfortable. He sat still a moment, shifting every once and awhile then reached behind himself and scratched his back. After he did this he shook his head, like he was coming out of a daze and stood up.

"Alright, the sooner we get there, the better." Paradox said while standing up.

"Exactly what I was thinking, you must be able to read minds." I announced, chuckling at how many times he was able to answer questions of mine without even my asking.

"It was strange." Paradox said, "But I felt like my energy was very slowly being drained, and I didn't want to move on any farther."

"Well, next time that happens I'll be sure to prod you." I said, startling me by his serious replying.

"You do that."

This made me think something was wrong, but everything seemed normal as we started trekking from our resting place towards the city. It was strange that Paradox had gotten tired, because I'd still hadn't seen him sleep. The only other time I'd seen him weary was after a strenuous battle and he had used his powers a great deal, but he hadn't used them once here.

I wiped some of the sweat from my forehead, and buckled under the sick crunch of the crust that had been covering it. Hmmm, Paradox had said that there hadn't been any survivors for over two hundred years . . . could he really be that old? *That's impossible!* I thought, looking him over and imagining an old man's withered face under the mask.

Paradox didn't sound old at all, in fact whenever he spoke it sounded like he was in his prime. There was certainly more then meets the eye here, and a lot he was holding back on. I watched what was left of the city grow closer, the small objects that glinted in the sky now appearing to be orbs moving about with little green lights flashing on their tops. It resembled a bee hive in peak production, the buildings taking the place of the hive, and the orbs as the bees.

I cast my eyes downwards to what was left of the plains before we would reach the city. Mounds rose up all around that were covered in the reddish crust. Upon closer examination it appeared that the mounds were bodies, not human but those of the creatures. It looked like the Recon Hunters were doing their job well at protecting whoever was inside the city. It was a good location, since the area was flat and the creatures couldn't hide and sneak up on whoever was there.

I felt an itch on my back, yawning and feeling drained as I fell onto my knees. Weird, I thought, I was just full of energy a moment ago. Paradox turned and looked at me, waiting to see if I would get up as I scratched the spot that was tingling and suddenly felt like I'd regained my energy. I stood up quickly, and Paradox started heading over to me and tilted his head.

"Are you alright?" He asked, looking over me and turning to go.

"Yeah, I just felt tired for a moment there." I replied and started walking forward once again.

We approached a small rise in the plain, making a very tiny slope that led upwards before leveling out to the city ruins. I grinned, hoping that there was plenty of food and cold drinks inside. We climbed up the small slope and I raised my arms in the air, relishing the sight of the city's gates. There was a wall connected to the gate, winding around the city. There were gaps and places where it was crumbling now, but it would probably still provide a little protection.

I grinned at Paradox who gave me both thumbs up then stopped dead in his tracks when he heard a distant beeping sound that seemed to grow louder. I looked towards the Recon Hunters; a couple of them had stopped and were now facing us. Their orbed bodies were larger then I had originally expected, almost the size of a car, and had two cylinders positioned on each side which was pointed up into the air. A slit appeared to be the scanner eyes on the front, as the ones that stopped to face us began to increase in number.

More and more of the orbs stopped their patrol, all beginning to beep in unison as the flashing green light on the top of their heads began to flash red. I frowned, not feeling good about this in my gut as the cylinders on each side started swerving downwards to aim in our direction. Paradox stiffened, and I knew that his posture confirmed that this wasn't right.

"Move for the slope." Paradox said who didn't hesitate in sweeping around and charging for cover. "Once you get to the slope, drop down immediately!"

I was pumped full of adrenaline as the Recon Hunters had all stopped now and were focused on us. I moved backwards, almost tripping over myself and finally managing to turn as I leaned forward and ran. The tiny slope dropped off in front of me, and I lunged down it headfirst as the ground exploded behind me in a rush of heavy munitions.

I covered my ears from the sound that followed right after the first shells struck, an incessant beating of a thousand large weapons blasting away into the top of the slope. Paradox covered his head as the crust rained down over us, blown to shreds by the thunderous strike it had taken. This continued for what seemed like a millennium, but lasted only a few seconds as the aggressors let up on their fire and scanned for the designated targets survival.

I held my breath, expecting the shower of rounds to start up again, but was relieved to find out that they couldn't scan us through the crust ridden ground. Paradox uncovered his head, and looked at me before peeking over the ledge. He sighed, letting silence fall upon us as our ears slowly regained their hearing.

"I don't understand. They shouldn't be firing upon us, if they are then why don't they fire upon the person they are protecting in the city?" Paradox asked the air, knowing he wouldn't get an answer as tiredness slowly crept into my mind again.

I yawned, not noticing the itch on my back, as Paradox reached behind him and began scratching his own back while muttering. This is good right here, I thought, this is as far as I need to get. Justin would be alright, he didn't need my help. Paradox could take care of everything anyways. Right now I just wanted to rest.

I laid my head on the ground and closed my eyes, feeling like I would sleep for a long time. Moments passed, and then I was struck in the face as I swung my eyes open and sat up, still feeling extremely tired but unable to ignore the pain. Paradox seemed to say something, but I was too tired to listen as I yawned again and got ready to lie back down . . . just as he reached back and sent a fist across my cheek.

"What was that for?" I asked stunned, not feeling as tired through the pain that now burned through my cheek.

"Are you itching anywhere? Tell me!" Paradox demanded as I nodded and pointed to my back. He reached out and pressed me down, holding my face to the ground where I saw some kind of dead creature the size of my fist lying. It looked like a brownish caterpillar somewhat, but with a circular mouth on the end filled with tiny teeth. I was ready to ask what he was doing when my back that was itching now sheered through with white hot pain. I struggled against Paradox, not feeling tired anymore as he let me bolt upright.

"What's the big idea?" I asked, grasping at my back where I was burning.

Paradox didn't say anything as he held one gloved hand in front of my face, holding tight to one of the caterpillar-like creatures. It gave little shrieks and repeatedly closed its mouth and opened it, trying to latch onto something. I jumped back, and Paradox closed his hand harder, crushing the little worm monster then dropping it to the ground once it was dead.

"I found one of those on my back, where it was itching. That's what was making us tired . . . when it bit us we were continually injected with venom that made us feel tired. It didn't affect me as much as you, because we're so different." Paradox said, stomping down on the already dead creature, and then turned back towards me. "This also explains why the Recon Hunters were firing at us. They had detected these things and couldn't allow them near the person they were protecting, another bug in their programming. Anyhow, we have a bigger problem now."

My back slowly stopped hurting, as I looked at my hands that had been grabbing at it. They had a very small amount of blood on them, and I wiped it off on the crusty ground. "Alright, what's the bigger problem?" I asked, hoping that he wouldn't say there was no way into the city, or worse yet . . . home.

"Look at this." Paradox said, lifting his duster coat so I could see where the caterpillar creature had bitten him. I couldn't see any skin, but dark matter leaked from his wound and slowly drifted up into the air before dissipating. "Since I have a leak, it's like I'm slightly using some of my power. I've just become a signal to every creature out there until I heal, whether they come or not depends on how strong this particular signal is, and how fast it will travel."

"Alright, that's wonderful news . . . what do we do now?" I asked, as I stood up looking at the orbs that continued to patrol around the city.

"We go into the city, since we don't have anymore uninvited guests on us. It's our only chance." Paradox said calmly, both of us hearing the shrieks and calls of the first creatures to notice the leak.

I couldn't agree more on this one, as we both stood up and started running for the city gates. I watched for any hostile reaction from the Recon Hunters, but none came and I finally felt like we were going to make it. The Recon Hunters stopped only for a moment, looking at us one by one then continued on their patrol. Probably scanning us, I thought.

The gates were drawing closer, my legs pumping as more creatures made their terrible sounds off in the distance, but closer this time. Paradox reached the gate first, not even out of breath as he slammed open a keypad that was positioned next to it. I caught up, and looked at the strange symbols on the pad as Paradox's fingers flew over them. It was a language he apparently knew.

I looked the way we had come from, watching the first of the creatures rise over the slope. It was a Rethagin, it gave a shriek and charged towards us, and more following that started as a trickle and was growing every moment. The leader gave another bloodcurdling cry and was cut off in the middle of it as the first heavy rounds ripped it to pieces and black oil looking blood splashing the ground.

I looked up and saw the Recon Hunters starting to fire while forming into large groups. The first group flew forward out of the city, unloading their rounds into the approaching masses. I cheered them on, not caring if they could understand me or not, and turned to see Paradox still working on the keypad. Firing rang up from the other side of the city as well, and was soon heard from all sides, meaning that we were totally surrounded.

"What's going on Paradox? Talk to me man." I shouted over the noise, as he seemed to finish putting in whatever code he was typing, the keypad giving a denied buzz, and his gloved fingers flew over the symbols once more.

"I have to put in the right code for the area." Paradox shouted back, looking behind him at the carnage then continuing on with the symbols. "It's got to be one of twelve."

Although the dead creatures were piling up, it looked like there were far more still alive with others arriving every moment. The Recon Hunters stayed a safe distance away from them, and continued their attack, propelling themselves all around to get different firing angles for maximum effect. Still, it wasn't enough and looked like they were only slowing down the quivering ocean of twisted muscular bodies that covered most of the plain.

"I got it!" Paradox said, finishing up on the last code. Nothing seemed to happen at first, when a small recorded voice played from a speaker positioned over the keypad saying something I couldn't understand, as the gate rolled heavily open.

Paradox and I rushed inward past the gate, which slowly started to close when Paradox punched in one of the strange symbols on a keypad placed on the opposite side. The heavy chatter of weapons continued on outside the wall, still very loud but dulled a tiny bit because of the wall blocking the sound waves. The city sky was pretty clear except of a few Recon Hunters that zipped back and forth.

I stared at the scene before me, taking it all in and feeling cold inside. I didn't know why I'd been expecting something good to eat, and a cold drink . . . because it held a post-apocalyptic view about it. Paradox looked each way, and then started down the main street. Slowly following him I looked at what were obviously vehicles scattered about not much different from our own, covered only lightly by the crust and easy to tell which were military and which were civilian, some of them still displayed fading colors.

The buildings weren't much better. What looked like it'd once been magnificent stood twisted upwards to the sky, slowly rusting away; pieces falling from the concrete, some of them looking like it had been a miracle they were standing at all. The signs that I could see all had the strange symbols on them, so I was unable to read them. Paradox would stop at these signs, and look at them awhile before moving on, sometimes turning left, sometimes right. I had no idea where he was going, but I didn't have any other choice but to follow him.

The air above us started to fill with the Recon Hunters once again, their orb bodies floating effortlessly above the ground. Outside the firing had slowly started to cease, and I wondered if all the creatures had been killed. Paradox didn't seem to think so, at least. He kept moving on and didn't stop, unless it was at a sign. There was one difference though, and it was that he was now watching the Recon Hunters every moment.

"So do you think they are all dead out there?" I said to Paradox, trying to make a little conversation after the whole ordeal of getting into the city.

He stopped, looking at another sign, then at the Recon Hunters and plotting his course before speaking, "No. I'm pretty sure they just pulled back for now, they aren't friendly with each other, but they aren't stupid either. Anything living is high on their 'To-Eat' list and working together is one of the ways they can achieve that."

To think that the creatures had that much intelligence frightened me. When Paradox had explained how they avoided the mines, and outwitted the hunters, I'd thought that it was just an animal instinct that they'd gotten over time. But this showed that they could think and solve problems that were rather complicated. Hopefully we won't be here long enough for them to come up with a plan, I thought.

Paradox was moving again, and I followed him to one of the buildings. This one was in considerably better shape then the others I'd seen. It was only one story tall and looked like it would be a convenience store but for the fact that it had no windows, and two of the large Recon Hunters sat hovering at either side of the wooden door that served as an entrance. I went cautiously forward with Paradox towards the door, neither of the large Recon Hunters moved as we grew closer. Finally I grasped the door knob when Paradox placed his hand on my shoulder.

"The gateway to our world is around this location." He said then placed his hand on the building's door and nodded to the Recon Hunters. "I'm also certain that whoever is alive is inside here, due to the obvious."

I didn't say anything in return, and opened the door slowly. Inside was dark. The only item producing light was a strange glowing oval of energy that hung downward from the roof. It was only one room, but crowded because it was crammed full of shelves that held what looked like food. I couldn't understand the symbols displayed on the packages and cans, so I decided not to take anything off the shelf.

"Hello?" I called out, receiving no answer from the quiet shelves of food.

Paradox moved past me heading down a row of the shelves and barely making any noise, listening for sound. I shrugged and started moving about without any stealth. I expected that if anyone was there they would have responded to my call. Paradox looked at me, and I was easily able to tell that he was annoyed with me when I saw movement on the opposite side of the shelf he was standing by.

Lone Survivor

*B*efore I could warn him the entire shelf of food was pushed over, crashing down into him as he was knocked to the floor. I ran over to help Paradox, who was still coming to terms of what had just happened. I looked up, raising my fists and ready to fight when I saw a young women standing before me. My mouth dropped, with fists falling to my sides as I looked at her.

She was sixteen, or maybe seventeen years old it looked like. She wore a loose brown uniform that was kept in good condition, with brown combat boots, but it was how she looked that stunned me. Her body alone was more beautiful then any other girl that existed on Earth, with skin as white as snow. She held a delicate looking hand over her mouth; eyes that burned golden were wide in surprise at what she thought she was seeing herself, other survivors. Long dark blue hair cascaded down her back and ended near her waist, and her ears were slightly longer then someone's from Earth, and ended in a gentle curve.

I started stuttering, when she suddenly ran over to me and wrapped me in an embrace, her arms moving around me tightly as she buried her head into my chest and started crying gently. Regardless of everything else, this made me blush heavily. I could feel the blood rush to my face as I awkwardly hugged her back, not saying anything because I had no idea what to say. Paradox made a growl as he shoved the shelf off of himself, causing her to step away from me and turn to him, tears still streaming down her face.

She started speaking to Paradox in a language that I couldn't understand, and it sounded like crystal clear water trickling lightly down a waterfall, angelic. I felt foolish now, because if I had said anything she wouldn't have understood me. Paradox sat up a bit and eyed her as she finished speaking. He nodded and started speaking back to her in the alien language, making me feel left out as she wiped the tears from her eyes. When Paradox was done speaking to her she turned my way, her golden eyes making me go rigid as they studied me, as if waiting for something.

It looked as if Paradox was going to start talking to her again, as I reached out my hand and didn't even think as I blurted out, "My name's Aaron."

Paradox went silent, and watched as she took hold of my hand and looked me in the eyes. A moment passed, then she smiled, almost causing me to blush again as she said unsteadily, "Hello . . . my name is . . . Ethia."

"Ethia, that's a wonderful name, if I do say so myself." I forced myself to say, my eyes locked with her eyes that gleamed a brighter golden when she smiled.

"Aaron, is a wonderful name, if I do say so myself." She said more fluently in response to me.

It was amazing how well she could mimic me. She even replaced the word 'that's' with 'is', I thought. She tried to make her own sentence. She leaned closer to my hazel colored eyes, and looked a little confused as she let go of my hand and turned back to Paradox. She pointed at me and was speaking very rapidly, when Paradox held up his hands and shook his head. She looked exasperated, and Paradox began speaking to her once again in the language that I didn't know.

When Paradox finished speaking she looked over towards me a little curiously, hope burning in her eyes, and giggled a laugh out that made me blush. She grinned and winked at me, then turned back to Paradox and said something that made them both laugh out loud. It didn't last long however, as Paradox went straight back into serious mode and started talking to her. At first she looked horrified at whatever he was telling her, and then tears began brimming out of her eyes again.

"What did you tell her?" I asked Paradox, as he grabbed my shoulder and moved me into a back corner of the store away from her. "Please tell me what you told her before, and after you made her cry."

"Well, first off, when I was climbing up from the shelf she pushed onto me, she was saying she was sorry, and that she didn't know there were any other survivors on the planet. I told her that it was alright no harm done, and that's when you blurted out your name." Paradox said, as he watched my expressions flicker through different settings.

"What about it?" I said, wondering what Paradox could have against that.

"Her race, they were adept at learning things . . . especially languages. As soon as you spoke she instantaneously learned those words." Paradox told me, as I realized that she hadn't mimicked me, but had actually formed her own sentence with the words provided.

"Well, that isn't bad, is it?" I said while Paradox placed his hands on his goggles, like he was tired.

"No, that wasn't exactly bad. She asked me about you, because you were different. Your eyes are what really gave you away . . . this race didn't have hazel eyes." Paradox said, looking back over to the girl that had sat down and was quietly sobbing into her arms. "Anyway, when she asked me about you, I told her that we weren't from this dimension. This got her hopes up."

I looked over at her, she wasn't crying anymore but was just staring at the ground. Her golden eyes had lost the brightness that had made them glow moments before. I turned towards Paradox and shook the image from my mind and said, "So tell me what you told her that made her so sad."

Paradox seemed to think it over and shrugged, as he stated, "I told her she can't come back to our dimension."

"Please," Her beautiful voice washed over me, as I turned and looked at her. Her eyes looked at me, a little hope still there as she said, "take me with you."

"Sorry . . . we can't." Paradox bluntly said making more tears brim out from her eyes and roll down her face as I looked at him incredulously.

"Why can't we?" I demanded more then asked.

Paradox turned back towards me, sternness brimming through his mask and voice as he said, "Imagine what could happen to our world and culture if she is brought with us."

"I don't care what would happen. You're supposed to be a hero, and you want to leave her here to die!" I roared out, smashing an accusing finger in front of his face, "What kind of hero are you?"

The room fell very quiet at this, everyone staying still as I controlled my breathing and forced myself to calm down. Paradox didn't move, his mask never leaving my eyes as time passed us by. I wouldn't let him beat me this time. I kept my eyes locked with his goggles, willing myself not to look away first. He shifted, and then turned away, head lowering so that his hat's brim would conceal his mask.

"I won't stop you from bringing her, but she's your responsibility... along with any other consequences that she brings. This is your choice." Paradox said before walking towards the door.

"One more thing," I said, for once feeling in control of the situation. Paradox stopped and waited for me to ask him the question. "Why did she look at me and laugh?"

"It's when I told her that you were eighteen, because she said you looked quite older then her." Paradox said, then started heading out the door but not before adding, "She's over one thousand years old, but still very young for her race, of course."

I felt myself rock back and forth at this new information, and turned towards Ethia. She stood up and clasped her hands together behind her back as she stood in place, swinging back and forth. I walked slowly up to her, her golden eyes following my every movement as I looked down on her perfect face. She smiled and looked away, giggling again as I felt my face heat up.

"Come on." I said, putting my hand on her shoulder. "Let's take you home."

Ethia looked stunned, then smiled and burst into more tears, but this time of joy. Once more she hugged me tightly, pulling me close to her as I realized that she was much stronger then I was. I breathed in and out, making sure she hadn't cut off my air supply, as I smiled and hugged her back. She seemed surprised at first, her body becoming rigid then loosening as we held each other for a moment more.

I let her pull away first, watching her as she pushed some of her hair over her shoulder. Ethia grinned at me, then turned and started heading for the door as she said, "Come on!"

"By the way, I have something to tell you." I said, causing her to stop and turn around, looking at me in question. "I wanted to say, that for being over a thousand years old, you're wonderful looking." Ethia blushed at this, and she turned around and continued walking as I grinned.

I went after her, walking next to her side and trying to spot anything at all I could look at instead of her. I started whistling, and noticed out of the corner of my eye that she kept glancing at me. It's probably because she hasn't seen anyone in two-hundred years. I reminded myself, as we walked out the building and looked at the last of the suns setting in the distance. Paradox was moving along the side of the building, muttering as he kept his gloved hands flat on the wall.

"It feels like the portal is underneath the building." Paradox said, while continuing alongside it.

The two Recon Hunters followed behind Ethia, flanking both of her sides like car-sized metallic bodyguards. I chuckled and tapped one of them, as it said something in an alien robotic voice that sounded like it was protesting. Ethia laughed at whatever it said, and I wondered what it could have possibly been. I looked at Paradox who was now standing away from the building, hands balled into fists and pressed to his sides.

I was about to poke fun at him, when I heard Ethia say, "This is bad."

Paradox and I turned to look at her as she started speaking quickly in her native language and pointing to the sky frantically. We both looked upwards, and saw that there were no Recon Hunters in the sky ahead; they were all in groups positioned around the wall once again. I listened for any sound of firing, but nothing came to me as Paradox spun around looking from building to building.

"Why aren't they firing?" I asked, "Are they out of ammo?"

Ethia turned to one of the Recon Hunters, and spoke to it quickly. I hated not being able to understand as it said something back in its robotized voice.

"They have ammo." She told me when she turned back around.

I wanted to think about how Ethia was able to learn the English language so fast by hearing the words, but I didn't have the time to do it now. Paradox seemed uneasy, as he glanced about the buildings, then turned towards us and held a gloved hand to his scarf, the one finger sticking up showing us to be quiet. He knelt down, and turned his head to place his ear to the ground. I almost went crazy suddenly thinking I'd get to see his head when he removed his hat, but was dismayed to see him bend the rim rather then take it off.

Paradox held his head to the ground for a moment, then jumped up waving at Ethia and I, "Move, move!" He yelled out, but wasn't fast enough as the ground burst upwards in front of Ethia. The creature that burrowed out of the ground let out a bone shattering roar as it started to fall apart. Bits of it hit the crust ridden ground, sprouting legs and hopping up towards Ethia who was too terrified to move, fangs gnashing for her throat as I jumped against her knocking her out of the way.

I spun myself as we both headed for the ground so she wouldn't hit it, the Recon Hunters started beeping and signaling the others. Slowly their weapons turned downwards towards the monsters, while the creatures dashed over and tore into them, metal and claws screeching throughout the air. I helped her up, while standing myself, as Paradox shouted something incoherent over the sound. I turned to look at him on top of the buildings roof we'd found Ethia in, a ladder nearby and motioning for us to come on.

"Are you alright?" I asked Ethia as we rushed towards the ladder, and she started climbing it.

"I'm alright, and you?" She said, casting me a golden eyed smile amidst all the chaos.

I nodded and was glad that we hadn't left her behind. The Recon Hunters started swarming above the air as we made it onto the roof, with heavy munitions pounding at the street below. I ventured a look over the side, and drew back when more holes erupted from the street and creatures started pouring out of them. Paradox was sitting down in the middle of the roof. I knew that he was thinking hard for a way out of this situation, when Ethia screamed.

I turned to see her running past me as the different creatures poured onto the rooftop, their lifeless eyes and monstrous jaws snapping as heavy rounds pounded into them from above. For every one that died and gave up life, two or three more replaced it, causing the wave of death to grow closer towards us. I ran to the center of the building's roof where Paradox sat as he brushed himself off casually while watching the onslaught approach.

"Well then, I didn't expect this many to show up . . . especially during the day, but now it's almost night." Paradox said calmly over the monstrosity's shrieks of rage and pain. "It looks like I have no choice."

The last sliver of sun disappeared under the far horizon, as Paradox finished speaking his last words, covering the entire land in a deep darkness.

The only light there was now were the bright flashes that appeared as the Recon Hunters continued to blast away at their enemy. Paradox held one arm with the fist balled up in front of his face, the black matter that he controlled spilling out from it as his power grew from the night that covered the planet.

"Hold on ladies and gentlemen." Paradox spoke quietly as he stood up and opened his hand, the black darkness swirling and pulsing into a ball that grew ever larger, "It's going to a big one."

Ethia grabbed onto my arm, the first of the creatures lunging into the air at us as Paradox held up both of his arms in front of his body. A swirl of darkness flew from his back, striking the creature away from us, while dark wisps now seeped out from both of his arms. The creatures weren't deterred by his show of power, pressing forward towards us when Paradox dropped to one knee and slammed both palms onto the roof.

Blackness emitted from him that was visible in the dark night, racing in every direction from Paradox and engulfing the monsters racing towards us where their shrieks ceased immediately. He lifted his hands from the roof, the blackness rising along with them above our heads. Still more creatures started making it onto the roof, although the Recon Hunters were firing away.

Somewhere inside I knew Paradox was grinning, as he clapped his hands together and the blackness above us began spinning rapidly like a funnel. At first I thought it was going to suck the beasts in, but it didn't . . . instead a large black tendril emerged from the center of the swirling abyss that Paradox had opened above our heads. It twisted about, like a deadly snake ready to strike when the first of the creatures reached Paradox.

With a roar the monstrous beast opened its mouth, displaying jagged teeth located randomly inside. The dark tendril shot forward, enveloping the monster and swallowing it whole. The creature's shrieks were garbled as the tendril moved it up towards the spinning funnel, finally siphoning it inside as a second tendril appeared. Ethia and I watched on as Paradox shaped his hands together to resemble the funnel and moved them forward, controlling the dark funnel's movements, the black tendrils whipping out and grabbing any creature within range.

For each creature that was pulled in, a new tendril sprouted, making it multiply in danger the more enemies it pulled inwards. Paradox started moving the twisting mass down into the streets, walking forward so he could get a better view of what he was doing. Soon the spinning funnel was positioned around the holes, the tendrils snatching up anything that dared come out. Paradox counted the holes, memorizing their locations as he broke his hands apart, and pointed downwards towards each hole with a finger.

The swirling blackness exploded apart, splitting into separate strands and flying into the holes that had been created by the creatures. We could hear the massive rush underground slowly cease and Paradox dropped to his hands and knees, breathing heavily and coughing out his dark matter. I walked to the edge of the building and looked downwards towards the openings in the street. Black wisps of Paradox's power trickling out from them, and even made its way through tiny cracks in the ground.

Ethia walked over to Paradox, kneeling down next to him to pat him on the back. Her look of concern touched me, seeing that she was so quick to forgive the man who wanted to leave her there to die. The Recon Hunters were speedily moving about, checking for any other signs of hostile activity, then returned to their usual patrol patterns. Paradox shrugged Ethia's hand off, and stood up looking out towards the Mesa we had started on.

"You doing fine, Paradox?" I asked, walking over to him and Ethia.

"Well, are you doing fine, Aaron?" Ethia said, looking at me with her golden eyes, care showing on her face.

"Yeah, but what about Para-" I was cut of by Paradox snapping his arm upwards.

He turned towards us quickly, and then stated, "We've got to go . . . now."

A thunderous cracking sound rolled throughout the air, emanating from the mesa. I looked out towards it, Paradox already on his way down the ladder and Ethia stalling to see what the noise was with me. The mesa was cracking all over, fault lines running everywhere along it and chunks falling off. Through the bits that fell I could see something squirming in the center of the giant formation. Whatever it was, the mesa had been holding it, but now it was breaking loose.

"Hurry, I woke that thing up and it's not going to be in a happy mood." Paradox said to us, then entered the building.

Ethia and I looked at each other, and then raced to scramble down the ladder and into the building. We listened to the rock shatter altogether outside, along with a roar that shook the very planet. Ethia looked grim, watching Paradox move about the inside as he started shoving the shelves of food away from the center. The ground started quaking, a steady rhythm that was caused by something very large moving this way. Outside the beeping of the Recon Hunters sounded off, they had obviously spotted the approaching thing.

It will be here in a minute or so with how large it is, I thought. Ethia started quivering, a fear in her eyes that she may never even leave this planet after all. I placed a hand on her shoulder, causing her to jump a little and look at me.

"Hey, it's going to be alright." I said, as Paradox yelled out in victory.

"I found it! It's a hatch, like the ones on Earth. Everyone inside, we're getting out of here." Paradox announced, holding the top of it open.

Ethia seemed a little nervous to climb down in, so I went first, once touching down inside I backed away, so she could follow. The sounds of weapon fire starting were barely audible from here, but it was noticeable. It's already here, I thought. Ethia climbed down, looking frankly surprised that she had never known about this place. Paradox jumped in, his duster flying upwards until he landed. I noticed that the second blast door didn't have a keypad, so I pushed it open and walked into the familiar Main Area.

"Get ready to run." I told Ethia, who was visibly nervous.

"No time to run." Paradox said, as he ran over to the generator that was running the lights inside. "We teleport, it already knows we're here. Hold on to her."

I turned to Ethia who was already clinging to me by the time Paradox had finished his sentence. I grabbed on to her, just as Paradox kicked out the generators cord sending the lights off into darkness. Then I felt him grab me and we were flying through the air. Whatever was outside let loose another earth trembling roar, and smashed into the underground facility.

All I could see was the things gigantic mouth moving towards us through the earth, devouring everything that got in its way in a gamble to devour us along with whatever else it caught. I was thankful that Ethia had her eyes closed. The giant mouth vanished before my eyes, and I felt like I was being torn to pieces once again and shoved through a small hole. Dang it, not this again! Paradox must've teleported straight into the vortex, I thought as I wondered how Ethia was fairing.

Then it was over. I was staring up into a clear blue sky where the vortex was throbbing, no longer in pain as I sat up and saw that I was in a lush field. The grass was really tall, and flowers bloomed throughout it. A stark contrast to all the color was Paradox, black clothes from head to toe standing in one place and making a sign with his hands while facing the portal. He slowly closed his hands inward, and then broke them apart as the portal vanished. Good riddance, I thought.

I stood up and walked over to him, patting him on the back as he breathed in deep, and let it out slowly. Paradox looked about him, lingering on the flowers and grass as he chuckled ever so lightly.

"What's so funny?" I asked, and partially expecting the answer.

"This . . ." Paradox said waving his hand lazily over the field and flowers, "is definitely not my style."

I laughed as he took his turn and patted me on the back, feeling like we'd just performed a job well done. We heard Ethia make a slight sound, and hurried over to where she was lying in the grass. I smiled, happy that I'd brought her from that nightmare, as she slept peacefully with a smile of her own on her face. It was her first time through a vortex like that after all. Paradox shrugged, adjusting his duster and gloves as he turned to go.

"Where are you going?" I asked, still not believing that he wasn't tired or didn't need sleep.

"I'm going to look for a phone, to call the number on the back of Justin's photo." He said as he continued walking off, not turning back.

"Do you even know where we are?" I asked, never knowing what he actually knew.

"Nope, I don't." He said plainly.

"Then how do you know you're going the right way?" I asked again, plopping down next to Ethia and swishing a bee away that had landed on her.

"Maybe it's because I saw a sign." Paradox replied pointing ahead, where a gas station sign was barely visible behind the tree line. "You can wait here and rest up if you want. I'll be back as soon as I find a phone."

I watched Paradox continue walking away, knowing that he was either telling the truth about not needing sleep, or just plain old stubborn. *Perhaps both,* I thought. Looking at the comfortable grass I thought about choosing my own place to sleep, rather then next to Ethia. I got ready to stand up and go then stopped, looking back at her and smiling again.

"Don't leave." Ethia said in her sleep, making me smile wider. "Take me with you." She said, making me hope she wasn't reliving the entire nightmare while asleep. I guess I'll stay here, I thought, laying down next to her and closing my eyes as she rolled over placing her arm over me.

I laid there on the ground, my eyes closed as I slowly drifted off to sleep when I heard Ethia whisper into my ear, "Thank you." It was the first person that I'd saved, and I felt like a hero.

Epsilons Ambush

*P*aradox walked into the small gas station, looking about for anything off at all. It seemed alright, nothing amiss as he walked towards the cash register, heavy boots thudding against the floor. He examined the man attending the register, not really attending it but watching the T.V. set up in the corner of the store. Paradox waited a moment, not moving at all as the short man continued watching the T.V., his balding hair getting twirled around his fingers while he watched a commercial.

"Excuse me." Paradox said, as the man crashed backwards into his chair while spinning around.

"Goodness!" He said, his tiny beady eyes in his round facing eyeing Paradox up and down. "Don't do that, there's enough strange stuff going on around here!"

"Like what?" Paradox asked as politely as he could, looking the man in the eyes and forcing him to look away.

"You know . . . people have been disappearing. They've found the bodies of a few, and also of some strange critters running around." The short man said, his face turning red a little from being forced to look away in his own store.

"Interesting, I'll take note of that." Paradox said, thinking it was probably some Rethagins or something that had made it out of the portal he'd just closed. "If you don't mind me asking, where am I?"

"Why, Oregon of course!" Said the man, looking at him a little suspiciously now, "Why you asking? You lost?"

"Not lost." Paradox said, the leaned forward towards the man, making him nervous, "Just didn't know where I was, that doesn't make you lost . . . does it?"

The man shook his head no, as the door to the gas station rang out. Paradox turned to see me walk in with Ethia, who had woken up and was too excited about where she was to go back to sleep. I grinned, shrugging at Paradox who turned back to the man and backed away a little. I wondered if he'd asked about a phone yet, when I heard Ethia ripping something open. I turned and saw her with an open bag of chips, stuffing them in her mouth as I chuckled a little.

"We'll pay for that." Paradox told the man, who just nodded in response while staring at Aaron. "By the way, do you have a phone?"

"It's for employees only." The man said, puffing his chest out then looked down at the one hundred dollar bill that Paradox slipped out of his sleeve.

"It will be worth your time." Paradox said, as the man stuffed the money into his pocket and led him around the counter to the phone.

Ethia walked over to me, the biggest grin I'd seen on her face yet as she chewed on the chips happily. I smiled, reaching up and wiping my face to show her that she had some crumbs on it. She reached up and brushed in the wrong place, and I shook my head as she stuck her head forward to let me wipe it off. I didn't do anything for a moment, as she raised her eyebrows, her golden eyes sparkling as she said, "Please Aaron?"

"Alright, if you insist." I said, then reached up and gently wiped off the crumbs, marveling at how soft her skin was which made me blush, and her to laugh a little.

Paradox loomed out from behind the counter, looking at Ethia and me before shaking his head and saying, "She's way too old for you."

"Of course, she's much more around your age." I said sarcastically while dropping my hand from her face.

Ethia grinned placing the bag of chips on the shelf next to her, wrapping her arm around my own then interlocking her fingers with mine. I stood straight up, not having expected this as she looked at Paradox with a smile before leaning her head on my shoulder and saying, "I don't think Aaron cares Paradox."

"Well, I do care . . . I mean I don't . . . I mean . . . ." I tried to explain as Ethia looked at me in confusion, her golden eyes looking worried as I finally shut my mouth.

"Aaron, Aaron, Aaron." Paradox said, shaking his head back and forth before walking out of the store. "You don't know what you've gotten yourself into."

"What do you mean?" I said following Paradox out the door as Ethia walked alongside me, her am still around mine and grasping my hand.

Paradox looked at me from the side of his goggles, and then looked at her hand grasping mine. "She's yours." He said, before continuing on quickly.

"What do you mean she's mine?" I said, as Paradox quickly placed distance between us moving past the gas pumps, and looked ahead like he didn't know who we were as he waved the back of his hand at us.

"It's something about her race. Once she chooses the man that she wants, she'll stick with him until the end of time. If you happen to die before she does, then she won't ever choose another man to be with her, and will be very sad for a long, long time. She'll also be, um . . . ." He said then muttered something else under his breath that I couldn't hear.

"She does know that I don't live near as long as she does, right?" I shouted to Paradox, who was still placing distance between us and walking alongside the road now.

"I guess that's your problem." Paradox shouted back, and stopped rushing forward but kept a steady distance between us.

I sighed, and looked at Ethia who was resting her cheek on my shoulder and gazing at me with interest as she said, "Don't worry, it's going to be alright Aaron."

"So I have no say in the matter, huh?" I said looking into her eyes, feeling lucky but not lucky at the same time. After all, if she was a thousand years old and still young . . . then I'd die and leave her all alone to who knows how many years of misery.

"Is it a bad choice?" She said looking at me, fear in her eyes that I wouldn't agree with her.

I faltered under her golden eyes that dimmed when she got nervous and carefully un-wrapped my arm from hers. She seemed to be about to cry, when I placed my arm around her shoulders and hugged her close to me, then reaching over with my free arm and grabbing her hand. The fear and sadness melted from her eyes, as they burned brighter than the sun and she said something in her native language I couldn't understand.

"I feel like it's a choice that I could never go against." I said, as I squeezed her hand tighter.

Out of the corner of my eye I could see Paradox looking over his shoulder at us, snorting at the scene before him. I hoped that he would tell me about any other customs that this race had, before I was surprised by anything else Ethia did. For now it seemed like this was enough for her as we walked down the street, together in each others arms. I just hope she doesn't suddenly want to do anything else that her race was used to, attracting attention, I thought as I tore my face away from hers to look ahead where the road turned out of view.

Paradox chuckled to himself as he moved along the road, leaving their view and thinking how interesting this was. Of course there could be very large consequences because he allowed Aaron to bring her to this dimension, but Aaron had been right. What kind of hero leaves someone behind to die? Oh well, good training for him, Paradox thought, only vaguely seeing the police car move past him in the opposite direction as his thoughts churned about, he may make a better hero then myself yet. Still, he had other things to worry about at the present time . . . not the far future.

I watched Paradox disappear from view, and shortly afterwards a police cruiser drove by, which slowed down and stopped, making a U-turn to head back in our direction. I didn't feel comfortable about this as the car moved past us really slowly. Ethia looked at the car a bit curiously, unafraid but interested in how it looked compared to her worlds vehicles. It pulled over to the side of the road, blocking our path as both doors opened and two officers stepped out from it.

"Well, look at what we have here . . . the little arsonist that set Central Park ablaze." The first of the officers said, grabbing his baton with one arm and holding a picture in the other.

I wondered how they could have thought that I was the one to cause the fire in Central Park, and even more so have a picture of me, when my mind flashed back to the ruddy faced man waving his phone. That must be it, I thought, who knows how many pictures he could've taken. Ethia looked at me with question burning in her eyes, her hand gripping mine tighter.

"I didn't set anything on fire." I said to both her and the cops. Ethia accepted my answer, and turned her golden eyes back to the police who didn't.

"Is that so? It couldn't have been you, eh?" The second officer said, his deep bass voice thrumming out from the large frame of a body he had. "Well, judging by this picture that was sent out . . . and the description given to us by the officer's who claimed to have caught you sleeping under a tree in the park at night, you must be the guy. So where's the other two? The one dressed in black, and the ragged uniform man."

"Paradox isn't here. As for Justin, you wouldn't believe me if I told you." I said loudly, hoping Paradox would hear me and help in some way.

"Paradox . . . I'm guessing that's the masked one, isn't it? Well . . . the call we received from the gas station employee out here reported the two of you in the area. He also said that some guy wearing all black wanted to use the phone." The first officer said switching his hand from his baton to the handcuffs he carried. "Anyways, we don't know if you flew, or what, to get to Oregon from New York so fast, but we're going to have to take you in."

"I don't have time for this you guys." I said, exasperated because they wouldn't believe everything if I told them about it, and that I needed to find Justin quickly.

"We'll make time." The second officer boomed out.

Both of the men took a few steps forward then stopped and looked at Ethia for the first time, who was nervous and a little confused as she said, "Please don't take Aaron."

One of the officers took off his pair of sunglasses he was wearing, narrowing his eyes at her while the other leaned towards his partner. They looked uncertainly about her, and then at the paper that must have had my picture and the descriptions on it. The second officer shook his head, and then whispered something to the other before he lowered the paper and looked at Ethia again.

"Well, you're not in the descriptions . . . but your eyes. You're seeing this too, right Frank?" The first officer said, as the one called Frank nodded yes.

"Yeah, she could be on something . . . I've never seen eyes like that." Frank said then pausing a moment, looking at her, then saying, "Anyways, we've got to bring this guy Aaron in, and we could run some tests on her. What do you think it is?"

"I don't know." The first officer said as he started moving forward again.

"She's alright, there's nothing wrong with her, no drugs . . . just leave her alone." I said while Ethia almost crushed my hand with her grip. I'd forgotten how strong she was.

I took my arm from around her shoulders, and looked at Ethia. She was looking very confused now, and more nervous as the officers both marched up to me and her. I placed my free hand softly on the one she was crushing, and she loosened her grip. The officers waited a moment to see if we would let go of each other's hands then sighed.

"Please place both of your hands behind your back." Frank said waiting for us to comply then made a frustrated noise as Ethia took me into an embrace. I smiled and hugged her back, closing my eyes as I did so and feeling warm inside.

"Alright, move them apart from one another." The first officer said, as he grabbed me from behind and Frank grabbed Ethia, trying to pull us apart.

They tugged against us, slowly managing to succeed in tearing us away from each other. Ethia started sobbing, her golden eyes dimming greatly as she watched me yanked from her arms. Frank didn't seem to care at all, grunting while he struggled to pull her back away from me. I strained my neck to see if Paradox was coming, but there was still no sign of him as the officer forced my arms together and cuffed them.

"You're under arrest." He said before dragging me towards the cruiser.

"No! Aaron! I won't leave you." Ethia shouted, no longer sobbing but screaming in her own language now, sounding like someone was torturing her to death.

"Hey ma'am, cool it." I heard Frank say while my head was slammed face first against the cruiser going numb.

Ethia saw this and went limp, her body hanging from Franks hands as she started trembling with her face towards the ground. I struggled against the officer who held me down, thinking that Frank had done something to her when I felt it. The air seemed to compress in the area around us, as Ethia slowly lifted her head. I couldn't move when her eyes locked with mine, they were burning golden, but this time it was fueled by rage.

"I said . . . leave Aaron alone!" Ethia roared throwing Frank off of her, causing the cop to stumble backwards and try to keep his balance. In an instant she jumped upwards, dark blue hair flowing behind her while delivering a spinning kick with such force to his cheek that it created a ripple throughout the air, sending the receiver off his feet, through the air a small ways, and onto the ground where he lay unmoving.

"Frank! What the heck?" The first officer said, releasing his grip on me and turning to face Ethia. He grabbed his baton and removed it from his belt while she turned to look at him, her eyes narrowed in anger as the officer rushed her, the baton raised above his head to strike.

The officer smashed downward with the baton aiming for Ethia's head, making a surprised gasp when she reached up and took the blow with her hand, stopping the black weapons descent by grabbing it. He tried to pull it back, but it was held firmly in place by her sheer power. Finally he let go of it, reaching for his pistol when Ethia dropped down and swept the officers legs out from under him with her own. In the same moment, before he hit the ground, she threw a flat palmed strike forward that connected with his gut. The officer's eyes seemed to bulge, the air shuddering from the blow, before he flew away from her and smashed into the cruiser next to me, leaving a sizable dent.

Looking back and forth between the two officers, Frank was lying totally still. I couldn't tell if he was breathing or not, and the first officer next to me was alive but had been either seriously injured or knocked out. Ethia stood in one place, facing the unconscious man before exploding forward towards the cruiser with inhuman speed, eyes glowing violently as she shifted her hand behind her and aimed for the unconscious man on the ground.

If she hits him again it will kill him for sure, I thought then called out to her, "Ethia, please stop . . . enough of this!"

Ethia's eyes widened a little at my voice, and started slowing her run when she felt something grab her cocked back arm. She twisted around, throwing her free hand at Paradox who stood his ground. Paradox didn't budge an inch, still holding her arm as the other stopped a mere inch from his mask.

"Have you calmed down yet?" Paradox said his arm quivering a little from gripping her own.

I watched her begin breathing in and out heavily, as she quivered and fell to the ground. Paradox breathed a sigh of relief and caught her, setting her down gently before walking over to the officer and taking all of his keys, then moved over and undid my handcuffs. He turned and looked at Ethia a moment more, before he headed to the drivers side of the vehicle.

"What I said . . . is that she'd also be very protective." Paradox spoke quietly to me, opening the door and surveying the scene. "We're taking the vehicle, I'll explain why on the way. Come on when you're ready, don't worry about them, they're alright. When they wake up they probably won't remember what happened, is all." Paradox finished then climbed into the car, shutting the door on my surprised face.

Walking over to where Ethia was lying, I knelt down next to her side. Her golden eyes were opened slightly with tears leaking out of them. I could hear her whispering something, and when I put my ear near her mouth she was saying, "I'm so sorry, Aaron. So sorry, that was bad. I couldn't let them take you away from me."

"Hey," I said, brushing the tears from her face and lifting her from the ground so that she was resting in my arms. "It's okay, and I've got to explain some things to you anyways. Thank you for protecting me."

Ethia smiled slightly and finished closing her eyes, falling asleep as I placed her gently into the back of the cruiser so she'd have room to lie down. Closing the door I made my way to the passenger's side and climbed in. Paradox was looking straight ahead, and started the vehicle before pulling away from the curb and driving down the road. I watched for signs, trying to figure out where we were heading to, and finally gave up.

"So you want to fill me in about where we are going? Who's phone number that is written on the back of the photo? Why we are stealing a police car? Oh, and of course, fill me in a bit more about Ethia's race, because what I saw back there was incredible." I said sounding a little demanding, but also like I had the right to know.

"I'll start with the phone number." Paradox said calmly, taking a turn and passing another car that immediately slowed down when it came into view of our vehicle. "Whoever picked up was a lady . . . most likely the one from the picture. I asked who it was, but she refused to tell me, asking who I was. Of course I didn't tell her who I was," Paradox said, pointing to his mask, "but mentioned Justin. She grew very quiet, and then asked what I knew about him. I gave her his description, and she almost sounded like she didn't believe me until I told her about the photo. She asked where

I was, and I told her Oregon. She offered to meet with us back in New York, and I agreed."

"So we left where we needed to be." I groaned, and looked out at the trees whirring by. "So that answers two of my questions, but what about stealing the car?"

"Here's where it gets a little complicated." Paradox said, looking at me before turning back to the road. "Justin said that little device he wore could track my teleportation and allow them to replicate it, but he didn't say how large of a range the main device could detect had, for all we know he didn't know. It would be too risky to teleport straight to New York during the night, because they could pick it up and send in troops to stop us."

"So we stole this vehicle to drive us there?" I asked a little skeptically.

"Unless you would rather walk to New York, then yes that's why." Paradox said.

"But why steal a police car? We could have rented a car, at the least." I tried to reason, while Paradox shook his head no.

"First of all, we don't know how far the nearest town was, and second, in a police vehicle the Twilight Core will be less likely to notice and engage us in combat. After all, they are pretty low profile. They wouldn't want trouble with the authorities."

"Do they really have that many men?" I asked a little paranoid, wondering if anyone I'd known in my life was one of them.

"I don't know, but I've seen plenty of them. You can never tell who might be one or not." Paradox stated then said, "And with the normal authorities after us, you can bet they are using this as an advantage to keep their eyes open for us."

"Alright, you win." I said surrendering to Paradox, and knowing that it was just about impossible to change his mind once it was set. "So tell me a bit more about Ethia, well . . . her race anyways."

Paradox huffed out, looking at me then back at Ethia who was still sleeping soundly. "As I've already told you, her world was much like ours. They are almost identical to our race, as you can see, but had a few different characteristics." Paradox paused a moment, looking at his hand and moving one finger up after another as if counting. "The first is their eye color. They could have anything from black to gold, but never any multiple colors in their eyes . . . just one. Then there are the ears. They are slightly longer then ours, kind of like an elves but not pointed, it still curves like ours do and they have better hearing then us."

"Does that have anything to do with their learning speech capabilities?" I asked intrigued by what I was learning.

"No, that would just be their mind. Please, let me continue." Paradox said looking annoyed at being interrupted. "Then there is the hair color. Yes, they had all the same colors we do, but they can also have different natural hair color. Ethia's is dark blue, very rare in most of her race actually. Needless to say, most of those from her race looked angelic compared to our own. Last but not least, is their strength . . . even I would be afraid to make one angry, and it took a lot for me to try and stop her from killing that officer. They have a way of focusing their energy. Rapidly using it but augmenting their strength, speed, perception making them a superhuman to us, pretty much."

"So that's all that's different between us?" I said with more hope sounding in my voice then I'd wanted.

"Besides her being able to live multiples of thousands of years, and what her race was used to and accepted different from our own . . . yeah." Paradox said, still not sounding too thrilled to be speaking about this.

"Then why'd she choose me?" I asked him, and he shrugged in response.

"Who knows? They have their ways . . . you can look at it either as a good thing, or bad . . . you choose." He said, signaling a turn and hitting a freeway that I didn't recognize.

I grinned, smiling and leaning back in my chair slightly before I said, "I think I've already chosen how to look at it, and as long as she likes me I'm cool with it. I've still got to explain to her what's going on."

"We'll see how it turns out." Paradox said, watching the vehicles pass us by and setting the cruise control.

I looked out the window, slowly growing tired at the passing scenery and not looking forward to the long drive. Who knows what's going on with Justin, I thought. Do we even have the time it will take to drive to New York? I closed my eyes, figuring that I could get some sleep on the way. I hadn't gotten much, and now seemed like a good time.

I woke up from a dreamless sleep, happy that I hadn't had any dreams at all especially of nightmares. The radio was on, and Ethia was sitting in the backseat listening to it. She gave me a smile through the hole that had been carved carefully through the Plexiglas that separated us as I sat upwards. Paradox was looking at a map, while driving at the same time, tapping his fingers against the steering wheel and moving his head back and forth between the road and the map.

"Good morning Aaron!" Ethia said looking really cheerful. "Did you sleep well?"

"Yeah, I did, thank you." I said, watching her beam at my simple words and noticed that she was now speaking English rather well. I focused on the cut away Plexiglas, and tapped away near the hole. "So what happened here?"

Ethia giggled, and Paradox stiffened at my question before he roughly said, "She wouldn't stop berating me while I was driving until I had cut out enough Plexiglas so that it wouldn't, in her words, 'Keep her away from you.' I finally gave in, and once it was cut away she kept on asking me to teach her English. I finally drowned her out in the radio. It's a good enough teacher for her."

"Quit being so uptight Paradox." Ethia said, flashing her eyes at him. "You're just mad that you don't know where we are."

I looked at Paradox who was staring straight at the road now, and crumpling the map in one gloved hand as he threw it back at her. She held up her hands and blocked the attack, grabbing her hand and pretending Paradox had broken it, saying, "Ouch, Paradox! You big brute, how could you hurt a lady?"

"So sue me because I can't read a map." Paradox grunted, avoiding her taunts as he added, "I usually teleport around during night if I have to travel."

"I guess I can see your point." I said, making Ethia look a little disappointed that I hadn't sided with her. "So what's the plan then?"

"Going to stop at the next town, and we'll figure it out from there." Paradox said while turning the radio to a rock channel.

"Then maybe Aaron can show me around." Ethia said excitedly, clapping her hands together and reaching her hand through the opening of the Plexiglas to squeeze the back of my neck tenderly. I still wasn't used to the attention she was giving me.

"Remember, Aaron was my student before he was your . . . whatever you want to call him." Paradox snapped at her.

"Lover?" Ethia said lightly.

"Whoa, whoa, whoa," I said, grabbing her arm which had begun massaging my neck and carefully moved it away. "I don't think we've hit that yet, we're just . . . close friends."

"But-" She began, then was cut off by Paradox who interrupted.

"I really liked it better when you didn't speak English so well, if at all." He cut in sharply then turned up the music a lot, causing her to snap her mouth shut. It was obvious she was angry with Paradox and not me as she watched him, her golden eyes burning, but I didn't say anything. It was probably better that I wasn't involved in this situation.

It wasn't long until we turned onto an off ramp, and made our way to a no name town, that was moderate in size. Located in the middle of a desert region with small shrubs everywhere, I could feel the suns heat beat down on me when I exited the car after we'd pulled into a restaurant. Paradox tossed me the keys so that I could let Ethia out, who was patiently waiting for me to open the door, while he strode towards the door of the establishment.

I opened it and she jumped out, stretching her arms and legs while tossing her head back and forth making her dark blue hair shine in the sunlight. I looked around and didn't see anyone around who seemed to care. I swallowed and shrugged, making the first move this time as I reached out and grabbed her hand when she finished stretching. She looked a little surprised at this, then leaned against me looking into my eyes and smiling.

"So what do you want to do, *close* friend?" She asked me, causing me to blush.

"Well, what do you want to do?" I asked her, making her eyes glow brighter as she looked around and at the restaurant that Paradox had entered.

"I don't know there's so much to see, so much to learn! I can't decide." She said, then frowned and turned a little, looking at a delivery man who was watching her and walking by with a small package in his hand. She looked slowly back over to me, and said, "I just want to be with you."

"Well you are." I said, noticing the man also, who had finally looked away and was going around a corner of a building.

"I just don't know where to start." Ethia said, and then tugged on my arm towards the restaurant.

"I have to explain some things to you, and what we're doing before we can actually spend some fun time together." I said, as she just about reached the door.

She stopped and looked at me, finally understanding that Paradox and I were on a mission, and that we'd found her on the way here. "I understand . . . but after that you can show me your world, right?"

"Right." I said, opening the door for her and touching her perfect nose with my finger as I said this.

The doors bell rang out to quite a few people inside, all of them talking at once creating a constant buzz throughout the air. Ethia was quiet, turning her head this way and that, listening to all the words that she could. By now she probably has most of our language down, I thought, looking at her and noting that we needed to get her some less conspicuous clothes for her to wear. Paradox sat in the back corner of the building, waiting for us to head over as the smell of food drifted throughout the air.

Ethia's stomach rumbled, followed by mine. I remembered that I hadn't eaten for a day, much less drank anything. On the other hand, who knew how long it had been since Ethia had eaten a full course meal instead of a prepackaged food? She was looking in the direction of the smell, and grabbed her stomach before looking at me.

I wonder what she eats, I thought, recalling all of the food that had been labeled under her language. She ate chips at the gas station right down. Paradox waved his hand at us, perhaps thinking we hadn't seen him, although he was very obvious amid all the discussions going on. I looked at Ethia, her face was contorted into a tortured look after smelling the food.

"Don't worry, Paradox will take care of the food. He doesn't eat, so this is obviously for us." I said, as she looked doubtfully towards the masked man sitting in the corner.

"I already ordered for you both." Paradox said when we approached him. "Take a seat."

The food arrived just as I sat down. He must have ordered the meals before we came in, I thought. Mine was a plate filled with scrambled eggs, bacon, toast and jam. Ethia looked at it curiously but hungrily, and then turned to her meal, which consisted of a ham omelet, cinnamon twists and a small bowl of soup. She scooted in next to me and grabbed the fork provided to her, twirling it in her hand before cutting into her food, and quickly eating it.

Her table manners were surprisingly good, and I decided now would be the time to explain what was going on. I spoke to her as she ate, periodically she'd carefully dab her mouth with a napkin while listening intently. She didn't say anything, but her eyes would grow wide when I hit some of the suspenseful parts, sometimes accompanied by a little gasp. I could tell her interest shot to the highest point when I explained our trek across the barren wasteland of her home world, to her city.

I started wrapping up some of the details in the story when a bus pulled up to the diner, and a group of about twenty men entered. The sun was setting, and they all looked at it, as if judging the time, before crowding their way to the seats around us. Most of them had military style haircuts, but we didn't pay them any mind, and I finished the story. Paradox nodded, as if satisfied with the explanation, leaning back and staring at the roof.

Ethia finished scraping her plate down and turned to me, wiping her mouth down one more time before saying, "I'm glad you're okay, to go through that and . . . ." She stopped, trailing off as she frowned and turned to look behind her. I twisted in place to see what she was looking at, and I joined her in frowning when I saw that the same delivery man with the small package was sitting across the area staring at us. Paradox whistled slowly, still looking up at the roof.

"It appears that we are surrounded." He said quiet enough that only we could hear him, after he'd finished whistling.

"Surrounded?" Ethia and I whispered together, looking carefully around at the other tables.

The other tables that held the other men were filled with food that hadn't been touched. All of them sat quietly, once and awhile glancing at us. So these are Twilight Soldiers undercover, I thought. They were all very fit, between that and the hairstyles they had, the men otherwise looked like ordinary people. They all wore jeans and long-sleeved jackets. One of the men, who were looking at us, had his jacket undone, and I could see part of a symbol that resembled the Twilight Cores flag insignia from my dreams.

"Epsilon Force trained for quick and clean assassinations." Paradox said, moving his head from the roof to the real family's and people in the diner, who were slowly leaving. "I've faced them a few times, and barely managed to escape. They'll make their move either when we get up to leave, or when most of the people have left."

The sun finished setting, and the world grew darker as I looked at Paradox and said, "Well, since it's not too bright outside now they won't be such a problem, right?"

"They chose this location to fight me because they know I won't use my powers largely in a public setting." Paradox said standing up along with the last large family in the back of the restaurant. "But that doesn't mean I can't fight back, anyone can."

Ethia stood up and moved out of the way, so that I was able to get out from the table. Almost the entire group of assassin agents was watching us now, and Paradox started walking towards the door the family left through when they all stood up calmly. I was still getting up from my sitting position when I watched them all rush quickly at Paradox, who was now in the center of the group.

Gleaming blades emerged from under the sleeves of their jackets, shining under the dim lights when the first assassin reached Paradox and stabbed at him. The knife never reached its mark as Paradox moved around the thrust, grabbing the assaulters arm and throwing him into a few of the others on their way. Two more assassins reached where he was standing, duel blades sprouting out from under each of their sleeves.

Paradox didn't have much time to react, having both of the soldiers move in on opposite sides of him. The first soldier swung one of his blades towards Paradox's head, while the other man swung the reverse direction for his abdomen. The blades drew closer, and Paradox back flipped through air, moving between both the blades which passed through the air harmlessly, nipping through his clothes like butter. Paradox landed on both feet, and was assaulted with all the assassins rushing forward.

Paradox held his arms outward and created two blade-like figures from the dark matter that poured from his wrists. He started parrying the attacks, unable to jab out and make his own attack for fear of leaving himself open. Slowly the attacks were drawing closer, and soon I knew that he would be struck unless he did something else. The blades rang out, connecting with each other when the dark matter forming Paradox's blades started something new.

The black matter was splitting away when they now blocked an opponent's blow, sending dark pinpoint projectiles at the two nearest assassins next to the one who struck out at Paradox, forcing them to block and giving him more time to react.

"Come on, you guys, you can do better then this." Paradox chortled out, making a few of the soldiers give angry shouts.

It was a stalemate for now, Paradox was unable to do anymore then he was able to right now, and the soldiers were being forced to counter his attack created with each blow they made at him. Ethia watched this, looking impressed with what was going on before her. I gripped one of the heavy plates on our table, and turned towards her. She looked at the plate, and then at each of the soldiers.

"These are the men that are after you?" She said, turning back towards me as I held the plate in a Frisbee stance and took aim.

"Yeah, these are the ones." I said, and looked into her golden eyes. "I've got to help Paradox, you should stay back here."

"No." Ethia said plainly, grabbing my shoulder and her eyes burning ferociously. "I can't allow you to get hurt, I'll help."

I was ready to argue when she touched her fingers to her lips, and then placed them on mine. I shivered, feeling a strange energy pour into me as she said affectionately, "We can argue later, if that's what you'd like."

She turned before I could respond. The air broke around her with energy and propelled her forward like a rocket. Some of the soldiers must've felt the force moving towards them, and turned to face it. To Ethia they probably looked like they were moving in slow motion, because the assassins hadn't even made it all the way around before she'd closed the distance between them and launched herself from a nearby table. She tilted sideways in the air twisting gracefully, her leg that had provided the lift off still pointing down towards the ground while she faced me, her back to the soldiers.

The first of the soldiers finished his rotation towards her, unable to lift his blades up and defend his face that was struck hard by the back of Ethia's elbow sending him through the window, while simultaneously the heel of her other leg glided sideways through the air and smashed against the second soldiers temple and blew him past the others. She finished by landing on the one leg positioned towards the floor, and using the gained momentum she'd received to twirl in place like a ballerina to deliver a fist into a third soldiers back which I could hear shatter.

Paradox grunted his thanks, and started working his way closer to the soldier's still striking, dark matter trickling out from his body and grasping at the air about him. Five of the men broke off from Paradox, after receiving a nod from one of those that were sparring with him, and faced Ethia.

"Hey there pretty lady." One of the soldiers said cracking his knuckles, and looking her up and down. "Why don't you hang out with us real men?"

Ethia looked away for a second to the soldier with the broken back lying on the ground before saying, "You don't seem like men to me." The soldiers snarled and prepared to rush forward towards her when she stamped her foot on the floor, causing it to crack all around her and making the soldiers pause. She stood her ground, not moving forward or retreating and added, "Also, from what I can see, and how you're treating Paradox . . . although he can be rude at times, I'm happy I chose the person to be with that I did."

My face flushed as Ethia took the time to glance back at me and wink. All five charged forward, four of the soldiers striking out at various points on her body that would kill her quickly as they moved towards her. She dropped backward, allowing the blades to fly over her. She then palmed the ground, lifting her legs to deliver two jaw shattering kicks with the boots she wore into two of the soldier's chins. They rose from the ground, and almost struck the roof before gravity took them back to the floor.

Two of the three still standing reached out and grabbed her legs, lifting her from the ground before she could gain any leverage. She struggled against the men, but it looked like they were managing to hold each of her legs still. The third soldier raised his knife to cut her straight down the middle as she clawed out, unable to reach the two soldiers lifting her by the legs.

"Thank you Aaron." Ethia mouthed, closing her eyes and ready to die for my sake, as I swung the heavy dish plate from my arm and caught the third soldier in the throat.

He gagged, lowering his knife and gripped his throat trying to breathe. I grabbed an empty beer bottle that one of the soldiers had used from the nearest table, and shattered it creating a sharp weapon. The third one was still huffing, and I ran at the two still holding Ethia, forcing one of them to let go of her leg to face me. He held his blades up with experience, a serious look on his face no matter who his opponent was.

"No Aaron, don't worry about me, don't fight him!" Ethia said before getting thrown to the floor by the other soldier who didn't want to hold her up, then stepped on her gut, holding her down.

I watched Ethia, who looked like she was trying not to cry, when I felt my own anger brim from inside myself. I controlled it, and said out loud to her, "How can you be willing to give your own life for me, but I can't for you Ethia?" She opened her mouth to speak but only made a strangled noise as the third soldier moved next to her and booted her in the face before stepping on her neck, but not pressing down hard enough to break it.

"Come on Harold, take this kid out and we can maybe have some fun with her before we finish the job!" The third soldier exclaimed, as the serious man facing me gave a nod while the other two laughed.

"Hang on Ethia, I'm coming for you." I said walking towards the one named Harold, while the two other soldiers started making bets on how long they thought it was going to take Harold to kill me.

I wasn't sure how to approach him, and I forced everything out of my mind that might distract me. Paradox had always told me to expect the worst, and so I was. There were three of them, not just one. If I managed to beat him, or even start to beat him the others would jump in. In that case, I'd have to be ready to deal with all three of them. I stopped, a little away from Harold, who waited unmoving. It was apparent that he knew his striking range, so he didn't bother swinging out.

He was trained, and experienced in knife fighting . . . in all reality I didn't think I had a chance, but I had to save Ethia. I didn't have much choice, and ran straight at him. I could see his eyes widen, but only slightly, perhaps he hadn't anticipated this. His right hand surged forward, and I knew it would strike me first, so I fell forward under it.

As I hit the ground I grabbed his leg, and shoved the broken bottle into it before he had time to do anything else. Harold roared in pain, and lifted his boot to stomp down on my head. I looked over to Ethia whose mouth was trickling what looked like purple blood down her cheek, her eyes were tiny slits, but I could see the horror in them. I rolled on the ground as hard as I could, smashing into his injured leg and causing him to lose his balance. Harold toppled over, and the two soldiers holding Ethia down yelled at him, then the second ran off in the direction of Paradox.

The third soldier turned, looking down at Ethia he raised both of his blades to strike downwards to kill her. I crawled over, twisting onto my back and placing myself between her and the soldier's blades as they were stabbed downwards. My arms reacted automatically, and shot up and around the blades, grabbing the hands of the soldier and fighting against him. I could fill the adrenaline mixed with my anger, keeping his blades away from us both. The soldier gave a startled gasp of surprise, and then disappeared from view as he was jerked from my hands, the blades cutting my palms as they slid through quickly.

I sat up, ignoring the pain and watched him lifted up into the air. Paradox was standing between all of the soldiers, all of them surrounded by the dark power that he possessed and suspended in the air by it. They were struggling, but couldn't break free as Paradox finished wrapping the last soldier he'd grabbed and turned to me.

"Are you two alright?" Paradox said, not noticing the man with the package in the back of the diner still watching us.

I nodded, getting on my hands and knees to face Ethia. For all of the strength she had, now she looked very fragile. I lifted her back off the ground in one of my arms. Her eyes that were struggling to stay opened looked at me. I wiped the blood off the side of her cheek carefully, and could feel tears behind my eyes. I should have done something sooner to help her, and perhaps she wouldn't have been hurt this bad. I made a silent vow to never stand by while she fought for my sake again.

"Aaron." She whispered, trying to smile but seeming too tired to do it. "You saved me again."

"Quiet." I said, placing one of my fingers to her lips, while Paradox walked over to us. "You need to rest."

The man with the package watched us, sitting in a resting position and waving his foot. He looked at all the men hanging in the air and stood up, leaving the package on the table as he walked towards the door of the building. Paradox turned to look at him, and the man simply nodded to him with a smile before walking through the door.

"The package," Ethia said, her eyes opening very slightly. "That man with the package, there's something inside it. I can hear it, making a sound . . . tick, tick, tick."

I looked at Paradox, knowing it was a device that would blow up in some way, who snapped his head from the door to the package lying on the table. It started to glow from the inside, a bright light piercing through the thin layer of cardboard around it. Paradox ran for the door, and I wondered what he was doing. The package was now lighting up the entire room, and the soldiers who were bound up fell to the ground, the light forcing the dark matter to dissolve. The soldiers didn't even cast us a glance as they got up and charged out the door, a few of them even jumping through the windows and leaving their fallen comrades there.

I lifted Ethia up who was now limp and asleep, and started heading for the exit when Paradox crashed through the wall with the police cruiser. The package started vibrating violently along the table, and was heading for the edge of it while I opened the passenger side of the vehicle and climbed in. I didn't bother to put Ethia in the back seat, it would have taken to much time to do that, so I let her sit in my lap as Paradox smashed the car in reverse.

We had just cleared the restaurant when it went up in a white light. The light spun around quickly before shrinking back into itself, leaving nothing but the plot of land the diner had been sitting on. The soldiers were in the bus, watching us drive off towards the onramp of the freeway. Sirens blared in the nearby distance, and I was dismayed to see the police cars move past the bus and after us.

Paradox turned on the police radio, and we listened to the conversation going on between the patrol cars after us.

"Multiple reports of the young man who set Central Park on fire and the other in black clothing accompanied by a young lady in a stolen police cruiser heading down the freeway, we have a bus full of witnesses." One of the voices said, stating the situation and what was happening. "We've been told that they used something to destroy the diner and kill some people, consider them armed and dangerous."

"Copy that, they are in my sights and I'm in pursuit." Another voice sounded off, probably one of the police cars chasing us.

"What was that, that destroyed the building?" I asked Paradox, as I struggled with the buckle, placing it over Ethia who I was holding onto my lap to keep from sliding around while I did so.

Paradox twitched his head then said, "I don't know, I've never seen that before, but I can guarantee you that it was from a different force then Epsilon. They never use anything loud to get the job done."

"Well, even if they don't they were good at covering up and telling the police that we caused it." I said.

"Of course, that's what they do. The other soldier that left the bomb probably told the police before hand anyways, he didn't care if those from Epsilon Force died. I'm sure that the two commanders are going to be butting heads when both reports hit their HQ." Paradox said, navigating past cars as he continued to speed up to the patrol vehicles top speed.

"Can we get a chopper out here?" One of the radioed voices requested.

"Air support is on the way." A very cold and indifferent voice said, sounding very different then the original speaker who had provided the situation.

"Who is this?" One of the police vehicles inquired, and was met with silence before the radio went out.

"This isn't right at all, their being jammed." Paradox said when the first of the patrol cars exploded in a white light behind us.

The other patrol cars stopped their chase, and I turned just in time to see a swarm of missiles crash into the others, shards of metal flying into the air caused by the brief blinding explosions. In the night sky I could make out a hovering figure in the air, lights flashing on and blinding me. A helicopter sent out after us maybe? No, this wasn't making any noise at all as it sped up over us.

"The Twilight Cores Air Force, they were listening into the radio conversations and tracking us too." Paradox said, swerving past a semi that was struck by a small object, and exploded into a white fireball.

"Which Force is this?" I asked, trying to keep Ethia's head from jerking about too much from the driving being performed.

"Charlie Force, I believe. At least they didn't bring anything larger then this . . . and only one of them, but this is going to be hard as it is." Paradox cracked out, as he threw the steering wheel to the left, pulling us in that direction as the ground exploded where we had been moments before.

The aircraft flew directly behind us, the light piercing in through the back window as Paradox looked behind him. I couldn't tell what was happening, but I heard a whining noise start up, and I thought it might be a helicopter after all. The whining grew louder, and Paradox swerved around, trying to lose the aircraft, but it stayed easily behind us.

"Get down." Paradox said as I cringed as low as I could, positioning Ethia the same way.

Bullets flew through the roof of the car, transforming it into Swiss cheese. I could feel the pointed rounds flying over my head, barely missing me. The chatter of a chain gun or two was unloading behind us, and now I knew what the whining sound had been. Paradox looked over at us, crouched down low as he slammed on the brakes and the aircraft blew through the top half of our vehicle.

It spun out of control, and crashed along the side of the road. Paradox didn't stop, but kept driving past it. The cold night's wind whipped through my eyes, barely allowing me to hear over the engine and speed we were traveling. Ethia stirred, and tried to shoot upwards but was restrained by the seatbelt. She cried out flailing her arms wildly, and I wrapped my arms around her to keep her still.

"It's alright, Ethia, you're safe." I yelled as loud as I could over the wind and engine.

She stopped struggling, and settled against me. I could tell she was still very tense, and she was forcibly pacing her breath as she shouted out, "What happened?"

"We ran into an aircraft, it attacked us but we got away." I said, squeezing her gently and then loosening my hold.

She placed both of her arms over mine, resting her hands on my interlocked ones that I was still holding there, and slowed her breathing. Paradox was driving with one hand, holding his hat with the other, and scarf wrapped around his face blowing behind him. He still wasn't slowing down, and I wondered why when large beams of light shot down from above and encased us. I looked up and uttered an exclamation, while Ethia was now gripping my arms tightly in terror.

Above us was the silhouette of a very large aircraft, larger then any I'd ever seen. It had to be around two to three football field lengths in size. The large lights that shone down us never wavered, no matter how much Paradox swerved.

"One of their cruisers," Paradox groaned outwards over all the sound and looking at an overpass coming up, "Forget this."

I could see several large turrets covering the ship as it soared above us. They were much larger then the ones on the tower and many of them were swiveling about, taking aim at our vehicle. Many of their barrels started to glow an eerie pale blue inside, and I knew what was coming next. Paradox didn't bother to swerve anymore, and leaned forward as we moved under the overpass.

The massive cannons fired off, causing all the ground to erupt under the flying vessel. The overpass and road disintegrated within a second, and nothing remained of the police vehicle. The captain of this particular ship sniffed outwards when he saw the destruction below, and then turned to the radar control operator, who reported incoming aircraft: the police chopper.

"Enter stealth mode and return to base. I need to make a full report for the commander, he will be pleased. This is a proud day for Charlie Force!" The captain announced, the men cheering at this proclamation. The large aircraft's lights turned off, causing it to vanish in the night's sky as it turned about and headed off in the distance, leaving the police chopper to survey what was let of the area below.

—— ∞ ——

Nanoplicity

I don't know what hit me first, the realization that Paradox had teleported using the overpasses shadow to block out the light from the Twilight Cruiser to move from there to New York right before the area was vaporized, or the cold concrete roof of the building that my body struck. My limbs felt sore, and when I moved them it was like I was moving heavy logs that broke off from my body leaving massive splinters. It was almost like I'd felt Paradox's teleportation the first time, but this was different, it hurt.

Ethia was a few feet away from me, moaning a little as she tried to stand, shivering from her own bodies weight that pressed down on her no doubt aching limbs. She probably feels much worse then me, I thought lying in one place and watching her finally make it to her feet. She stood where she was for now, her legs wobbling under the pressure put on them. She looked like she was in a mixture of pain, and worry . . . and I probably matched her feelings.

Sitting up I heard Paradox cough, one large heavy cough. I twisted my neck the other direction and saw him standing on the edge of the skyscraper that we were on, looking out over the city. It was a brilliant and awe-inspiring sight. His duster flowed out behind him, his arms at his sides against the backdrop of the city's lights. He really did look like a hero at the moment. The rest of the roof was bare, except for what looked like a small maintenance shed, a few metal bars strewn about the place, and roof access doors set apart from each other.

"Are you okay?" I heard Ethia say while placing her arm around my shoulders.

"Yeah, it's just that it's never felt like that to teleport with Paradox before." I said while she helped me stand up.

"I apologize about that." I heard Paradox say. "I didn't have much time to focus under the overpass, much less time before we could have been turned into atoms."

"It's alright." I said, then thanked Ethia for helping me up and walked over to Paradox, while she crouched down and grabbed her head shaking it. It really looked like it'd been rougher for her. "You had to do what you had to do, otherwise we wouldn't be here."

"Just keep in mind, one day you may have to make many split-second decisions like that, Aaron." Paradox reminded me.

"I'll remember that." I mused, working out the remaining kinks in my arms and legs. "So I guess we are going to call that lady now?"

Paradox looked up at the stars and answered, "Not quite, I'm going to go scout around a bit. Perhaps find us a place to call home while we work things out, we can't stay here on this roof."

"You don't want us to come?" I said, looking at him. I could tell by the way he was talking it's what he wanted.

"I'll be quicker alone, you rest up for once." Paradox said before he stepped off the building and vanished into the night.

"Wow!" Ethia breathed out while walking over next to me. She looked out over all the lights then leaned over the side of the skyscraper to look down. "It's so big . . . but most of all beautiful."

"Be careful about doing that." I said, grabbing her by the waist and pulling her back from leaning over.

She complied with my tug, stepping away from the edge and pressed her back up against the front of me. I thought about what was going on, and clasped my hands around her, allowing her to place her hands and arms on mine as she relaxed. Both of us stood together, looking over the bright cityscape, cherishing the moment of silence.

Slowly Ethia turned around in my arms, facing me now and looking up into my eyes. She smiled and drew her face closer to mine. Her chest moved in rhythm with mine, moving up and down as we both breathed. I could feel the beating of her heart, which was growing slightly faster the closer her face moved towards mine. I knew what was coming, and I couldn't seem to take my eyes off of hers. Soon I could feel her breath lightly dancing over my lips, and the fragrance about her was like nothing I'd ever smelled before . . . something wonderful.

I closed my eyes right before her lips were about to touch mine, their perfect texture finally pressing softly against my own. I held her gently, while she moved one of her hands to caress my neck, the other wrapped around my back. It lasted only a few seconds, but it felt like a lifetime. She leaned away from me very slowly, so that I felt her lips slowly leave the presence that they had just given.

As her golden eyes radiated out, her smile only complimented what they were telling me. She moved the hand positioned on my neck to my cheek, sliding it along the way and running her hand along it tenderly. I started moving towards her again, and her smile widened, eyes sparkling as she pressed tighter against me. No words needed to be spoken as we grasped each other firmly, moving forward quicker so that our lips might touch once again. The sound of someone's throat being cleared made us part before it happened.

We both turned, looking in the direction the sound had come from while a bunch of thoughts tossed about in my mind. I wondered if it was a good or bad thing that we were interrupted. I also wondered who it was that had been watching us. *Maybe it was Paradox,* I thought, but somehow my gut knew it wasn't.

A high pitched mans voice that wasn't unpleasant, but sounding rather technical and educated, emanated from the tool sheds shadow. "Pardon me, if I was . . . interrupting anything important."

I couldn't see much, but I could see there was someone standing in the darker area of the shadows, where not even the starlight was touching. The only thing we could see clearly of whoever it was, was a single red robotic eye gleaming out from the darkness. The eye swerved slightly back and forth between Ethia and me, watching us both. The man with the robotic eye waited, for what we didn't know, but he seemed to take his time. Perhaps he wanted us to speak.

"Who are you?' I asked, sounding angry but not meaning too, probably because of what he interrupted.

"My, my, temper, temper," The man said, his red mechanical eye not looking at me any longer but resting on Ethia. "Second in command of Zeta Force, Lieutenant Gerald Lyman at your service, although you may refer to me as Nanoplicity . . . if you would like to refer to me by the nickname the Core labeled me with."

Both Ethia and I gawked at what we just heard. I reached down and grabbed one of the metal bars near my feet. Ethia immediately moved into a fighting posture, standing sideways with one leg out in front of her and both fists up. This man Gerald Lyman, or Nanoplicity, didn't move at all except for the robotic eye that watched the metal rod I picked up from the ground, and then observed Ethia's posture. A single moment passed, and we didn't know if we should make a preemptive strike or wait for him to come at us.

"Now take it easy, I didn't come here to fight." Nanoplicity said smoothly, the robotic eye once again staring at Ethia.

"Then what did you come here for?" I asked while patting the rod in one hand. I didn't quite believe him.

"I'm just following orders from my Commander to gather data, and so far it's been at the least . . . interesting." Nanoplicity said like a scientist observing bacteria.

"So in other words you were sent to spy on us?" Ethia said unmoving, her stance seemingly set in stone.

Nanoplicity's red eye shuttered closed, and we could see the dark form shake his head before it opened up again. "No, that's incorrect, I wasn't sent to observe the boy at all," He said, his right hand emerging from the dark shadows, pointing at Ethia and looking very human, "only you, Ethia, I believe?"

I looked at Ethia who was slightly scared now. I could see the fear in her golden eyes, and Nanoplicity's laugh only confirmed that he saw it too. His arm dropped back into the shadows, and I wondered if he was just a normal man. His arm wasn't armored at all. Just a normal looking uniform had adorned it. Perhaps I should attack him, I thought, but that red robotic eye told me otherwise.

"So tell me, my fair lady . . . how you came by such an exquisite eye color?" Nanoplicity asked playfully, making Ethia start to quiver both in fear and anger mixed together. "Oh, and let's not forget that amazing hair color. It's not dyed, is it?" He continued on, probing her with questions as she let out a deep breath to keep her temper.

"Don't talk to him, stay calm." I whispered to Ethia, who nodded her head yes.

"Oh? You're not going to answer me?" Nanoplicity said hearing me, reading my lips, or seeing into my mind.

He waited a moment more then started speaking Ethia's language. I couldn't believe that he knew it, I thought only Paradox knew it besides her. Slowly she began shaking in rage, her eyes burning, fists clenching then unclenching, as Nanoplicity finished speaking and ended with a mirthful laugh.

"No!" Ethia roared out, ready to charge forward. "You won't hurt him. If you lay one hand on him I'll tear you apart!" I placed my free hand on her arm, and she turned to look at me. It was easy to see how aggravated she was through her eyes, but she slowly regained control as I looked back to Nanoplicity.

"Ah, interesting. You understood me." Nanoplicity said, with his eye turning away from us to face the tool shed's wall. "That's all I needed to know, thank you for cooperating."

"What do you mean by that?!" I yelled out, this time he was making me angry. "We didn't cooperate at all, what did you come to find out about her?"

"You'll know in due time." Was his response, as he moved along the wall and prepared to disappear behind it. "My Commander had me scramble the teleportation signal, so that no soldiers will bother you when I leave, for now. Oh, yes . . . by the way, Justin is turning out well, Aaron."

I was shocked that he knew my name, but more so at the mention of Justin. "What? What do you mean he's turning out well? Tell me!"

Nanoplicity ignored me as he took one last look at Ethia, the red eye swiveling up and down in the darkness as his last words rang out. "We'll be in contact, Ethia."

Preparations

nodded to Ethia, and we both went on the attack as he disappeared behind the tool shed. I went one way around it and she went the other, where we almost collided into one another. Nanoplicity was no longer there, like he had vanished into nothingness. He probably was able to teleport back to wherever he came from because he was the one who scrambled it in the first place. I dropped the metal bar, and wished Paradox had been there.

Ethia was a little pale, now knowing that the Twilight Core had their eye on her for some reason. The mood that hung over us was dreadful, the one before killed by the recent event, and she sat next to me quietly eyeing the ground. Her golden eyes looked almost dead as we waited for Paradox who arrived shortly after. Paradox was carrying two large trash bags stuffed full of something, and he dropped them on the roof when he picked up the mood.

"What happened?" He asked, looking around at the surroundings.

"We were met by the Zeta's Lieutenant, Nanoplicity." I said, and Paradox quickly rushed about the roof, checking everywhere as I pointed out, "He's gone now."

"What did he want?" Paradox interrogated, looking at Ethia who was huddled up into a little ball next to me now.

I scratched her back softly, thinking about what had happened and answered, "He wanted to know more about Ethia."

"That's just like the Twilight Core in general." Paradox vented out thoughtfully, "We'd better keep a good eye on her for now."

I didn't tell Paradox that he'd mentioned Justin also, he probably had enough to worry about. Paradox walked up to us, and looked over Ethia as if judging whether she would be fine or not before saying, "I've found a place to stay, although I had to clear a few pests out from it. It will be safe to operate from temporarily."

I stood up and helped Ethia onto her feet. She stuck tightly to my side, looking over to where Nanoplicity had been, while we walked behind Paradox who was carrying the bags to the roof access. He set one of the bags down and opened the door, and we followed him inside. It was a hotel. Clean inside and very expensive looking. A room attendant didn't give us a second glance as we trudged to the elevators and I pressed the down key, soon we were inside it heading for the lobby.

Paradox didn't seem to care who saw us, as we walked into the lobby of the hotel. Then again it didn't seem like many people gave us a second glance, if they even looked at us at all. We proceeded through the golden revolving doors that led out onto the streets. I looked for a sign that told us which we were on but wasn't able to see any. Ethia looked like she was doing a little better, probably because her mind was taken off of what had happened.

Paradox turned left, walking behind a large group of people that were making their way down the street. I placed my right arm behind Ethia's waist, and we both started following him. Wondering what was in the bags we didn't get far when Paradox made another quick turn and started heading down an alleyway on our left. We didn't immediately follow him because Ethia was entranced by everything she saw.

"Let's go." I said as she turned to look at me, wonder in her eyes. "I'll show you everywhere I can once we are done."

"I know." Ethia said, finally turning to head down the alleyway along with me where Paradox was waiting.

When we reached Paradox he started walking down an alleyway that was connected to the one we were in, and thinner in width. When we reached the end of this he seemed to disappear into the wall on his left side. I noticed an entrance barely large enough for us to fit through that he'd entered, and I climbed in after him, with Ethia trailing along behind me. Eventually we reached a room, not really a room, but where the buildings had been placed in such a way as to create it. The only way in and out was the way we entered. Paradox was sitting on a chair among other bits and pieces of refuge that were strewn about, along with tiny patches of grass that were sprouting around.

There was graffiti lining the walls, and the way the few pieces of furniture were set up made you think it was a local gang's hideaway. So that's what he meant by clearing out some pests, I thought.

"Come on over, make yourselves at home." Paradox said, motioning at the two chairs in front of him and patting one of the bags. "I've got some things for you both."

I looked at Ethia, and she practically skipped over to the chair offered to her and sat down. I grinned, happy that she was happy, and that Nanoplicity was out of her mind if just for the moment. Paradox opened the first bag, and brought out a black jumpsuit that actually seemed to glow slightly under the little light that the stars gave. He handed it to Ethia who looked at it with mild interest and then back to Paradox.

"I thought you were going to make me look less conspicuous." She said, and Paradox sighed in reply.

"This is for the operation we are going to perform. It's a special type of cloth that will help moderate your energy usage, so you can fight longer . . . or you can use it to boost everything to new heights, although that could be dangerous. Take it or leave it." Paradox grunted out, as Ethia smiled and hugged it to her.

"Well, for now it's alright, but we are going to need to get me some other clothes. I want to see what all your clothes are like here." She said happily, probably imagining all sorts of things.

"Trust me . . . most of them aren't that great." Paradox stated in a serious tone.

"Just because you like all of your clothes black and specific, doesn't mean all the others are bad." I pointed out to Paradox, who shook his head and looked at me.

"Not you too," Paradox said in exasperation. "Come here, I still have some things for you Aaron."

I walked over to him, laughing inside because of his air of surrender to the barrage of playful jabs that Ethia and I were throwing at him. I sat down, and he handed me the second bag. I opened it, my eyes growing wide in disbelief at what I was seeing. It was filled with clothes for me too, but ones identical in every way to Paradox's down to the heavy leather boots.

"You've gotta be kidding me." I said slowly, fingering over the items inside and watching Paradox stiffen at what I'd said.

"No kidding. Your training is almost over, Aaron. So I want to provide you with the clothes that you should get used to wearing." Paradox said, as I almost laughed out loud.

"What are you talking about Paradox? You haven't taught me much of anything. We've been chasing after these Twilight Soldiers and I don't even know a quarter of what you know." I said, watching Paradox whose shoulders seemed to sag at this.

He stayed that way, and I wondered if I'd actually hurt his feelings when he spoke saying, "Indeed I haven't taught you much, but in the end you have taught yourself a lot. The best teacher, or mentor, isn't someone who speaks to you, but yourself."

"You may be right, but I don't think I'm ready to wear anything like this." I said, setting the bag down and expecting Paradox to explode as he puffed his chest out.

"Suit yourself. In the end it won't matter." He said in his mysterious way, making me wonder what he was talking about but knowing he wouldn't give a clear answer even if I asked him. "So take your time and rest up. In the morning we're going to go call and meet this lady."

"Fine by me, so what are you going to go do tonight?" I asked, since he said he didn't sleep.

"I'm going to go patrol the area, stop some small crimes. There are a lot of them, especially during the night." Paradox said, while walking towards the opening that we'd entered between the buildings.

"What if Nanoplicity comes back?" Ethia said, sounding concerned but not too bad.

"I'm not going to teleport at all tonight, so he'd have a time finding you." Paradox said, and then left through the small opening.

Ethia shifted over to the bag that Paradox had taken her jump suit out of, and opened it. She brought out what looked like a large black tool chest, and set it to the side without opening it. Digging a little farther into the bag she took out a couple blankets, not very large but sufficient for the cool night's air. She walked over to me, and handed me one of the blankets before I stood up and choose one of the scarce patches of grass to lie down on. Ethia followed me, and lied down close alongside me.

"Aaron?" She said quietly, perhaps not wanting to bother me before I tried to fall asleep.

"What's up?" I asked, staring up at the stars in the sky before looking at her.

"I wouldn't ever do anything to hurt you." She said, her golden eyes looking saddened by something.

"I know you wouldn't." I said firmly, making her smile while I looked back up to the stars. "I wouldn't do anything to hurt you either."

"I won't let him hurt you." She whispered into my ear.

"Who?" I asked.

"Nanoplicity, what he said . . . some of the things. I'll make sure it never happens." She continued on, a slight fear in her voice.

"What did he say?" I asked, wishing she would tell me.

"It was . . . just some things to make me angry. That's all." She finished, sounding rather sleepy now and wrapping her arms around me.

I couldn't keep my eyes open any longer, and closed them while saying, "Don't worry about it, everything will be fine. Once we get Justin back we'll see the world together, and I'm sure Paradox can take care of anything that happens."

"I love you." I heard Ethia whisper, but I was already to far gone to respond. The last thing I recalled feeling before I slept was her lips brushing a kiss onto my cheek.

Justin was running from me again through the empty streets of the city in my nightmares, but this time it was slightly different. Paradox and Ethia were with me, all three of us were chasing after him. The dark clouds already covered the sky above us this time, but they continued to grow darker as we traveled on. Soon Paradox split away from the group, heading towards a large figure in the distance that stood waiting where the sounds of battle commenced.

He didn't say anything before he left, and the buildings soon blocked whatever was happening from view as I turned to see Ethia smiling at me. Another street junction came up, and this time it was her that broke off, heading down another direction that looked empty. I stopped and thought about following her, but I could see Justin growing farther away in the distance so I continued my pursuit.

I watched him branch off again to the left, and I knew it was the same alleyway that he had gone into before. Reaching the way he entered into I turned to see Justin facing me with head down, his back was to the blackness that he'd ran straightway into last time. He raised his head breathing heavily, face contorted in pain while gripping his chest. Before

I could say anything, or move closer, his eyes widened in terror as he was jerked from his feet into the blackness that totally concealed him from view.

The sky darkened, and out from the darkness that grew outwards, where Justin had been taken, a single red robotic eye watched me. Nanoplicity's cold laughter grew from its direction and I wished Paradox was there. Then he was, placing a gloved hand on my shoulder. I should have felt relieved, but then Paradox slowly disappeared, turning into strands of darkness that floated away. I could feel his presence about me, and most of all inside me.

The strands of darkness flew upwards into the sky, which now grew to a darkness that covered the land in a near pitch black. From the roofs of the buildings I shuddered as multiple red eyes leaned over from them to stare down at me, each one adding another laugh that was identical to Nanoplicity's. I shouted outward, and felt helpless as more appeared, and heard a whisper that sounded like Ethia in my ear, "I'm sorry Aaron."

Bolting upright I automatically wiped off the cold sweat and contorted every way I could until the memories of where I was returned to me. This had to be one of the worst nightmares I had yet, and I thought maybe I should confront Paradox about them.

Breathing in the crisp morning air I heard men shouting in one of the corners of the lot we were in. Ethia's voice cracked out like a whip when I realized she wasn't next to me.

I jumped up, and spun towards the sounds of combat. There were about ten men, big burly looking thugs with arms the size of a gorillas. They lumbered towards Ethia who had her back pressed against the corner's edge, defending against attacks and delivering combinations of blows to the men. She sent them off their feet, hitting the ground, only to get back up again. I didn't observe more then this, as I ran forward to enter the fray against probable members of the gang who once lived here.

Growing closer I felt a fuzzy feeling sweep through me as all the men paused, frozen in place, as a mechanical voice spoke.

"Another person has entered the combat area. Shall simulation be set for two?" It inquired from a small metal disc lying on the ground.

"It's alright." Ethia said, leaning against the back wall and slightly out of breath. "In fact, terminate the simulation for now."

"Affirmative, simulation terminated." Was all it said before the men became static figures, dispersing into the air.

"That was a simulation?" I asked, noticing that Ethia was in her jumpsuit and looking twice as good as she usually did, and then wondering when she had actually changed into it. The jumpsuit was different looking from when Paradox had given it to her. Metallic plates were placed on different places around the suit, protecting vital parts. On each of her wrists were two knives that slid into two sleek metallic bracelets for combat, much like what the Epsilon Forces had, and making her striking blows all the more dangerous.

"Yeah, it was pretty real looking wasn't it?" She said, hoisting herself from the wall and walking towards me, her lips pursed in thought. "Except the part where they stood back up, most men wouldn't be able to do that here . . . but I told it that I wanted some good training."

"Yeah, now that you mention it that is kinda unrealistic, I haven't seen one guy stand back up after you delivered a blow to him." I said, still examining her perfect slender frame in the jumpsuit.

She noticed this and her cheeks reddened only slightly when she smiled, spreading her arms out and twirling around the short distance left between us before lifting my chin so that I would look her in the eyes, winking at me and saying, "So what do you think?"

"I can't really find the words to describe how different you look." I said, as she gave me a playful punch in the arm. "Beautiful doesn't quite cut it."

"Beautiful, I like that word." Ethia said, looking up at the sky then back at me mischievously. "But I know you've always thought that about me, I could see it in your interesting eyes."

"Interesting eyes, huh?" I said then, poking her playfully in the side, "Well, I can tell a lot of things by the way your eyes are too."

She laughed and grabbed my arm before moving close to me, I gulped feeling her full figure now through the tight jumpsuit that she wore, unlike the loose brown uniform she'd been wearing. She started laughing a little about something, and backed away, still smiling but her eyebrows raised in a serious gesture.

"If you think I'm beautiful now, just wait until I can wash myself and put on some normal clothes." She said, poking me in the belly button then moving over to the disc on the ground and picking it up. She tossed it a few times in the air, and finally went and placed it inside the bag that had her things in it.

"So, Aaron, about last night before Nanoplicity had interrupted us." Ethia said, making me freeze in place and hoping that everything was alright. She looked at me sideways, smiling and brushing some of her hair out of her eyes. "What did you think? I mean, I hope you liked it . . . I felt like it was the right moment."

"Alright you lovebirds, time to get moving." Paradox interrupted, clapping his hands and stepping through the small entrance and changing the subject that Ethia was waiting to hear a response to.

I looked at her and grinned, mouthing that I would tell her later. She blushed red, and Paradox stopped immediately and stood near the entrance looking Ethia up and down, hand raised to his chin. I couldn't tell if he liked or disliked what he saw, but I trusted that he was thinking about the clothing that she was wearing and not her.

"What did you do to the jumpsuit?" Paradox said, walking over and examining all the metal plates and knives attached to it.

Ethia made a face, as if pouting a little and said, "It just wasn't my taste, I modified it a little using that tool case and items inside that you left here with us so that it would be better for the mission too."

There was a moment of silence, and I could hear some birds on the rooftops chirping away. Ethia visibly got ready to endure the assault of words that Paradox may give at any moment, as he leaned his masked face close to hers.

"Not a bad job at all." He stated then turned to go as Ethia breathed a sigh of relief, and I let out my breath which I hadn't even known that I was holding.

"What do you want to do with the bags?" I asked, motioning to both of them.

Paradox tipped his hat in thought and said, "Leave them here, we'll come back once we are done."

$$\infty$$

A Long Way to Meet

thia and I trailed behind Paradox as we left the area we'd stayed in. The alleyway turned back into the larger one, and soon we were out onto the street. People bustled along as we joined the stream and Ethia observed them, seeming to linger on a few overweight people with confusion on her face. Paradox once again seemed to know where we were going, so I enjoyed the time I was able to point things out to Ethia, explaining to her what restaurants were really all about, and stopping at a hot dog vendor, to Paradox's dismay, to get both of us a hotdog.

She was adventurous, getting everything she could on her hotdog, while I settled for just plain old ketchup. We both ate, holding each others free hands while following along. Paradox headed down into a subway station, and Ethia jumped onto my back while I started walking down the stairs. It was funny, and in most cases would have been embarrassing probably, but I didn't care as I wrapped my arms around her legs and piggybacked her down the stairs. She and I laughed all the way down, causing a few people to look at us before moving on their way.

Paradox stopped at the ticket booth acquiring three tickets and looking like he wanted to pretend he didn't know us again. He handed us out tickets, which Ethia grabbed from my backside and we headed in waiting for the train. Ethia slid down my back, and walked over to one of the maps located in the station reading over it. I sat down on a bench, watching her while Paradox sat down next to me.

"So you're not going to ask me where we're going? What's going on? Or anything like that?" Paradox said, making me look away from Ethia to face him.

"Well, it ran through my mind, but you seem to know where we're going, so I thought that was good enough." I said, turning back to see another guy around my age talking to Ethia. I was about to stand up and head over there, but Paradox grabbed my arm and nodded in their direction.

Ethia was shaking her head 'no', and then pointed to me, smiling in my direction and waving as I waved back to her. The guy glanced at me, shrugging then stalked off towards another girl that was a ways off. Ethia was walking back to me when the train's brakes started screeching throughout the tunnel, she fell to her knees and planted both of her hands against her ears to block out the sound as her mouth opened and let out a silent scream at all the noise.

A few people had already walked over to her, trying to figure out what the matter was, when I was on my feet and over to her in a second. Looking a little better now she shook her head as the train came into the station. Rolling to a stop as the automatic doors opened people began spilling in and out of the train. The group dispersed as I helped her stand, only one individual remaining.

"Is she alright?" The man asked. He was taller then me, and had a wiry body that adorned an expensive business suit. His eyes gleamed behind large spectacles with a quick looking light about them, and he held his hand out for me to shake it, the other holding a suitcase. "David Jacques is the name."

"Yeah she's fine." I said, absentmindedly shaking his hand. "Are you a doctor or something?"

"I'm afraid not. I am part of the public relations branch for my company. Are you sure she's alright?" He said then asked, turning to look at Ethia.

"Yeah, everything's good." Ethia said, rubbing her ears and leaning against me. "The noise just caught me off guard. We've got to go now."

"Alright, you two take care." The man said before boarding the train with the other people.

Paradox walked over and practically pushed us towards the open door of the train, making Ethia stumble a bit because she seemed to be off balance slightly. We got on and found empty seats near the back of the train, and sat down on them.

"What happened, Ethia?" I said, rubbing between her shoulder blades while she leaned forward shaking her head.

"The sound just caught me off guard. I didn't have time to adjust my hearing." She said, stretching out along the seats and laying her head on my leg. I traced my finger lightly along her face, when Paradox shifted uncomfortably on the other side of me.

"It's my fault." He said, "I should have warned you."

"It's okay, it's over now." She said, turning onto her back and letting one leg drop down to the floor and closing her eyes as my finger traced between them.

I leaned forward a little, and looked into the train car ahead of us. There were various people inside, and at the head of it was David Jacques. He looked at me, speaking on a cell phone and waving his hand smiling, before getting up and heading into the next car forward. I didn't think much of it, and leaned back against the seat, resting my right arm on Ethia's stomach, and brushing her hair with my left.

"Who was that man?" Paradox said, his legs stretched out in front of him and hat tipped down like he was trying to sleep.

"I don't know, some guy named David Jacques, said he was public relations for a company." I said hearing the sound of heavy machinery draw closer. Probably just something on the train, I thought.

Paradox was on his feet in a flash, picking both Ethia and I up into the air tucking us each under as arm and running for the next car ahead of us as the back end of the train car exploded in twisted metal. Ethia screamed out that she couldn't see what was behind us, but I could because Paradox was carrying me backwards. I really wished instead that I was looking ahead instead of facing what was coming up from the rear.

It was a large armored vehicle that took up the tunnel behind us. Rows of metallic teeth twisted in different directions, devouring the back end of the train as it slowly moved forward. A tiny slit served as a window, and I could see the masked faces inside watching us. Bright floodlights flashed on, bathing the inside of the train and tunnel ahead with light as the vehicle slowed down to match the trains speed. Two doors lowered from each side of it onto the remaining car, creating a platform that bridged the vehicle with the train.

The people in the car ahead started panicking, tripping over each other to get into the next car. Paradox wasn't able to move any farther for the moment, and dropped both Ethia and me to the floor, in an attempt to face the monstrous vehicle behind us. From out of each door that had opened on either side of the vehicle, Twilight Soldiers poured out of it with rifles at the ready. The first soldier touched down onto the platform and opened fire, crossing onto the train and forcing all three of us to take cover behind the walls separating the two cars.

"How'd they know we were here?" I shouted out over the grinding metal and bullets being fired.

Paradox shook his head and pointed to his ear, showing that he couldn't hear me from across the car. The firing stopped, and I knew they were getting ready to move forward, if not already. He started letting the darkness seep out of his body, forming it into a sphere about him, but smaller then usual because of the floodlights that shone through the door. The soldiers once again started firing, bright bullets piercing the black matter that they could see. It didn't look like they wanted to take any chances of Paradox moving into the same car with them.

Ethia pointed with her finger at the small strand of darkness that Paradox was feeding through the sphere. It worked its way between the two train cars, avoiding the light issued from the bright lights and snaking its way into all the small crevices. One of the soldiers started shouting something incoherent. Perhaps he had noticed what was going on before it happened.

The sound of scrambling men became evident as Paradox shifted his two hands apart. The cars shook and squealed, finally breaking apart from each other. I heard the radioed screaming before it was encased by the shredding sounds of metal getting blended up. I peeked around the corner and saw that the back car was totally gone in the gaping maw of the shredding machine. A few pieces of cloth were seen swinging round the metallic teeth, but not much. It let out a whistle of pressure, and was once again moving forward towards the train car we were in.

These guys don't give up, I thought, while Ethia stood and tugged on my leg before I jumped up also. Paradox was already heading into the next train car. When we entered it there were a few people inside that had been watching the ordeal. Everyone crammed into the next car ahead, it was getting crowded now, and I could hear the mechanical vehicle start working its way through the second car.

"If you want to live," Paradox shouted out, "get me David Jacques now!"

Screams and shouts passed along up the line at this statement, people were pulling out their licenses and showing it to one another. Soon from the front of the car a shout of protest was heard. A large man came carrying David over his shoulder, who was shouting and beating on the man's back like a little child. The man threw him into one of the seats, and Paradox reached out and lifted him off the ground, his mask looking up into his face.

"Stop them, now." Paradox said to David, who was red in the face and looking rather angry.

"What are you talking about? I don't know what's going on at all!" David said, as Paradox dropped him to the floor and started dragging him by the collar of his suit into the next car back.

The machine had finished chewing through the second car, and tore the third back end off the next to the screams and pleas of the civilians inside the train. Paradox continued dragging David towards the maw that was spinning in circles, tearing chunks of metal away and spitting it out the back end. Paradox grunted, and held David by the back of the neck so his face was only a few feet away from the machine's teeth and growing closer.

"Stop them now, or you die first." Paradox said, holding him steady.

I thought what he was doing was pointless. Paradox knew that they didn't care at all for their fellow men, so why would they stop for this one? David's resolve for resisting quickly melted away with the metal teeth nipping at his face. Soon he was digging into his pockets, grabbing his cell phone he hit redial and was shouting stop into it. The two soldiers operating in the vehicle looked at one another, and then one reached up and pulled a lever down as the machine squealed to a stop.

It grew smaller in the distance of the tunnel, and disappeared when the lights were shut off. David was breathing heavily, and dropped his phone to the ground where Paradox flattened it. He lowered his arm, setting David down who was trembling in place, before turning away from him and walking back to us. The people cheered, patting Paradox on the back and thanking him when the train finally started slowing down for its next stop.

"How come they stopped for him, but not the other soldiers, and why didn't you send him to wherever you sent the others?" I asked Paradox, who looked at me and pointed a thumb over his shoulder to David.

"He's a public relations guy, they're harder to come by then grunts, and they work with the public to gain favor with the Twilight Core. If I made him disappear we'd probably be in more trouble with the police. So he's got to find a way to explain his way out of this situation to the authorities, and people who witnessed the situation." Paradox explained, while Ethia bobbed her head in agreement and I shrugged it off.

$$\infty$$

Lover's Last Call

We exited the train and left the subway quickly, leaving a great many people with surprised looks that their ride had about half of its mass missing. The sun was nice to see outside, and I felt depressed when I saw Central Park down the street. We traveled all the way back to where we started, I thought. A second thought almost entered my mind, thinking that we didn't have to go to the other dimension in the first place, when Ethia grabbed my hand. I looked at her and decided that it was a very good thing that we'd done.

Paradox scanned the area, and then we all headed for the park as he said, "I contacted her this morning, she said she'd meet us in Central Park."

"Its funny how stuff works out that way." I said as we approached the vibrant green of the park.

We didn't run into any police as we entered the park. This was much easier then I expected. I kept thinking that we were going to be ambushed again. Ethia was at ease, looking at all the people splayed out around the grass and trees with a smile. Paradox didn't do anything, but kept walking in whatever direction he chose, moving farther into the park and eventually reaching a small space with a picnic table set on the grass.

Trees surrounded the area, not too tightly, and the open sky sat right above the table. Sitting on one of the tables benches was the lady from Justin's picture. She didn't notice us approach her, and was slightly startled when she turned our way. She stood up, and backed away eyeing us for a moment and holding her hands up.

"You're the ones that set the park on fire!" She yelped, one of her hands pointing an accusing finger at us.

"No, neither of them set anything on fire." Ethia said calmly, her golden eyes watching the women's movements.

The women didn't seem to listen to her, and she dropped her hands balling them into fists as she said, "What did you do with Justin?"

Paradox whipped out the photo Justin had left from the inside of his coat, and walked over to the table, sitting down and placing it there. She cautiously moved in while Ethia and I hung back. Tears welled up in her eyes as she took the photo into her hands, Paradox made no movement to stop her.

"How did you get this?" She said softly, looking over the photo and then up at us. "I remember Justin carrying it with him all the time."

"We have a lot to talk about." Paradox said, nodding for her to sit down. "What we are going to explain will sound just about impossible to believe, but if you help us, we can help you find Justin."

She nodded, and sat down while Paradox explained what had happened. It sounded a little different from what I would have told her, but it was from his point of view. The lady wiped the tears from her eyes, looking a little speculative on some parts, but keeping silent especially during the parts where we described Justin. Paradox finished what we needed to tell her, and she breathed in, then out slowly while thinking it over.

"I'm Anna, Anna Cantrell, Justin's wife." Anna began, looking at each of us while Ethia frowned and shook her head.

"What's a wife?" She blurted out, causing Anna to look at her with curiosity.

"Wife, you know . . . Justin's my husband." Anna said, looking confused at Ethia's blank stare.

"Does that mean you're my husband Aaron?" Ethia whispered to me, and I looked down at the ground and patted her hand.

"I'll explain later." I whispered back, and Ethia didn't seem quite satisfied but went back to silence.

"Please, continue Anna." Paradox said, his mask never leaving her face.

"The part where you said he'd been making trips to the communications room," She said, looking away from Ethia. "That must have been when he was calling me. The first time he called I didn't believe it was him. It had been three years since we'd last spoken to each other."

"Why was it so long?" Paradox inquired, leaning forward slightly as if in interest.

"It's because he was kidnapped, or that's what conclusion I came to." She said sadly, "The company he worked for called one day and said he didn't show up to work, or call in. The police investigated, and could only come up with that."

"I see . . . so about the calls?" Paradox asked, grabbing the photo and looking at it again.

"Well, he just talked to me, said he'd be home soon. Then on the third call he sounded frantic, and I could hear other people in the room with him. They said something about calling headquarters, and one of them said the comm. was already in use. That's when it was shut off. That was the last call he made." Anna said, watching the photo in Paradox's hand.

"Aha!" I shouted startling everyone, and throwing one of my fists in the air. "I told you he was innocent Paradox, and you thought he'd betrayed us."

Anna looked from me to Paradox, who didn't move at all and said, "It's true. I suspected he sabotaged one of my sanctuaries."

"So, if I believe all of this." Anna said while standing up from the bench, and closing her hands together. "What do I have to do to get Justin back?"

"All you have to do, is point us in the right direction." Paradox said, tapping one finger against the table.

"And where would that be?" She asked, looking at us questioningly before adding, "And what will you three be able to do?"

"The first part is, show us where he used to work. The second . . . we'll figure something out." Paradox stated while standing up, and cracking his knuckles.

"Alright, I'll do it if it will help get Justin back." Anna said, turning to go and saying, "Follow me."

We all followed her, and she called a Taxi for us to get into once we had left the park. The three of us sat in the back while she was in the front, the driver tried to make conversation but it was difficult for him to do that with a masked man sitting in the back, along with a dirty boy and golden eyed, dark blue haired girl.

The car ran through many different streets, and I didn't commit them to memory since I was horrible with things like that. The car lurched to a stop, and Anna paid the fare before we got out onto the sidewalk. Before us was an apartment building, with a very large office building down the street. The apartments cost themselves were probably higher then a lot of homes back where I lived in the west. She led us inside and up a few flights of stairs, when I saw the elevators 'Out of Service' signs, opening the door to a roomy apartment.

Two children came rushing from different directions, both around the age of eight years old, and excited to see their mother. They slowed down, looking at Paradox, then at me, and finally ending on Ethia. After registering each of us they continued on to their mother who scooped both of them up in a hug. I heard Ethia giggle, delighted by the young children and poking me in the back. I winked at her, which made her blush and look away as we entered the living room.

"Justin's workroom is this way. I haven't touched anything in there for three years. I guess I just hoped I'd find him someday . . . and I guess that hope's paid off." She said, leading us to a closed door and opening it.

Inside was a small room, dust was everywhere but it was easy to tell he'd been an engineer. Mechanical drafts were strewn about in an organized way, and pencils lay alongside various tools. One of the drafts on the wall was that of an office building, one that he hadn't drawn but was studying what it looked like. Anna pointed to it, and all three of us gathered around as she flicked on a single light.

"That's the building down the street." I said, while Anna nodded.

"Yeah, that's the building he worked at, only for a few weeks before he disappeared. He said there was something that wasn't right about it, like the design inside was different then what it should have been. He spent a few days mulling over that chart that he'd gotten, but claimed that even it didn't match what it was like." Anna said, while Paradox turned towards her.

"So what did he settle on, what it looked like, I mean." He questioned Anna, who thought about it.

"It was a day or so before he vanished, he told me it wasn't an office building at all farther inside, but industrialized . . . military." She said, nodding in confirmation.

"Then this is the building we are looking for." Paradox said, ready to move out then stopping when he heard my stomach growl in protest. "Of course, we can go after you two eat."

"Oh, you must stay. I'll make you some food." Anna said and hurried off towards the kitchen.

The two children stood in the doorway, wide-eyed looking at Paradox and Ethia. Paradox grunted to them and moved along to the kitchen, while Ethia approached them both and bent down so that she was eye level with them. She smiled and both of the children laughed and smiled back, pointing excitedly at her eyes. Each one grabbed one of her hands and pulled her from the room as she threw back her head and laughed looking at me.

Failsafe: Green Light

J left the small workroom, heading into the living room where Ethia was sitting with the two children who were busy competing in trying to keep her attention. I sat down on the couch near a window, and watched as the young boy pulled a game console from underneath the television set and turned it on, excitely pulling a controller over to Ethia so that they could both play. I smiled at the little girl's expression, which was one of dismay that Ethia was playing with her brother and not her.

Ethia was confused, and didn't know how to play whatever game the little boy was playing. It looked like she was getting beaten horribly, and she managed to press the pause button on the controller in her hands while the little girl pulled on her arm whispering something about telling a secret. The boy wanted to keep playing, and kept making over exaggerated sighs as the little girl whispered into Ethia's ear whose face darkened.

"What's wrong Ethia?" I asked as she stood up and walked towards the window, both of the little children were silent now.

She looked at me, leaning against the wall the window was set in, and leaned over peeking through it making a little gasp and quickly leaning back before saying, "Aaron, come here."

"It's something bad, isn't it?" I said, getting up from the couch and moving to the other side of the window while Ethia nodded.

I looked through it to the street below. Everything seemed normal, just a street with a bench to sit on. A man with a newspaper was sitting on the bench browsing through it, and was about to lower the paper when Ethia pushed me back out of view.

"It's that man on the bench, Helena told me that he's been there almost every day since her father disappeared." Ethia said nodding to the little girl, who must have told Ethia her name, and speaking quietly, as if the man with the newspaper could hear us.

"You are thinking he's a Twilight Soldier keeping tabs on Justin's family?" I asked Ethia, who walked away from the window.

"Yes, it makes sense doesn't it? What better leverage to make someone do something then with their loved ones." She said, moving for the kitchen where the smell of eggs and bacon were drifting out from.

We entered into the kitchen just as Paradox was about to leave it. He stopped, nodding to us and moving his hand behind him in a sweeping gesture to allow us through. I thought we should talk to Paradox about what we'd learned, but Ethia was heading straight for Anna who had set the table. Paradox must have told her he didn't eat, because only two plates were set. Anna turned to see Ethia walk right up to her, and fold her arms.

"Is something wrong?" Anna said, looking a little nervous about Ethia's attitude.

"Why didn't you tell us?" She said, wanting a clear answer.

"Tell you what?"

"About your apartment being watched by Twilight Core members, they could have spotted us." I stated while Anna seemed to shrivel under the talk and accusing stares.

"I didn't think anything of it." Anna said, looking towards the window. "They've never bothered me, and if they didn't see you it's fine, right?"

"They saw us." Paradox said, hidden with his back on the wall between the kitchen and living room.

I looked at Ethia, who was looking worried now. Anna was trembling, and she headed for the window, looking out of it. Paradox came around the corner and watched Anna return from the window.

"So why haven't they attacked yet?" I asked Paradox, who was still observing Anna.

"Deciding how to act, like which Force or Forces to use against us most likely." Paradox said, sounding alert and letting dark wisps of matter trickle out of him, making Anna back away a little.

Ethia frowned, and shook her head then tilted it as if listening to something. "What is that noise?"

I strained to listen, knowing that her hearing was far better then ours. It sounded like a slight whirring, and it was growing louder into an incessant whine. It sounds just like that one night in the police cruiser when we were being chased by that small aircraft right before . . . . I thought as my eyes widened while Paradox ran over to Anna. One of the small aircraft hovered down outside the kitchen's window, both of its large chain guns spinning rapidly.

"Aaron, get out of here, I'll take care of Anna and the-" Paradox shouted out but was cut off by the whirring turning into the quick chattering of the two heavy weapons firing. Hundreds of bullets tore in through the window and wall as Paradox teleported away with Anna in the nick of time.

Both Ethia and I dropped to the floor, covering our heads as debris and munitions tore everything away above us. I tapped her leg in front of me, and she turned to see me start army crawling towards the living room door. She started following my lead, and then we were out of the kitchen. The firing weapons died down, but we could still hear the whirring of the weapons moving in our direction. Paradox was nowhere to be seen, along with Anna and the children, so we rushed for the door. Out of the corner of my eye I could see the aircraft strafe into view and the pilot inside press down on the buttons to open fire.

Ethia knocked me down into the stairwell, and we tumbled down a few steps as bullets ripped through the area where we'd just been standing. My thoughts raced quickly through my mind, as I stood up carefully when the hail of bullets ceased once more. I helped Ethia onto her feet and looked down the few flights of stairs where orders were being barked from, to see a steady stream of troops with weapons ready, rushing into the entrance.

"Up it is." I said grabbing Ethia's hand and pulling her along with me up the steps after the aircraft's weapons couldn't be heard anymore.

I hoped that no one else staying in this apartment was getting hurt because of us, but there wasn't anything we could really do right now. I listened to the shouts of the soldiers clearing the destroyed apartment below us, while trying to come up with a plan once we got up top. It was a tall building, somewhere between thirty and fifty stories in height it seemed. My legs screamed at me to stop running up the stairs, but the sound of heavy boots continuing up was enough incentive to keep going.

Gunfire erupted in the streets below us, and I guessed that the soldiers had entered a firefight with the police. There were a few explosions, and I wondered how long the Twilight Soldiers would battle in the streets before retreating. Finally we reached the top, bolting through the doorway entrance to the roof, and looking for anything to block the door with. There were large cooling vents covering the roof, big enough to find cover behind, but nothing that could be used to barricade the door.

We ran over to the opposite side of the roof, ducking behind some of the cooling vents when we heard the door burst open. The running stopped, and I listened to a few of them walk over to the edge of the roof where the fighting below was ringing up from. One of the soldiers muttered something about time, and then I heard whoever was in charge start to shout.

"Alright, sweep the roof. Flush them out of hiding and terminate any of the targets on sight." The person ordered, the boots spreading out and moving in groups of two in our direction.

I felt a brush of wind, hearing only the faintest noise but still enough to make me look behind us. My stomach plunged as an aircraft hung in the air above us, aiming downwards as racks of missiles bloomed from its sides. Dark clouds drifted over the sun as the soldiers on the roof backed away a little, moving behind some of the other ventilation ducts I knew they were pointing their weapons in our direction.

"Targets confirmed." I heard a radio blare out from one of the soldiers then state, "Engaging."

One of the missiles roared out from the rack it was positioned in, flying in our direction as we both dove in separate directions. The vent we were hiding behind was no more, consumed in a blazing inferno that licked at my skin created by the missile. Across from me was Ethia, who stood up to move back towards me and was met with the soldiers firing at her . . . forcing her to stay where she was as the aircraft positioned itself to make her it's new target.

It would be the end for her once it fired, but it never got the chance to, as a plume of black matter, which could only be the doing of Paradox, rose from under it. It grabbed the aircraft and bent back like a pitcher getting ready to throw a baseball before throwing it forward at the soldiers on the roof. It spun wildly, the pilot trying to regain control but was unable to before it flamed into the troops positioned across the roof from us.

This act disorganized the remaining soldiers on the roof, stunned and not sure what to do as Ethia rushed onto the ventilation duct in front of her and flipped through the air towards the nearest one. The soldier raised his weapon to fire, but it was kicked down by her left foot where it shattered from the blow. Her right foot followed after her left landing down on the top of his head where he crumpled to the roof.

She instantly tallied the number of remaining soldiers to five, and ran towards the group with her arms trailing behind her, faster then I'd ever seen her move. The roofs heavy cement tiles broke apart under each of her steps. The first soldier was met with a lightning quick backhand blow to his cheek, sending him toppling head over heels while Ethia moved past him to the others that were still standing. The second was still halfway in his turn towards her, by the time he completed his turn he was over the edge of the building from the flying kick she had planted in his chest.

The third soldier had dropped his rifle and had a knife in his right hand which he thrust at her. She stepped around it without slowing down, grabbing his arm and picking him up off the ground. Spinning him in place Ethia released him into the stairwells door which shattered into multiple wooden pieces. The fourth soldier only wielded a knife also, and had approached Ethia as she had released the third soldier, slicing down at her.

Ethia finished her spin, moving in close with her back to the soldier's chest and using her right arm to grab the soldiers arm and stop his downward attack. Her left leg lifted out behind her as she pulled on his arm, propelling the soldier over her shoulder and meeting his back with her right knee before dropping him to the ground. The fifth soldier had moved away from her, rifle at the ready and was in the process of pulling the trigger when I mashed a metal bar into the underside of his arms.

He let out an enraged cry, his weapon firing into the air as his arm lifted upward from the hit I performed. I knocked the back of his leg out from under him, and then knocked him out with a blow to the head. I turned to see Ethia walking towards me as I dropped the bar, wondering how many of the men she attacked were able to move after she did so. She held her arms out, and I happily hugged her, then lifted her light frame up and spun her in the air.

"You're amazing." I said to her, setting her down and hugging her again.

"You didn't do too bad yourself." She said, nodding to the soldier lying next to us. "If it wasn't for you I might not be standing because of him."

"Yeah, well . . . if it wasn't for you then I wouldn't have been able to get past those guys, I'll admit it." I said, brushing her hair from her face and making her laugh.

"Someone's coming." Ethia said and stopped laughing, concern showing on her face. The fighting had stopped on the streets below, and she looked towards what was left of the door to the stairs.

Paradox stepped over the soldier that was halfway through the door, busting out pieces of the door with his boots as he emerged and we both breathed a sigh of relief as he said, "If it wasn't for me, neither of you would have made it this far."

"So did the soldiers pull back?" I asked Paradox, who was busy taking pieces of wood off his black clothes.

"I'm not sure." Paradox said with sincerity. "I've never seen such an operation happen during midday, especially in the city. They might have pulled back for now though, of course, they left no traces for the police down on the street to find. I'm sure they'll find this interesting up here."

The clouds that had blocked the sun finally moved away, allowing it to cast its rays over the city once again. I grabbed the soldier's rifle that had been knocked out and relieved him of some of the clips he kept on himself. The sun darkened once again, probably from another cloud, and I looked at Paradox who was looking upwards.

"So are we going to wait for the cops to get up here before we leave?" I asked, as Paradox grabbed Ethia and me, teleporting quickly away from the building.

There was a green flash as massive blasts fell from the sky, and the building disappeared in a second, along with all the buildings around it in a burning oven of flames. I looked up through the dark of the quick teleportation and saw what was blocking out the sun. It was another, if not the same, Twilight Cruiser that had pursued us on the freeway. When I witnessed the destruction it caused I felt light headed and nauseous, thinking that it could have been us.

The ship seemed to vanish in the sky, and the sun once more reigned supreme in the heavens. Paradox landed on a roof a mile or so away from the devastated area, coughing as he did. News helicopters buzzed about the sky, and I felt crestfallen.

"All those people in that area . . . gone in the blink of an eye." I said to myself, as Ethia stepped up to my side, wrapped her arm around my waist, laid her head on my shoulder, and looked out in the same direction that I was.

"There was nothing you could have done." Ethia said, trying to comfort me.

I was grateful that she cared, while on the other hand Paradox was back on his feet not saying a word. It was strange how he always kept his cool, no matter how bleak the situation was. He scanned the sky, looking for any more possible threats, I guess, and then gestured for us to come with him. We headed down through the building, exiting onto the street where masses of people where gathered and pointing at the destruction.

No one seemed to care that I was carrying some strange looking rifle as we worked our way through the people to the other side of the road. We could hear a radio somewhere on the street informing the people, that there had been a terrorist attack. More like a tactical strike to get rid of evidence and us in one attempt, I thought. It was probably their failsafe, like the bomb at the diner.

Paradox entered into another building, this one was another hotel but not nearly as fancy as the last one. Striding past the receptionist we headed for the elevator and climbed in, where Paradox pressed the button for the twenty-first floor. I leaned against the wall, breathing in and out slowly. Halfway up the power went out to the building, and I froze as a small emergency light clicked on inside. We waited a minute, and then heard footsteps step lightly on top of the boxcar.

"Looks like they tracked me here." Paradox whispered, listening to the movement outside.

It didn't sound like they were trying to get in, and another minute passed when Ethia asked the question on my mind saying, "What are they doing?"

The elevator car lurched in response to her question, and then I knew what they were doing. They were cutting the cables holding us up. Paradox crushed the emergency light with his gloved hand, and turned to the doors as the boxcar lurched again. He moved his head forward slightly, and brought his arms back as dark matter surged out of him and blew the door outwards. Then we were falling, I watched the floors rush past us then in the next moment we were standing on the twenty-first floor.

"That was close." Paradox seemed to yawn out, then head down the hallway. He knocked on a door, and no response came. After waiting a moment he knocked on it again, an almost imperceptible voice that belonged to Anna responded by asking, "Who is it?"

"It's us." Paradox said as the door locks were turned on the other side.

"I'm sorry. I'm just worried, what happened to the power?" She asked while opening the door, some sunlight streaming through from a window. It was a small room, and I heard her two children whimpering under the bed.

Paradox shrugged and stepped inside with Ethia following him. I was about to enter when I heard metal being forced open. I turned to see the elevators doors open slightly, and two pairs of green night vision eyes staring back at me.

"Paradox, we've got company coming from the elevator!" I said, wielding my rifle around, about to fire a few shots. They were faster, and I saw a barrel already pointing at me before I dove into the room. Bright bullets shone through the dark hallway where I'd been standing. "They've got silencers." I croaked out on the floor, using my leg to slam the door shut.

"Anna, you lock the door, and then everyone stay back." Paradox commanded while Anna did so then backed away.

I heard the two men move stealthily up to the door, but not quiet enough for us to miss them. I could see Paradox's black matter move under the door, and one of the men outside the room muttered something. Large flashlights flashed on in the hallway, and Paradox recoiled. His power dissipated back into the room, and he pulled back a fist. The darkness formed into a large club around Paradox's hand, and he threw it forward in a sharp jab. The darkness smashed into the door like a cannonball, sending it off the hinges and into one of the men outside.

The other soldier shone his flashlight into the darkness, but it didn't disappear quickly enough. Paradox shoved his hand in the direction of the soldiers light, and it was crushed by the blackness. The entire hallway was flooded with Paradox's power in an instant, and choked gasps were heard before it vanished, leaving no trace of the men at all.

"We've got to get out of here right now, before they initiate countermeasures." Paradox said, throwing the bed against the wall with his power and grabbing the two children.

He means the failsafe, I thought grimly. There were so many people around, and there was no way to save all of them. The lights flashed back on inside the building, and Paradox coughed a little. Ethia opened the window, letting a flood of screams in. She looked down, then up, before reeling back in and grabbing Paradox.

"Go, go, go now Paradox!" She shouted out, as the green flash emitted seconds before the destruction outside.

Then we were moving through the air, all six of us. This was taxing Paradox a lot, and he was moving slower then usual. The building erupted behind us, and the screams of the people below suddenly ceased when the area around the building went up into dust. I could feel the very air get ripped apart by the blasts aftershock, causing windows on buildings farther away from the destruction to quake and shatter.

Paradox moved for the street, and when we touched down he could barely stand. A steady stream of his matter poured from his mouth through his scarf, but even still he pointed through the coughing that was making his entire body bounce, to a sewer lid in the street. We all understood that's where he wanted us to go. It was probably one of the only safe places that we could go for now.

I slung the rifle onto my back, moving over to the lid and grabbing it, trying to pull it up and out but it was sealed to the pavement. Ethia walked over, reaching down with one arm and grunting as she ripped the lid upwards from the street and stood aside, waiting for us to climb in. Anna went first, followed by the children. Paradox heaved a few more times, waiting for them to reach the bottom and get out of the way before simply jumping in.

I looked at Ethia who had a serious look on her face, the lid still gripped in one hand as I said, "Thank you."

The seriousness melted away slightly, and she nodded. I climbed down into the sewer and waited for her to follow. She came in last, replacing the lid in its place before moving all the way down. Once she reached the bottom she looked around in disgust, and plugged her nose.

"What's that smell? What is this place?" She asked, swishing her hand in front of her nose.

"It's called the sewer, and it's where all of our waste goes." Paradox said simply, then thought about it a moment before adding, "That is, where your waste goes."

"This is one part of your dimension I wouldn't mind missing." Ethia said, covering her face with both her hands now.

"Well, get used to it. We're going to be traveling through here until we get to someplace better, and secure." Paradox said a little unkindly, causing Ethia's golden eyes to sparkle slightly.

All of us walked into the dark tunnel, the only light provided by the small service bulbs. It was different down here, much quieter. Paradox was once again leading, and I hoped that he knew his way around the sewers as well as he did other places. There was still something uncomfortable in this dank darkness. A feeling, like we were all still being watched by someone, or something.

Evil Worse than Twilight

*E*veryone was on edge as we continued down the tunnels that brought a whole new meaning to the word stinky. Paradox had slowed down, and was moving with silence in his steps now. Everyone was alert. It was a different feeling from when the Twilight Soldiers had been around, this was like walking amidst a sleeping behemoth. The air seemed to be electrically charged, making the hair on our arms stand up. It definitely wasn't your normal sewer tunnel.

Ethia stopped, and Paradox halted also. Both of them stood still, except for Ethia moving her head around. I looked at her and she turned towards the wall on our left and moved her head closer to it, mumbling something in her language. Paradox was next to her in a flash, and he conversed silently with her a moment. Anna and the children had stopped, watching what was going on nervously.

Paradox finally finished speaking with Ethia, who nodded her head and turned to us saying, "There's something on the other side of this wall. Stand back, Paradox is going to make an opening."

Paradox was already at work, moving his dark matter between the bricks and pulling them out one by one. A blue flickering fluorescent light spilled into the sewer tunnel as the wall was torn down, revealing a room that had dull grey metallic walls. A heavy blast door was positioned in the center of the wall ahead with red glowing letters above it, and a single blue light that continued to flicker. Paradox was the first to walk forward, carefully placing his steps and making sure it was safe.

"It's all clear." Paradox said, reaching the other side of the room.

We moved in, and the electrified air became much higher, but not unbearable. Slowly we made it to the door, unsure of what was inside. It had no control panel, and was firmly sealed shut. The letters that were glowing above the door in red were more symbols, but these ones were different from the ones Ethia's language had been in. She studied them, while Paradox looked at the door with interest.

"I don't know what it says." Ethia said, turning to Paradox. "I've never seen this language before, have you?"

"No I haven't, and there's no way to open the door from the outside easily." Paradox said, rapping his fist on it and receiving nothing. "It's very, very thick too."

"Could you open it?" I asked Paradox, who shrugged and walked back and forth in front of the door.

"Possibly, it's worth a shot." He said, placing his finger tips in the center of the door. The dark matter seeped into the small crack, and Paradox moved his finger tips away from the center like he was trying to pull it open. The door squealed in protest, and he got it open about an inch when we heard whispering.

Paradox stopped, holding the door open only by that inch, but not any farther. The whispers were accompanied by a mechanical burbling and gurgling noise, that sounded like some kind of language. It's effect was the opposite of Ethia's language, and created a sick feeling in the stomach. I saw her listening to it as Paradox started forcing the door open wider, and a red light pulsed from inside when the voice and whispers suddenly ceased.

"Stop!" Ethia cried out frantically as I ripped the rifle from my back, ready for action. Paradox lashed away from the door, expecting something to come rushing through, as it slammed back together.

The voice gurgled out again, only briefly this time and Paradox turned towards Ethia and held his hands up saying, "What was it? Why did you want me to stop?"

"The voice, when you were opening the door it said 'Warning. Breach in door three of Quarantine Containment, two of three doors remaining. Distress beacon activated." She said, and then continued as Paradox looked back at the door. "Sector one: Control room: Outbreak levels minimal. Sector two: Residential area: Outbreak levels extreme. Sector three: Military zone: Outbreak levels none. Recommend combat personnel only. Caution highly advised.'"

"What about when the door closed?" Paradox said, placing his hand on it.

"It said that door three was secure. No outbreak occurred in the area." Ethia answered, then walked up and took Paradox's arm off the door. "I think it's best if we leave it where it's been all this time."

"I agree." I said, still feeling bad in my stomach about being here. "Outbreak . . . It sounds like a zombie horror film."

Paradox shrugged and walked away from the door, as he entered back into the sewer and started walking away. "You win. We've got to move on anyway."

All of us but Paradox sighed with relief as we entered back into the sewer. It still felt like we were being watched, but not as bad as when we were in that room. The feeling slowly died away, and we emerged from the next manhole we came to. After we'd all climbed out into the setting sun I noticed that we were less then one block from the building that Justin had worked at. Paradox waved us away to a building nearby, and we went inside.

It was another apartment building, and we headed down into the basement without anyone noticing us slip in. It wasn't very large, and most of the space was taken up by the pipes that ran the various functions of the establishment. I dropped to the cold cement floor and yawned, grabbing my stomach because I still hadn't eaten. Ethia curled up into a ball next to me and almost immediately fell asleep, while Paradox spoke quietly with Anna then disappeared upstairs. Anna sat down against the wall across the room from Ethia and me, holding both of her children in each arm as we all fell asleep. Tomorrow would be a big day.

Into the Lion's Den

No dreams or foreboding feelings as my eyes swung open, and the aroma of eggs, sausage, and biscuits drifted around me. Ethia, Anna, and the children, were gathered around a blanket spread out on the ground. Paradox stood a little way off watching them, and I stood up and stretched before leisurely walking over to the group. The blanket was assorted with large plates full of not only the three items I'd smelled before, but pancakes and waffles too.

"Who got all this?" I asked, as Paradox tilted his head up a little and waved once with his hand before placing it behind his back.

I sat down and Ethia scooted over next to me, smiling while chewing on a piece of bacon and handing me a plate. There were forks, spoons, and knives placed about, and I grabbed a pair before shoveling some scrambled eggs onto my plate. It looked like there was more food then everyone would be able to eat, but I was surprised that by the time everyone else was full Ethia was finishing off what everyone had started.

"Wow, most girls that I've known would be worried about their weight." I said to Ethia, who raised her eyebrows in response.

"What do you mean? Why should I worry?" Ethia said as Anna looked at her with startled amazement.

Paradox stepped forward, and looked at the remaining food as he said, "Ethia won't get fat. In fact, Ethia can't get fat. Her race uses so much energy they burn it up. That's one of the reasons they look so much . . . better . . . then some of our race."

"I see." I said, as Ethia finished off another biscuit and patted her stomach.

"That's good, I'm full now." She said, while Paradox waved his hand over the food and it seemed to fall through the floor into a dark portal he'd opened.

"We have a big day ahead of us." Paradox said, resting his gaze on each of us one at a time. "I think it would be best if you just stayed here Anna, it's too dangerous for you to get involved . . . especially for Justin's and the children's sake."

Anna nodded, and the children understood too. I stood up and twisted a little in place, taking the rifle from my back and realizing how sore it had made my muscles from sleeping with it on. My pockets were jammed full from the couple clips that I'd gotten from the now deceased soldier, and I didn't know how many rounds one clip held. Ethia stood up and stretched down to her feet, and tested the wrist blades which slid out then back in. Paradox waited for us to finish our checkup, and then we headed upstairs leaving Anna and the children alone.

It was getting late outside, and I didn't have any idea what time it was as we headed for the Twilight Cores building. There were still quite a few people out, a lot of them chattering about what had happened that day. A few of the people who walked past us eyed my rifle, and hurried along without doing anything else. I'm sure if the police saw me they'd have some questions, and ones that I wouldn't be able to give.

The building loomed over us as we drew closer to it, a feeling of sinister presence drifted in the air. It's probably just our mind playing tricks on us, since we know who actually owns the building, I thought. We hid behind some planted bushes and observed that there were no guards at the entrance. It resembled a normal office building as people moved in and out through twin revolving doors. I wondered how many of those people were actually in the Twilight Core, and how many didn't know what they were working under.

"So how are we going in?" I whispered to Paradox, who was looking up and down the building slowly.

"It looks like the front door." He said in reply, as he stood up and casually strode towards the revolving doors with his gloved hands in his pants pockets.

Ethia went rigid as she hissed out, "What is he doing?"

"I don't know he always does something crazy like this." I said, readying my rifle and charging out of the bushes to Paradox's side.

I heard Ethia sigh, the rustling of the bushes telling me that she was coming too. As the doors got closer some of the people looked at us with mixed reactions. Some started running. Others just looked at us with question, and some with a blank expression. People stopped moving through the doors, and dispersed until only we were in the area. I reached for the first door, and pushed to move it. Slowly it started to turn then locked in place and didn't move any farther as bright lights flashed inside the lobby and a man in a security shirt tapped a speaker console.

"This is the security of the EngineerTek Corporation. The doors have been sealed due to reports of a weapon attempting to be brought inside, authorities have been contacted. Have a nice day." A one way mechanical speaker reported from between the two doors.

"Heh, they're still role-playing inside." Paradox said, as he too tried the door.

I lifted the rifle, taking aim at the glass and firing a small burst of rounds into it. To my surprise the bullets ricocheted off of it, almost striking me in the process. Ethia ran over to make sure that I wasn't hurt, as I sat stunned at almost killing myself. Paradox knocked on the glass, which gave the same sound normal glass would before he stepped away.

"It's some kind of new technology that the Twilight Core either created, or stole from someone else." Paradox said raising both hands above his head and gathering a concentrated ball of darkness between them.

"Incoming." Ethia said, tapping me on the shoulder and pointing behind us.

I turned around and saw well around fifty of the small aircraft zipping in our direction. I knew that when they had contacted the 'Authorities' that they sent out an alarm signal to probably every branch of the Twilight Core. Paradox turned slowly, carefully lowering both arms. His right hand now held the ball of concentrated dark matter, and he watched the approaching fighter planes.

Still a good mile away, I was able to see them all launch missiles haphazardly in our direction as I said, "They must be crazy, they'll hit their own building!"

The three of us made a run for it, the ball of dark matter still growing in Paradox's steady arm. We were about to make it around the corner when the first warheads struck the front of the building, smashing against the side and exploding as others rained down on the area we were in. I was blown off my feet from the multiple impacts, flying diagonally around the corner and spinning through the air before hitting the ground as Ethia braced herself against the shock.

The explosions ceased, and I crawled to the corner and looked around it, trying to focus my eyes through the smoke to see the damage done. Impossible! I thought, looking at the building that was untouched from the impact against it. Paradox ran out from behind the building with a sphere of compressed dark matter the size of a large beach ball, with the fighter's now less then half a mile away as they unloaded another salvo in his direction. Ethia and I moved farther away from the front of the building, down the side as the explosions once again took place.

Paradox created a wall of darkness that grew from his back, blocking the warheads and explosions that hit near him. They needed to get inside, and he could do it. His back exploded in pain as he brought the large sphere of darkness to the glass and funneled it inside. The light began working on it, slowly shrinking it down, but since it was compressed it would take longer for it to totally dissipate. He looked to his left and shouted for me and Ethia, as he finished moving it inside.

I barely heard Paradox's shout over the screaming missiles and explosions that crashed about. It was now or never as I grabbed Ethia's hand and we ran together into the swarm of explosions. I kept my eyes straight ahead on Paradox, whose shield behind him was about gone. Out of the corner of my eye I could see a single warhead trailing its way through the sky straight at us, and in the next second before impact Paradox threw his left arm out and blocked it with a thin wall.

The detonation destroyed the wall, and sent Ethia and me into the buildings wall together. Luckily it wasn't enough to injure us, and we finished our trek to Paradox. The gunships behind us were near enough now that we could hear the whining of their chain guns starting up. Paradox made the compressed ball inside uncompress and expand. It started quickly disappearing in the light, but it made contact with Paradox and that's all he needed as we teleported inside of the buildings lobby and bullets thudded quietly off the glass from outside.

The aircraft ceased fire, knowing it was useless to keep firing against the building and ventured off into the night's sky. The security guard growled at us, slamming his hand on something underneath his desk and pulling out a pistol from the drawer in front of him. Paradox took a step forward then fell to the ground gripping his chest, hacking fitfully as I lifted my rifle and opened fire. The bullets struck the security guard, and he fell back into his chair no longer moving as I swept the area and Ethia headed for the desk.

Paradox continued to cough, making his way onto his feet. I followed after Ethia, keeping my sights swinging from side to side to the hallways on each side of the room. There was a staircase that went upwards on each side of the desk to a new level, and elevators could be seen a little way down the hallway that was running under the staircases on our level. Ethia reached the desk as I came up behind her, she bent over and looked for whatever the guard had hit. She sighed, standing back up straight and looked at us both.

"It looks like he triggered an alarm." She said, looking around and listening for any sound.

"If he set off an alarm, then why can't we hear anything at all?" I asked, when one of the elevators announced its arrival to our floor.

Paradox ran from out of view as a group of Twilight Soldiers poured out of the elevator and opened fire. Ethia and I moved against the wall, staying out of sight as the soldiers drew closer. The first soldier to enter the room fell forward at Ethia's kick to his shin bones. The rest opened fire, chewing at the wall separating them from us as the soldier that she had attacked crawled back down the hallway in pain. Paradox walked over from the other hallway and pressed himself against the wall next to us.

"The other hallway is clear, no soldiers yet." He said then chuckled out, "We need a plan."

"Oh really?" I said to him, shaking my head from the debris created by the bullets eating into the wall. "I thought if we just walked up to the front door they'd greet us with milk and cookies."

"Alright, Aaron, you move down the other hallway, and see if it comes back around. If it does you can get a clear shot at the soldiers. At the least it will distract some of them, and then perhaps Ethia can do the rest." Paradox said strategically as I nodded and ran down the hallway that was clear.

"How many did you see Paradox?" Ethia asked him, hoping he knew the number of the soldiers.

"I only saw six. Elevators have weight limits you know." Paradox said, brushing off his hat when a rifle sounded off down the hall. "That must be Aaron."

Paradox was right, the soldiers weren't watching their backs, probably because they'd been expecting other's to be in the hallways adjacent to the one they were in. I fired off and caught one in the back, causing two of them to turn my way and open fire. I jumped back behind the wall as the bullets barely missed their mark. At least I wasn't so helpless now.

Ethia charged around the corner, a bullet glancing off one of the metal plates on her jumpsuit as she jumped into the air and launched onto two of the soldier's heads that were next to each other. Her feet scrapped against the ceiling as she spun over them and planted their skulls one against the other where they fell to the floor. I turned the corner, taking aim and fired off another volley of shots against the ones fired at me.

Ethia rolled onto the ground, grabbing and lifting up the soldier that probably had two broken shins, from off the ground and throwing him at one of the other two men turning her way. The other man concentrated fire on me. They both made radioed yelps of pain as they crashed to the floor together in a heap. The last one turned to face her but was met with a few bullets piercing into his back before he fell to the ground.

I lowered my weapon, watching the last soldier fall as I ran down the hallway towards her and Paradox as they emerged from around the corner. Ethia had walked over to the two soldiers still alive, and knocked the soldier that was able to stand to the ground and ripped his weapon from his hands. She snapped it in half in front of his face, and then ripped his mask off.

"Where is Justin?" She said over the moans of the other soldier who was grabbing his shins.

The soldier had a bloody nose, and only grinned before spitting in her face. Ethia closed her eyes and wiped the spit off of her before delivering a solid knockout blow to his temple, then moved onto the next soldier and asked the same question.

"I—I don't know any Justin." He said, as Ethia reached down and grabbed one of his broken shin bones, tightening her grip. The soldier howled in pain as he reflexively beat on her arm to no avail. "You'll never win, you cannot defeat the Twilight-" is as far as he got roaring through the pain before Paradox kicked him across the face.

"No time for this. You can bet there are more soldiers on the way most likely." He said then walked over to the elevators.

I emptied my clip the way I had watched Justin do so during the battle with the Urthigeon, and placed one of the soldier's extras in its place. Ethia and I nodded to each other as we walked to the elevator that had stopped for us, and Paradox closed the door. We looked at all the buttons, and wondered which of them would lead us to the floor Justin was on. Paradox reached out to press one and Ethia grabbed his arm, tilting her head and listening.

"I hear alarms." She said, looking up then down, and nodding. "It's coming from below us, but there are no buttons to go any lower."

I looked at the controls once again, and she was right. The only thing other then the controls was a metal box with a keyhole that had 'Electrical Maintenance' labeled on it. Paradox reached over, a light coating of darkness covering his hand as he grabbed the metal box and ripped it off, revealing a new set of buttons that had coded meanings. Only the soldiers knew what each of them meant above the buttons.

"Let's choose . . . this one." Paradox said stabbing his finger at a button in the center called AB-1.

The elevator lurched to life, and we headed down a long ways when the elevator finally made a satisfied beeping noise and the doors slid open. We all froze as we saw a very large wide open room expanding out from the area, and columns of soldiers stood at attention ready for action. The alarms blared out as the soldiers turned their heads from their attention at the elevators announcement of arrival, looking at us and seeming equally stunned.

"Um, wrong floor." Paradox said, pressing the next button down as the soldiers scrambled for their weapons and the doors slid closed.

"Yeah, that was definitely bad." Ethia said, and I nodded in agreement hugging my rifle.

This time when the door opened we weren't greeted by soldiers. It opened into a military styled hallway, bleak and devoid of anything but what looked like a map. We moved out into the hallway and looked at the map which showed the different levels of the 'Alpha Force' complex. The bottom of the complex ended in a generator room, which must be where the building was getting its power from. A few floors above that was the detention area, where Justin must be, I thought.

I pointed it out to the others, and we turned to go as my eye caught where we were on the map, the control level. The elevator slid open and I climbed inside with Ethia, but Paradox halted at the familiar sound of a heavy combat suit stomping down the hallway. I held the elevator door open as Paradox turned around and faced Gear-Crusher who was applauding as he came around the corner of the hallway, shining armored hands clanging against each other as he stopped and viewed us through his helmet.

"I must say, Paradox, that you really are impressive." Gear-Crusher said, lowering his arms and chuckling. "Just to get inside this complex is a feat for you on a whole new level. Who thought that you would go so far for one of my men?"

"Justin isn't a traitor!" I shouted out at him, aiming my rifle for his armored suit and ready to pull the trigger.

"Ah, the little maggot . . . and accompanied by a little girl that has to protect him, how interesting." Gear-Crusher said, taking a few more steps forward down the hall then holding his arms away from him after seeing the rifle trained on his armor. "Go ahead! I'll give you as many free shots as you want, but once you're out I'm going to do what I said back on that planet you escaped from."

"Don't worry about him." Paradox said, tightening his gloves and rolling his head. "I'll take care of him."

"How dramatic, the hero lays down his life for the weaklings. I'll enjoy picking them apart slowly once I'm through with you, Paradox." Gear-Crusher crowed out, smashing a hole into the wall with his fist as if to prove his point.

"You can't beat me." Paradox stated, and then whispered to Ethia and me. "Aaron you go save Justin. Ethia, I have a request to make."

"Name it." Ethia said looking like she was ready to fight if needs be.

"I want you to go take out the power generator. I might be able to beat him if you do that, no arguing. Go now!" Paradox shouted the last bit, and started running at Gear-Crusher.

Gear-Crusher crouched down and tore down the hallway for the elevator while roaring out, "You're not going to get away! Whatever you have planned will fail . . . victory for the Twilight Core, glory for Alpha Force!" He finished as the elevator door closed and started moving downwards once again, when I realized Ethia had pressed the button.

"Ethia, we can't leave him there to fight alone!" I shouted, as the elevator stopped at the detention area and the doors opened for me.

Ethia looked at me, her eyes sparkling as she placed one hand on my cheek and said, "Paradox said no arguing, and you've got to save Justin. This is your stop."

I paused for a moment then nodded realizing that she was right, as I turned and ran out of the elevator while saying over my shoulder, "Just get that generator down."

"Good luck." Ethia whispered, as the door closed between us and she pressed the button for the lowest level, sending herself in the elevator grinding downwards into the depths of the complex.

The Clash of Titans

*G*ear-Crusher grinned as he approached Paradox and pulled his fist back to deliver a blow. He was going to finish what he'd started back on the living planet, and nothing could stop him. Paradox knew this was a grim situation, and slid down onto his back at the last moment. He dodged the heavy punch thrown at him and slid under the heavy armored legs, wrapping black matter around them like a rope and pulling as hard as he could.

The back pull combined with Gear-Crusher's forward momentum cause him to topple forward, smashing into the floor. As he climbed back up, Paradox jumped into the air, a sharp form of dark matter pointing from his right hands' closed fist and aiming for the back of Gear-Crushers armor. Gear-Crusher spun around, his arm catching Paradox in the side mid-fall and throwing him into the wall. Paradox gasped out as he hit the floor and stood back up, backing away from Gear-Crusher who was now also back on his feet.

"Impressive durability, that would have killed most men." Gear-Crusher said as his right arm's weapon popped up and fired a streaking bolt of white lightning in Paradox's direction. "Any other interesting secrets you have?"

Paradox threw both of his arms upwards, and blocked the blast with a shield of darkness that encased him, absorbing the electricity before dissolving. "More then you could ever know in your lifetime."

"We'll see if they're enough to keep you alive." Gear-Crusher said angrily, firing another blast while running forward and swinging his right arm at Paradox as his shield blocked the initial strike once more.

Paradox ducked under the right hook, which shattered through the concrete wall's corner. He rolled around Gear-Crusher who kicked out at him, almost connecting but missing from the erratic movement Paradox gave him. Paradox stopped rolling and stood up, racing for the elevator as he heard the crunching of the floor behind him from the heavy suit. He reached for the button but wasn't fast enough, and Gear-Crusher tackled him into the elevator door, busting through it and falling rapidly downwards.

"Trying to run were you?!" Gear-Crusher said excitedly, holding Paradox by the waist with one armored hand and veering downwards.

Come on Ethia, get that generator, Paradox thought as he forced a black bubble around him and disappeared out of Gear-Crusher's grasp just as he smashed into the bottom of the shaft headfirst. Less than a second passed, and Gear-Crusher was jetting upwards with flames firing from his back as he collided with Paradox who'd just reappeared. He grabbed Paradox by the leg, and flew quickly past the wrecked floor that they'd been fighting on up to the next one before punching in the elevator door and flying inside to where all the troops waited.

"Open season boys!" Gear-Crusher announced, swinging Paradox over his head and releasing him over the hundreds of soldiers who raised their weapons to take aim. "Take him down!"

Paradox didn't have many options. That is until the lights went out inside the complex, casting the particular room he was inside into pitch blackness. The soldiers opened fire, spraying everywhere up into the air for a chance to hit their target. Only in the bright flashes of the rifles and glowing bullets could you see Paradox teleporting at speeds faster than any of the projectiles, and with each teleport deliver a blow to a soldier that would take him out of the fight.

Moments passed, and none of the soldiers were left standing. Their weapons were strewn about the floor as they laid in heaps, and Gear-Crusher flashed on two lights that emerged from his armors chest cavity to observe the situation. Thank you Ethia, Paradox thought as Gear-Crusher's lights fell on him. Paradox stood defiantly in the center of all the soldiers that were littering the floor, and Gear-Crusher finally seemed slightly nervous about facing him.

"The only way you could have beaten me was when there was light all around." Paradox said, striding towards Gear-Crusher who took a step backwards and raised his right arm, firing off another blast of white lightning. But Paradox wasn't there any longer.

"Where did you go?" Gear-Crusher demanded, his scanners finally picking up that Paradox was behind him.

Paradox waited for him to spin around, and made an uppercut motion. The blackness swelled underneath Gear-Crusher and crushed him into the roof that cracked from the impact, as Paradox said, "You have no hope when you're in my turf."

"Fool, you still don't get it, do you? I'm indestructible!" Gear-Crusher shouted, spinning around with his jetpack and firing out from a weapon that emerged from his lower arm.

Paradox hadn't seen this weapon before, and it spewed out a continuous stream of flame instead of a fireball like his left arms top armament. The area around the fire was lit up somewhat, and Paradox dodged to the side as Gear-Crusher moved his arm and followed him. Paradox created a small shield of darkness with his left hand, diverting the flame away from him as he moved away. Gear-Crusher watched the black matter begin to funnel his flames back at him, and then stopped firing in case it would block his vision.

His sensors indicated that Paradox had retreated farther into the dark. His lights moved about the area, locating Paradox who had black matter pouring out from him in all directions. It grew around him, forming what looked like a gigantic creature of alien origin. Its massive eyes could be seen spewing out more dark matter that rose into the air like smoke, and hands formed outward from the ground which ended in black claws that gleamed in the dark. Large teeth could be seen where a vague mouth appeared, opening and closing slowly as if testing its jaws. The body totally encased Paradox, and when he spoke it came from the creature, but sounded raspy and hollow.

"So you want to test my real power do you?" The creature of black matter that Paradox had created rasped out. "So be it, but I cannot guarantee that you'll survive."

For the first time Gear-Crusher felt a cold chill inside. The black eyes that watched him didn't blink, and he watched the creature lean forward, as if to get a better look at its prey. Gear-Crusher shook his head, and beat his chest as he stood up straight and lifted both of his arms, looking into his armored palms. The creature created from dark power tilted its head to one side, as if wondering what he was doing.

"You really are a demon, Paradox." Gear-Crusher laughed out raucously. "But I am a commander of the Twilight Cores Alpha Force . . . and I will not be defeated by the likes of you." He said, lowering both of his arms as rocket pods emerged from his shoulders and fired away.

The rockets surged forward towards the creature's face, as the creature lifted its left hand and blocked them with the back of it. The explosions lighted the area, but seemed to have no effect whatsoever on the creature Paradox had summoned. With an eerie shriek the creature thrashed its left hand away from its head, a wave of darkness rushing towards Gear-Crusher as he took to the air. He didn't get very far as the wave collided into him, knocking him away and trying to rip his armor off as it passed by.

Gear-Crusher hit the wall near the ruined elevator door, steadying himself while he dropped back to the ground. His armor wasn't damaged, but the creature was now clawing its way towards him, digging the massive black talons into the ground and dragging itself forward quickly. Paradox was nowhere to be seen inside the monstrous image, as Gear-Crusher activated his right arms side mounted weapon that resembled a mini-gun, and then took off for the elevator shaft.

He flew up it, hearing the wall explode below him as he looked down and saw the monster racing up after him, with its clawed hands easily piercing the walls and pulling itself up at unbelievable speeds. He pointed his right arm down, firing brightly lit rounds into the snapping maw that was glowing closer when he blew through the roof of the building and into the sky. The sun was still up, but lingering low over the horizon as the black creature blew upwards from the hole making it larger.

It shrieked again as the sun struck it, and it started dissolving away. The maw continued to move closer to Gear-Crusher, open to receive the meal before it as Paradox emerged from behind it. He held his hands to resemble the mouth, and was moving his hands forward, trying to consume Gear-Crusher before it was gone. Gear-Crusher held open his left hand. The armor on his palm clicking open and creating a blinding flash of light that shot out of it.

The mouth of the beast was struck by the light, disappearing as Gear-Crusher shot towards Paradox and grabbed him by the arm. Paradox was helpless, unable to teleport quick enough in the sunlight as Gear-Crusher placed his other armored hand on his side and jerked his arm. There was a ripping sound, and Paradox fell to the ground gripping where dark matter was pouring out from the hole where his left arm once was. Gear-Crusher landed a little ways off, and looked at the limp duster coat's sleeve in his hand and dropped it to the roof.

"I see." Gear-Crusher said, nodding his armored head and looking at Paradox who was writhing on the ground, the black matter rising into the sky and vanishing, while getting slowly onto his knees. "You aren't even human! No wonder you could withstand my blows . . . it all makes sense now."

Paradox stood onto his booted feet, looking back at Gear-Crusher as he leaned over gripping his wound while saying, "I was human once . . . a very long time ago."

"All in all it won't matter once you are dead." Gear-Crusher said, walking forward leisurely and gripping Paradox by the neck and lifting him up off his feet. "Why don't you fight back?"

"I will, until the bitter end." Paradox said, watching the sun sink a little lower over the horizon. "I just want you to know, that you can never actually kill me."

Gear-Crusher grabbed Paradox's head with his free arm, crushing his hat and started to pull lightly. Paradox let his right arm fall to his side, and then shot it out towards Gear-Crusher's chest where a rotating ball of black matter struck his opponent. Gear-Crusher's hands were ripped away from Paradox as the ball of black matter spun him away and over the side of the building. He was turning so quickly in the air he couldn't activate his back thrusters correctly.

The next thing Gear-Crusher knew was that he was embedded into the pavement, struggling to get himself out as he watched Paradox leap off the building, heading down at him and forming his body into a dark point that gravity pulled towards its mark. Seconds passed away, and Gear-Crusher couldn't help but feel like grinning when Paradox struck him in the chest and the area exploded out from around the impact zone.

A Multiplying Problem

*E*thia had made it about halfway to the power room when the lights went out. Strangely there were no soldiers on this level of the complex, and since she wasn't the one that had sabotaged the power, then, who did? She inched her way along the hallway, encountering a red pulsing emergency alarm light every so often as she continued towards her objective. At least once she got there she'd be able to find out who had saved her the trouble of disrupting the power.

Up ahead she could make out the door that led into the power room by a lone pulsing red light. Two figures were lying next to the door, and as she grew closer she registered them as Twilight Alpha Force Soldiers. Whoever had been through here got past them, and bullet prints marked the hallway she was currently walking down showing signs of a fight.

She wondered who it could have been, and shuddered as she reached the two soldiers. Through their masks she could see looks of horror sunken into withered faces, like they'd been drained of any and all fluids present in their body. The skeletal figures in uniform still held to their rifles, and she forced herself to move past the corpses. On second thought, maybe I don't want to meet whoever it was that did this, She thought.

The heavy door to the generator sat slightly open, and she was surprised how easy it moved when she opened it the rest of the way. The room was large, and a massive cylinder generator sat in the middle of the room stretching from the roof to the floor, a single red light pulsing slowly in the darkness. A good thirty bodies or more were strewn about the room. Uniforms covered the corpses that resembled the ones outside, the arms of them resting on nearby weapons. Ethia looked at the controls covering the walls, most of them smashed into pieces, when she heard a noise.

She spun around, holding her arms up in defense as she saw a soldier hanging in the air, suspended from his back by what looked like a rigid metallic pipe, emerging from behind the generator. It throbbed as the soldiers skin crumpled like a packet of juice running low on liquid, and she gasped as the pulsing arm stopped and the soldier dropped to the floor. The pipe quivered, seeming to move and reform itself into a humanoid arm that disappeared behind the generator.

"Who's there?" Ethia demanded feeling unnerved but keeping ready for a fight.

"My dear Ethia, it's too bad that we had to meet at such a . . . unpleasant time." A cool, almost friendly sounding voice said from behind the generator.

Ethia went cold inside, her heart thumping as her mind recalled the glowing red eye in the darkness, and knew that the voice could only belong to that same individual as she said, "Nanoplicity."

"The one and only." Nanoplicity said, stepping around the generator casually and leaning his back against it. "I'm flattered that you remembered my name."

Ethia finally got a look at the man before her in the pulsing light. He looked like he was somewhere between eighteen and twenty-one, and wasn't the bulkiest person around. In fact he was more on the lean side when compared with most of the soldiers she'd fought. He had the usual flattop that most of the soldiers had, and she thought his hair looked white, but it was hard to tell in the red light.

Most of his body appeared human, and he was wearing a uniform that shined in the light. His right arm was normal, but his left looked mechanical, and shifted about ever so slightly. He would have had a handsome face, which adorned a smile, but the mechanical arm climbed up the left side of his body and neck, ending in the left side of his face being mechanical where his red robotic eye sat looking at her.

Ethia wondered how he was able to defeat all of these soldiers, and wondered why as she looked around at them then shouted, "Why did you kill your own soldiers?"

"Not my soldiers." Nanoplicity said, smiling wider and holding a finger up. "Only Alpha Force's soldiers. So Gear-Crusher's I believe."

"Does that make a difference? You didn't have to kill them!" Ethia said, clenching her hands and shivering in anger.

"Perhaps so, but I wanted to have some fun." He said simply, folding his arms and still smiling at her.

"You're sick if this is your idea of fun." Ethia said, then tilted her head a little and asked, "Why did you sabotage the power?"

"I'm afraid I can't tell you that." Nanoplicity said, his smile never leaving as he pulled a cloth from his pocket and breathed on it before wiping down his robotic eye.

"So then what now," Ethia asked, "Watching the cloth and thinking it was some sort of trick before he placed it back in his pocket. "You're going to kill me too?"

"Oh my, no, no, no," He said, raising both of his hands and waving them back and forth, as his eyes closed while smiling at her. "I just want you to come with me."

"Right, I'll just do that. No thanks, I think I'll stick with Aaron and Paradox." Ethia said her eyes flashing angrily as Nanoplicity stood up from leaning against the generator. His smile was really getting annoying.

"My commander predicted that you would say something along that. If you did, I'm supposed to take you with me by force, are you sure you want me to do that? It would be very pleasant if you just came along with me. We could talk and get to know one anoth-" Nanoplicity started saying, his arms behind his back when he was interrupted by Ethia blasting forward and delivering a solid and powerful left hook to his human cheek, which sent him flying into the shattered controls and flailing to the floor.

"How's that for an answer?" Ethia seethed out, and turned to go when she heard movement and turned to see him standing up, mechanical arm hanging from his side and smiling at her while he rubbed his right cheek with his other arm.

"That was quite a powerful hit." He said, still rubbing his cheek then moving his hand to the back of his head and scratching as he tilted it and continued to smile like nothing had happened. "Powerful and beyond beautiful . . . especially when you're angry, your eyes give you away. It's really too bad that you chose Aaron to be with you, I wouldn't have minded."

Ethia was mixed with shock and fury. It was incredible that he had gotten up from the punch she had delivered so easily, especially one with more force in it then she had used on the soldiers. Her fury stemmed from how he was talking to her, so casually and about him being with her instead of Aaron! And that stupid, pasted on smile! She thought as she found herself rushing at him again, one of the knives zipping out from her wrist and aiming for his head.

Metal rang against metal as Nanoplicity moved his mechanical arm up very fast, and the hand transformed into a flat shield that the knife pierced into. Ethia held her arm straight, breathing in and out as Nanoplicity moved the knife away to the side. She struggled to pull the knife out, fighting against him and realizing that his strength surpassed her own. The knife started to slide out of the shield, and then stopped as Nanoplicity continued to smile at her and the shield started creeping down the knives blade towards her arm.

She reached up and tried to undo the bracelet with her free hand, as Nanoplicity reached up and brushed her cheek with the back of his own as he said, "This is your last chance to come nicely."

Ethia screamed out in rage, unable to get the bracelet off. She pulled back her free hand, tears streaming down her face as the metal from his shield continued to draw closer. She shoved her hand into his gut, lifting him off his feet as the bracelet was torn off from her wrist along with the metallic arm that was grabbing it. She stumbled backwards, gripping the pain that took the bracelets place, and looked towards Nanoplicity.

He stood back up from the second blow, the smile still in place as the bracelet was absorbed into the arm. It returned to its humanoid looking state, and he laughed a little before flexing it and saying, "Do you know how I got the name Nanoplicity? It's because my arm and part of my face is constructed out of nanites, small little machines that can replicate themselves. That's not all though."

Nanoplicity started trembling, as his human eye widened and his smile was replaced by a look of pain. His body seemed to widen, and rip apart as another pair of arms emerged, along with legs, body, then finally head. Suddenly there were now two Nanoplicity's looking at her, both of them exactly identical, and both of them smiling at her. He's able to multiply? Ethia thought while backing away and removing the bracelet on her other wrist, not wanting it to get in the way.

"Don't look so shocked." Both of the Nanoplicity's said in unison and smiling as one lifted its arms in a shrug, and the other placed a hand to its chin. "I thought my name would give it away. I guess not."

Ethia knew she was going to have to go all out if she wanted to out of this situation. She crouched down into one of her fighting positions as she waited for Nanoplicity to finally come at her, but he kept on talking instead as he said, "I'm sorry it has to come to this. I'll try to be as gentle as I can to take you with me, but there are no promises that you won't get hurt badly."

She had enough of this. Ethia became a blur as she homed in on one of the Nanoplicity's, and performed a chop to his neck. This one flew away from her strike, crashing into the walls as the second's arm extended in a cone like fashion towards her. She back flipped over it, landing on her hands and bringing her legs heavily down into the rushing mass. The nanites jerked and fell to the ground as her legs forced their way through, cutting them off from their host.

The Nanoplicity that had performed the attack only shook his head, smiling as Ethia stood up and backed away. The mass on the ground slithered towards him and crawled up, reattaching itself to his arm. The one she had knocked away was back on his feet, but with another identical copy next to it. Now there are three of them, Ethia thought, trying to figure out what to do. She raced over to one of the rifles and picked it up, aiming and firing in an arc at all three Nanoplicity's.

Their arms expanded around them, creating a shield that blocked and deflected the bullets as all three rushed forward. Ethia dropped the rifle and ran for the generator, narrowly dodging a clubbed swipe that the nearest Nanoplicity made by spinning around it. She was about to use the generator as a source to attack from, when a tiny pain shot through her legs. Ethia looked down, and saw tiny metallic dots running around as she batted them off, feeling numb spots wherever they'd been.

These ones must've latched on when I kicked all those nanites. They had to have injected me with something that numbed a small area around them, Ethia thought, just as she ran around the generator and a swarm of nanites flew through the air past her. The Nanoplicity's could use their nanites as a projectile weapon, as well as melee. They'd fling it at their foes, and even if they missed the Nanites crawled right back.

Ethia heard the first of the three Nanoplicity's moving around the generator, as she threw her leg around it and caught him in the side and smashed him into the generator. He wobbled for a moment, as another split of from this one she hit, tallying up the number to four. She made a break for the door, vaulting for it when she felt a cloud of nanites rain down onto her back. Immediately a prickling pain followed by numbness, they crawled down her injecting whatever it was they carried as she fell to the floor and watched one of the Nanoplicity's walk over and shut the door, and another walking over to her.

Her entire body was numb, and she couldn't move at all as she watched the little robots scurry off of her and back to the one that approached while the others gathered around. She couldn't believe what was happening, it didn't make sense. Why did they want her? Why did he sabotage the Alpha Force's power? Why was this happening?

"I'm sorry about the numb feeling. It will wear off over time." One of the Nanoplicity's said politely.

Ethia's mouth felt like a leaded brick as she managed to force out some words saying, "What about my friends?"

"Who knows? Perhaps they will survive, perhaps not. You can only hope for the best." Nanoplicity said while turning her head slightly so that she could see his smiling face. He talked like he would support whatever she thought and brimmed with optimism, although he probably cared less.

I can't allow this. No . . . I won't allow this, Ethia thought. Her body trembled as she used the jumpsuit she was wearing to funnel her energy into a concentrated form inside her body. It overrode the numbness, and she could feel again as she stayed on the floor. Ethia seemed to glow a little from the energy, and the air swirled with a slight tingle to its touch as she started twitching, her hair flowing a little off her body about her. What she was doing was dangerous and could end her life. She was going to risk going past her limits, rather then be caught by Nanoplicity.

All the Nanoplicity's leaned forward, their smiles finally disappearing as they watched her twitching. Then the air cracked and exploded with a sonic boom as she was on her feet, moving past the sound barrier in speed. Nanoplicity looked horrified at this, and was unable to react more then a change of expression as all four of him were colliding into the wall, and one of them breaking in half with a shower of nanites against the generator.

"No! Don't!" Nanoplicity shouted worriedly. "You'll kill yourself!"

The next thing he knew was that she was next to him, her eyes an inch away from his as she said, "You should be worrying about you."

Then he was in the roof, picked up from the ground and kicked with such force and speed that he hadn't known what happened. His other set of eyes watched her perform this feat, when he started to split into two more, when she was across the room and cut him in half before the process was complete with her hand. There was once again only one Nanoplicity which tried to shower her with nanites that seemed to vibrate off of her, and he felt Ethia's foot against his neck just as he performed his advanced multiplying ability.

Ethia could tell something was wrong as she kicked the last one in the neck, and he seemed to be standing in the same place as another one of him flew out from the blow. There were two of them again. She zipped over to the newly created Nanoplicity, and slammed down on his head with her elbow as he stayed where he was and another spurted downward to the floor from her blow. This is bad, She thought as her insides felt like they were just about ready to rip their way our from her body.

Nanoplicity had to stop her, he knew it . . . otherwise she'd be dead in a matter of seconds. He watched her tear a long piece of metal from one of the control consoles, and set about cutting his other self's in half, which promptly formed two new Nanoplicity's. He could see she was frustrated now, continuing to hack away and creating more. She was also in great pain, and her body was rippling, like it was about to shred itself apart.

Ethia threw the metal shard out of her hands, piercing one of the Nanoplicity's in the chest, and watching it dissolve into nanites that scurried to various others. That's it, Ethia thought, if I can impale them all quickly enough then I can get rid of them. She got ready to run for more metal when her guts wrenched inside, and she toppled to the floor screaming out in pain. There were at least seventeen Nanoplicity's that rushed over to her now as she lay on the ground squirming.

Nanoplicity had to act quickly, otherwise she'd be dead in a moment. He remembered how the nanites had vibrated off of her when he'd attacked that way, so this time he positioned all seventeen of himself around her. All at once they struck out with their mechanical arms, pouring on the Nanites from every direction and effectively cocooning Ethia. He could feel the vibrations die down inside the cocoon, but knew that she wasn't dead as he breathed a sigh of relief and smiled. His commander would be pleased, and although she put up more trouble then expected, she was well worth it.

Ethia felt the nanites cocoon her and obscure her vision as she closed her eyes and felt them all inject her at once, numbing the pain quickly inside as she felt herself drifting off into a sleep. She could see Aaron, and he was sad about something, sad about a few something's actually. She wanted to reach out and hold him although she didn't know what was wrong, but her arms wouldn't move. Suddenly he transformed, half of his face becoming mechanical and his arm following it to become Nanoplicity.

She wanted to lurch back from him, as he walked forward with the fake smile pasted on his lips as Ethia cried quietly out saying, "Goodbye Aaron."

The Breakout

*T*he elevator door closed behind me as I ran down the hallway, slowing so that I could hear ahead easier. I lugged my rifle up to my chest, resting it in the crook of my arm so it didn't seem as heavy. The hallway was just like the others we'd seen, cold grey cinderblocks lining the walls and bright lights parading down them. I wonder if each Twilight Core has a facility for each Force, I thought as I walked down the hallway quietly.

I heard the soldiers before I saw them because the hall twisted out of view. It was hard to judge how far they were, and their radioed voices made it difficult to pick out what each was saying. I peeked around the corner so I could see the men. There were two of them, facing each other and talking. One of them was going on about eating something and the other would shake his head yes or no then say something in reply.

It was a straight shot past them to a very heavy looking door that had 'Detention Area' printed above it. I could just make out a smaller door to the right of the larger one. The smaller one had a glass window next to it, so I was guessing that was the security room where they opened and closed the detention area's door. The question was how many more soldiers were on this level, and would be alerted if a firefight broke out. I made sure that the rifle I carried was ready, the glowing stripe along its barrel pulsing slightly, as I got ready to spin around the corner to enter combat when the lights went out.

I froze. The only light emitting now was from the barrel of my rifle. I took out the clip and the strip of light died away into the blackness as my eyes tried to adjust. The soldiers hadn't noticed me, and I could hear them muttering something about a faulty generator and how the technicians would get it back up and running soon. I leaned around the corner and could see the lights shining out from their helmets as they continued to look at each other, giving me an opportunity to start slinking closer through the blackness towards them.

It was slow going, but the soldiers didn't even bother to change what they were talking about. I got as close as I dared, about six feet away from them in the dark hallway as I tried to figure out how to get past them now without them seeing me. It didn't seem like I had a choice but to fight them, and at this range it would be hard to miss. I would have to catch them by surprise if I wanted to take them down before they took me.

I held the ammo clip in my hand that would activate the weapons light strip as soon as it was slammed into place. I licked my lips and listened to the soldiers going on about what movies were coming out recently, and I hated to do this. I rammed the clip in place and raised my rifle as the strip shone out. The two soldiers turned, either in shock or perhaps thinking that I was one of them when my weapon's fire resounded down the hallway and both of them fell into heaps.

Freezing I turned off my light and listened for any indication that others had heard the gunfire. Nothing changed in the hallway. No enemy reinforcements, no heavy boots moving down the hall from front or behind, no shouts or doors opening. After the rifle firing had created a thunderous racket, it was eerily quiet. I turned on my light and trained it on the security room's door, moving carefully towards it and stopping only to eject my rifle clip and replace it with a new one from the fallen soldiers.

Sidestepping in front of the window I looked inside. There were tiny holes in the glass, for talking through, so I guessed that if anyone had been in there they would have come out already. My light danced over some controls and a chair inside. Otherwise it looked just like a small security room with nothing special about it. I pressed the control on the side of the door to open it, and was surprised to see it slide open. It must have its own power source, I thought, a backup generator that won't last long if anything.

Inside the room only confirmed what I'd seen through the glass, nothing special about the room at all with a simple layout of controls for operating the heavy detention door. I pressed the one that was marked with 'Open' on it. The large metallic door grumbled as if in protest and started lurching sideways, sliding into the wall and opening the way into the place where Justin should be. I left the security room and trudged inside the larger door, my beam of light sweeping through the air and my rifle's muzzle following it.

It looked just like a prison block. Rows of cells lined the walls, the entrance to each cell not blocked by bars, but a thick metal door that had nothing but a window that was twelve inches in length and one inch in height on the door. Even though the windows were so small a fine net of mesh was set in each one, allowing me to peer in, but not allowing anything else. I moved from cell to cell, gazing in to see if Justin was there. Each cell had a person in it, sometimes more then one and I felt sick to my stomach realizing that the cells weren't even that large inside. Some of the people glanced over towards me as my light shined on them, illuminating starving bodies and wild eyes. Some of the people weren't in bad shape, but whether that was because they were recently captured or fed well I didn't know.

"Hey you, kid." I heard a voice say as I turned to see a man peering at me through the mesh of his cell. "Yeah, you, come over here for a second."

I cautiously moved towards him, and he backed away from the mesh so that either I could see him better or so that I wouldn't feel threatened. He was a very large man, muscles rippling through his clothes. His face had a wild beard, showing that he hadn't been able to shave in some time. He wore a dull grey uniform with a number on it, no doubt his detention serial number.

"What do you want?" I asked him, as he looked me up and down, scratching at the beard on his face.

He paused a moment, then looked to either side of him as if there was someone there then said in a rough voice, "The names Buck, and you aren't one of those Twilight punks." He said spitting on the ground heavily on the last two words as if he had to get his point across.

"How do you know I'm not one of them, Buck?" I asked, looking around at the other cells where people had begun gathering at their meshed windows and whispering to others and themselves while looking at me.

"Oh, I don't know. The way you dress, the way you came over when I called you, the way you kept glancing over your shoulder . . . take your pick. I know you aren't one." Buck said while his beard seemed to move a little as he talked.

"Alright, granted that I'm not one, what do you want?" I asked again, part of me wanting to get on with looking for Justin.

"I, no not just I, we want you to break us out of here. Some of us have been here for years. We haven't done anything wrong, we were normal people. They took us off the streets and placed us here for some reason. Sometimes they come in and take one or two of us, but where they go we have no idea." Buck said, his rough voice almost breaking by the end and tears welling up in his eyes as he added, "You're the first person we've seen for a long time that's not a Twilight Soldier."

The realization hit me that all these people weren't actually criminals. They were just as innocent as I was, and had been swept away when no one would notice. I didn't just have to save Justin . . . I would have to save everyone here. I looked for a way to open the cell door, but there was nothing at all. No lock, no handle, nothing.

"How do they open the doors?" I said, gazing at Buck.

"I'm not totally sure." He said, rubbing his beard thoughtfully as his eyes gleamed and looked at the other cell doors. "A few soldiers would come in and wait by a door, as it slid open to get the person."

The security room, I thought. As I turned and jogged away from Buck's cell and called out. "I'll be right back."

Within moments I had reached the security room, looking over all the panels and finally locating the one that controlled the doors. There were around a hundred of them, and I was getting ready to press them as quickly as I could when I noticed the release all. I chuckled to myself, marveling at this and wondering only for a second why the Twilight Core had it. I shrugged and pressed it, when a whirring shriek sounded throughout the complex and died down slowly. The backup generator had just used up it's life.

I heard cheers and shouts as I left the security room, and looked at the people bursting from their cell rooms and gathering into groups. Buck was organizing them with professionalism and turned to greet me when I approached.

"Great job kid," He said, placing a hand on my shoulder. "I heard the backup generator die. It could make it easier or harder for us. Depends on what happens. Anyways, we're ready to get out of here."

"Alright, my names Aaron by the way, do you know anyone here named Justin?" I asked as Buck shook his head no, and both of us started hurrying down the hall, the other's following us and salvaging any weapons they could from the bodies of the men I'd killed.

"People are coming and going from here all the time, he might be with us. I suggest you look for him once we are all out of here." Buck said, walking quickly.

We turned the corner, hitting something as we did and causing me to almost fall backward. A group of Twilight Soldiers stumbled back as we collided with them and everything seemed to freeze in time. Before anyone else reacted Buck let out a roar and charged forward, barreling through the soldiers and knocking them down as the rest of the prisoners mobbed over them. It didn't take long before we had some more weapons for other people, and they took up point with a few in the back.

We walked down the dark hall, passing a few doors where shouts and orders resonated from, a dull clanging coming from the other sides. Whoever was in there was trapped because the power was out, and probably wasn't getting out anytime soon. A few moments more and I had led them to the elevator. We pried it open and looked up and down. I knew that with the power out it wouldn't be operating, but I didn't expect to see it demolished on the bottom level where Ethia had been.

"It looks like we'll be taking the ladder up to get out of this place." Buck said, pointing to the service ladder running vertically in the shaft. "Its dangerous going single file, but we'll have to risk it. Are you the only one that came here?"

"No, there are two other's." I said, making Buck look unsure on how three people managed to get inside. "It's a long story, believe me."

Buck chuckled and jumped onto the ladder after a few of the others, and I followed him as he said, "You'll have to tell me about it sometime."

Progress was slow, and we were mostly silent as we crawled upward past elevator doors. I knew we were getting close to the level that had contained all the Twilight Core's troops, and my stomach lurched when we passed the door where we had left Paradox. Its twisted metal frame was definitely a sign that they had left that level, and I didn't know if it was a good or bad sign. My arms and legs were growing a little tired with our climb, when someone above us cried out.

Gunfire roared in the shaft, and someone above us fell from the ladder downwards. More gunfire and luminescent bullets were zipping up and down around us. There was shouting on both sides, the radioed shouts giving the location of the enemy that was on the ladder above us. I hoisted my rifle with one arm and leaned sideways on the ladder firing up at our enemy that had their lights shut off. It was a blind firefight, and we had to pretty much guess where the soldiers were along the ladder. Every once and awhile one of them would fall past us, or one of our allies were hit and met the same doom.

After some minutes of fighting the people on both sides had enough, and surged up the ladder, still firing at each other. I didn't have much time to speculate and think when we passed the second door that was shredded apart, leading into the large area where Twilight Soldiers were lying strewn about, either unconscious or dead. The soldiers above us cheered as they reached the main levels door, and pried it open, pouring out of the shaft. This was bad for us, the enemy would either look down the shaft and pick us off now, or they would take up defensive positions right outside the doors.

Buck seemed to be thinking the same thing, and pulled a grenade from his uniform. I didn't know where he'd originally gotten the grenade, but I didn't care as we continued to ascend upwards. He pulled the pin on the grenade, and counted under his breath. A few seconds passed, and he finally heaved the object over his head and into the open door, another second and an explosion emitted from the hallway, and we poured in from the ladder.

Weapons were raised and ready, but lowered in surprise as we looked about and noticed none of the soldiers were there. We carefully moved into the lobby and checked around, but still no sign of them. We came to the conclusion that the soldiers had decided to ditch the headquarters while we were still climbing the ladder, which we were fine with. I led them to the revolving doors, now unlocked and spinning, as I nodded to Buck. We both stopped for a moment as the people who were once prisoners started filing out the door into the setting sun.

"It's been awhile since I've seen sunlight." Buck said squinting his eyelids slightly at the sunlight, and then turning so we were face to face. "Anyways, you'd best hang out here and look for that friend of yours."

"So what are you going to do now?" I asked, watching him move into the spinning doors while I followed him, making our way towards the outside.

Before we were all the way through he shrugged and said, "Perhaps find a way to topple this place. We have plenty of witnesses now too."

Buck disappeared outside amidst the group lingering about, and I turned to scan the remaining people inside emerging from the doors when something caught my eye. I turned towards the movement and looked up, my brain registering in horror Paradox falling at an extreme speed in the distance. He was shaped like a spear point, aiming at something, and there wasn't much time to react at all by the time he had smashed down into the concrete, creating a black shockwave that rippled outward from the force.

Rebirth

J ran for the impact site that was created by the force of Paradox's strike. A small crater sunk into the street, and when I approached it I saw two figures lying inside. One was Gear-Crusher, who was moving and already getting to his feet. A sizable dent in his chest armor showed, but he didn't seem to mind at all. Paradox was lying almost completely still, moving slightly and looking like he was dazed. I realized that his left arm was missing, and blackness poured from it dissipating into the sun.

"Paradox, are you alright?" I called out, raising my rifle and aiming at Gear-Crusher.

Gear-Crusher turned halfway towards me, then back to Paradox as many of the freed prisoners rushed for the site as well. Paradox gazed at me, masked face holding still as Gear-Crusher rushed for him. I shouted, pressing down the trigger and firing as the hail of bullets bounced harmlessly of the armor that Gear-Crusher wore. Everything seemed to slow down as Gear-Crusher ignored my attack and raised his fist into the air, bringing it down with all the force he could muster right into Paradox's gut. Paradox didn't make a sound as he did this, and sagged from the blow as Gear-Crusher threw him up into the air.

I stopped firing, afraid that I would hit Paradox and hoped that this was part of some plan that he had. In the next instant Gear-Crusher's jetpack sputtered to life and he was above Paradox, smashing him out of the crater and onto the concrete. Massive amounts of blackness were pouring out of him now, and he didn't move as Gear-Crusher landed heavily next to him.

"All out of tricks, Paradox?" Gear-Crusher said, lifting his foot and stamping on his stomach over and over as the ground seemed to quake with each blow. "I thought you had plenty of tricks left? Hmm, how are you doing? Are you dead yet? For all I know you are. No movement, no talk . . . and of course you probably never had a pulse."

"Stop it!" I roared out, charging at Gear-Crusher as the people around me roared in agreement.

Gear-Crusher shot an arm out with lightning speed, encasing my head completely with one massive armored hand and chuckling, "Well, if it isn't his little friend. I'll take care of you in just a minute."

He angled me so that I could see Paradox, and I cried out as a weapon that was positioned on the right of Gear-Crusher's arm fired off a quick burst into Paradox. The black matter leaked out of the holes, and I was thrown to the ground with such force next to Paradox that I almost blacked out. I turned to look at Gear-Crusher and narrowed my eyes at him in defiance as he aimed the weapon at me. I couldn't believe it, he'd beaten Paradox . . . killed him. It almost didn't seem possible.

"It was almost enjoyable. Too bad it didn't last longer." Gear-Crusher sneered, as if reading my thoughts.

I knew I'd be dead in a few seconds, and waited for the shot when one of the people I'd saved jumped in front of the gun. This surprised Gear-Crusher and he moved his arm to swat the person away when he was surrounded by everyone. They were beating on his armor, trying to tear it off him, but to no avail. They didn't seem to understand that it was hopeless to stand against him.

"No, please don't, run." I said hoarsely, watching Gear-Crusher toss multiple people aside, and knocking them away.

I moved from my back onto my knees, and got ready to stand up when I felt someone grab my arm weakly and a light cough come from its direction. I turned and saw Paradox reaching over with his right arm, looking at me and trying to pull me closer. I moved closer towards his mask as everything else seemed to grow farther away. Then we were alone, in the empty streets standing across from each other. I looked around realizing that it was the streets from my dreams, but this wasn't a dream. Here I was with Paradox looking at me.

"Paradox, what happened? Where are we? What's going on?" I said in confusion as he folded his arms and continued to look at me.

"Your training is complete, well almost. This is the last thing we . . . or more I . . . have to do." Paradox said walking a little closer towards me and stopping.

I double checked his left arm to make sure it was there and then blurted out, "But how are you still alive? I watched Gear-Crusher-"

"Kill me?" Paradox cut in, then laughed a little. "I told him you can't ever really kill me. It doesn't matter though, my time was up anyway."

"What do you mean? This doesn't make sense . . . I'm confused." I said rubbing my temples as Paradox reached out his hand in a handshake gesture.

"It will all make sense soon. All you have to do is accept the final task." He said, still holding out his hand and waiting for me to grab it.

I eyed it, remembering back to when he'd first waited for me to make the choice to either go with him or stay at my house. He'd held out his hand and waited for me, never trying to force me to make the choice. Now it was similar to that, and as I stood there I only had one question burn in my mind.

"What's the final task?" I asked, as he tilted his head a bit and adjusted his hat with his free hand while waiting with the other outstretched.

"I can't tell you that. You can only find out once you accept." He said, nodding forward to his hand.

Inside I burned, and I weighed my choices. It was strange, but I felt like I had a duty to accept, that it would be the right thing to do as I reached out and grabbed his gloved hand. "I accept."

Behind his mask I knew he was smiling wider then he'd ever had while I'd been with him. The sky seemed to grow darker, as the world around me moved into blackness. The building's receded until I couldn't see them anymore, and the last thing to leave my sight was Paradox where I was left with complete and utter blackness. The whispers returned, and I felt power inside of me, around me. The whispers slowly ceased, and all spoke up at once in unison loudly and I could pick out my mentor's voice among them.

"The final task was," All the voices announced around me, "To become Paradox."

The Demise of One

My eyes shot open to the shouts of those attacking Gear-Crusher and his raking laughter. Everything made sense now, such as the dream where the soldiers had captured Paradox. It hadn't been a dream, it had happened in the past. He had used so much of his power to escape that he was slowly dying, and needed someone to take his place, that had been me. He'd once been human, like I, but over time his physical body disappeared, and left him with the manifestation of his power. That's why he never took off his clothes, I thought.

I looked sadly over to Paradox, and reached out towards him. There was nothing left but his clothes, the dark power finished seeping outwards from it and had disappeared into the sky as I thought, "He's dead."

"Not quite." I heard another voice announce inside my head as I shot backwards away from the clothes. I concentrated, and realized that I could feel another conscience inside my head besides my own. Not only that, but there were numerous others with it. They weren't intrusive. In fact I had to concentrate very hard to feel for them. One of them was easier to pick out from the other ones as I heard the voice say again, "I'm not dead. You can't ever really kill us. Perhaps I should explain some things you still don't get."

"Wait, wait, wait." I thought, looking at Gear-Crusher and the thinning crowd around him. "That's you in my head Paradox?"

"Yes, one of many Paradox's, I was your mentor, and I will still teach you through this way from now on." Paradox said, as I stood up and he added, "I was the one that was slowly dying. The coughing fits I had were signs of my nearing end. Anyway, when my mentor died, and I accepted the final task, his conscience was implanted into my head also, along with all the Paradox's before him."

"So all those other's I feel . . . those were all once people like me?" I asked in thought.

"Correct. I'm tired right now, and I need to rest. I haven't done that in a long time, but if you need any advice, just ask." I heard Paradox say, as his voice slowly dissipated and disappeared.

I shook my head, as if waking up from a dream. Gear-Crusher was almost through with the rest of the former prisoners, and I started trembling as I looked at the bodies of those who had fallen to protect me.

"Everyone, you've done enough, stand back!" I shouted out, and noticed that my voice sounded different. It sounded like my voice was being over laced by Paradox's.

Everyone stopped and backed away, many of those still standing taking off in different directions. Gear-Crusher turned towards me, and pretended to crack his armored knuckles as I stood defiantly before him with my chest puffed outwards. He chuckled and walked back and forth examining me. He turned and swung his boot out, connecting with one of the people on the street, and making them cry out, grabbing their ribs.

"You should have run while you had the chance." Gear-Crusher said, as he turned back towards me and I clenched my jaw. "In fact, I'm happy you didn't. I just remembered what I was going to do to you on that meatball planet."

"Try if you want." I said, holding both of my arms steady and trying to sound more confident then I felt.

"Oh I will." Gear-Crusher said as he rushed at me and swung out one metal fist trying to catch me in the side.

Something clicked in my mind, and I seemed to naturally dodge it, as if I'd done it thousands of times. Gear-Crusher snorted and charged forward, attempting to run me down as I felt the warmth of Paradox's power throughout my body. This time it was different though, and it felt like it was alive inside me, waiting for my command. I reached out with my right hand, clawing out its fingers and smashing it upward into the air as darkness surged from me in a torrent and caught Gear-Crusher by surprise, lifting him into the air like a doll and tossing him away from me.

"H-how?" Gear-Crusher stammered as he stood back up then seemed to regain his composure. "No matter, more fun for me, I'll crush you just like I did Paradox."

The sun dipped out of sight, and now the city was cast into darkness. Gear-Crusher reached over, ripping out a streetlight that had just come to life as he spun around and swung it at me. Before it could connect with me, my hand was up and black matter was holding it steadily in place no matter how hard Gear-Crusher tried to move it. He finally let go, and let out an angry roar as he charged at me once again. I stood in place as his massive metal arms encircled me and lifted me from the ground, but try as he might, he couldn't crush me.

The darkness around me was forcing his arms apart, and then we were both rising into the air through a swirling storm of darkness that blotted everything else out. It tore at Gear-Crusher as he spun around rapidly, trying to get his bearings while I folded my arms and watched him. His jetpack continued to try and activate, trying to get him out of the nightmare he was spinning in, but the black matter held him in place and caused it to sputter.

"There's no way you can beat me!" Gear-Crusher declared, and then pounded his chest through the chaos. "My armor is indestructible!"

"Everything has a weakness." I said, my eyes burning into his mask. "I've just found your's."

Gear-Crusher seemed startled, but didn't get a chance to speak as all the black matter around us forced its way into the jetpacks openings as it continued to try and start. There was a muffled creaking sound, and then through Gear-Crusher's helmet I could see the orange flash of an internal explosion caused by the built up pressure in the jetpack trying to find a way to escape. Gear-Crusher's armor fell to the ground and didn't move as I teleported next to it.

A second orange flash inside, and the armor split open. I stepped back from the smell, and couldn't tell what I was looking at until my mind filled it in slowly. The suit was all mechanical. There was no sign of a man inside whatsoever until the helmet opened up slowly. There sat a human brain, *well, almost human,* I thought. Part of it was mechanical, with various wires and bits of machinery making it up.

"W-who are you?" A mechanical voice that fluctuated between Gear-Crusher's and a monotone managed to get out.

I looked on as many of the spinning gears and lights started stopping and winking out as I said in a voice that now sounded exactly like Paradox's. "My name is Aaron, my mentor was Paradox."

The mechanical device emitted a laugh, which was disconcerting as it fluctuated between a man and machine. It attempted to move but only managed to pop some more gears out of place as it stated, "What have you accomplished here today?"

"I've defeated you. I've saved my friend Justin, and Paradox did what he had to do." I said firmly, as the machine laughed again, a few sparks showering out of it.

"F-fool." It stuttered, more from becoming unstable then fear or anything now, as the remains of Gear-Crusher continued, "You c-came for J-Justin. He was n-n-never here. He's b-been in another facility all al-along."

"Thanks for the info." I said, turning to go back to the building when his next words caught my attention.

"And that girl . . ." Gear-Crusher said, "Y-your friend, gone."

I sharply turned towards him, my fists clenched in rage as I said, "Ethia? You're lying!"

"Am I?" Gear-Crusher said, a mechanical chuckle emitting from him. "I-I watched him butcher my m-m-men on camera. Then h-he took her."

I had a feeling that if Gear-Crusher's brain could have smiled in triumph, it would have right there. "Who, who took her?" I shouted out.

The last of Gear-Crusher's mechanisms were dying out as his now fully mechanical monotone voice said, "Y-you don't understand. The Twilight Core will always succeed and conquer . . . conquer . . . conquer . . . conquer . . . ." It continued to repeat conquer, the voice box provided finally failing as I angrily stomped on it, crushing it under my shoe until it finally stopped repeating.

I fell to my knees, feeling drained, tired, and most of all sad. We'd failed horribly, they'd won, and there was nothing I could do. Bright lights illuminated the cities block, and I looked up to see one of the Twilight Cruisers hovering over the Alpha Headquarters, no doubt getting ready to disintegrate it. I contemplated just staying where I was, and letting the end finally come as the cannons began to charge slowly.

"You aren't really going to give up are you? The only time you lose, is when you actually give up. You can still save her." Paradox said, cutting through my thoughts like a knife.

"You're right." I said to him, standing up and teleporting away to watch the building disappear in a brilliant green. "It's time to do more then just save my friends. It's time to take down the Twilight Core and anyone allied with them."

"Now we're thinking." Paradox joked, poking fun at the way we had to speak to each other now as I disappeared into the night.

In the Light of Darkness

*D*im lights lit the room, but all the commanders of each force were standing back in the shadows, concealing themselves. A large screen was before them, reporting incidents and progress of various missions and objectives. The screen switched through, moving through each Force and displaying their goals. Alpha's screen was shown, and all of their objectives marked with a question mark at the end, confirming that something large had happened.

"Has Gear-Crusher reported in yet?" Someone asked, a thin light blue line shining from the darkness that served as their eyes.

"No, which is unlike him, since he was always here early trying to one-up all of us." Said another voice where a cascade of brilliant medals moved down a uniform, but his face was hidden by darkness.

Someone shifted in their seat uneasily, and then spoke out while thrumming their fingers on a table in front of them, "Any word on the missing Battle cruiser?"

"Nothing on that either." Said the voice with the blue strip floating in the darkness, as it turned away to face a red glowing eye in the back of the room. "Do you know anything about what happened at Alpha Headquarters, or the missing Battle cruiser, Nanoplicity?"

The eye blinked, as Nanoplicity simply stated, "No idea."

"Well, wipe that smile off your face. You'd be wise to think that it might make people suspect you're up to something. There have been rumors going about of traitors." Another voice said with hate unconcealed that made Nanoplicity chuckle.

"Calm down everyone." A voice said that seemed to be made of steel and ice. "My lieutenant is devoted to our cause in every way."

"He'd better be," Grumbled the voice which emanated from the body that had medals all over its uniform, "On to the other news that we have received."

"As you know, a distress signal was picked up from beneath the city. We sent in troops to find out what it was and came across a strange, and promising, facility. It took us some time to open the door, and our interpreters are still trying to decode the language that was being used." The voice paused, but after no one said anything it continued. "Our expeditionary force radioed in that they had set up camp inside a second set of doors. A day later they radioed that they were under attack by unknown hostiles and had been cut off from escape. After that, they never reported back in."

"Interesting, I'll send some of my drones to acquire what went on down there." The cold steel-like voice said. "Nanoplicity, if you would please."

Nanoplicity's red eye moved in a bowing motion and left the room as murmurs spread through the group. "What of Paradox, anything new on him?"

"Negative, nothing new on his whereabouts or what he's doing, and we need to find out." A female said as the back door of the room burst open and a soldier ran in.

"Pardon me, sirs! A report has just been received. Alpha Force headquarters are . . . gone. Pieces of Gear-Crusher have been found, so has bits of Paradox's clothing." The soldier reported smoothly and efficiently. Another wave of murmurs moved throughout the room, as the soldier stayed where he stood at attention.

"You are dismissed." One of the commanders said as the soldier saluted and left.

The light blue slit made its way around the room, turning slowly as it said, "This is quite disturbing." As most of the other commanders agreed with him and he stated, "Keep your guard up until the next meeting."

The commanders stood up, and filed slowly away from each other in the darkness.

Paradox

J sat on top of the skyscraper, staring out at the city lights that illuminated the night. It was indeed a beautiful sight, and to think that this was the same place that Ethia and I had first kissed only a day or so ago. Now she was gone, either dead or kidnapped by the same conglomerate that had taken Justin. The night air was nice and crisp, and I breathed in deeply. I would begin my search tomorrow for my friends, and a way of stopping the Twilight Core, as I heard a scream emanate from an alley below and I stood up and looked down, realizing it was going to be a long night.

There was a woman, and two thugs attempting to mug her. I stepped off the building and disappeared just as I started to fall. Appearing behind one of the two, I calmly asked in my new voice, "What are you doing?"

They turned around, jumping back at the sight before them as I stood there dressed in black boots, black cargo pants, a black shirt, a black duster coat, black scarf, black glasses, and black hat topping it off. Essentially the clothes that Paradox had given me, so that I looked exactly identical to the way he looked. The two men were stunned for a moment, one waving a small knife carefully in front of him and the other pulling a pistol on me.

"Look, I don't want any trouble." I said, holding up my hands as they stood their ground. The woman watched, pressing herself against the wall."

"Stay back you nut." One of the thugs said brandishing his knife, while I took a step towards him.

Suddenly the knife was wrenched from his hand by the blade and disappeared into darkness. It appeared again in front of him, crumpled into a small ball, causing him to yelp and run down the alley. His companion fired a shot off, the bullets whizzing through empty air. Blinking the man swore to himself that I'd been there a moment before. I tapped him on the shoulder, and he spun around, trying to fire a shot off before he disappeared into a wave of black matter. I turned to the woman.

"Sorry about that, I hope the rest of your night is pleasant." I said, getting ready to teleport to the second thug that had made his 'escape'.

The woman was scared a little, but she stood up straight and asked with curiosity, "Who are you?"

I smiled behind my mask, as I disappeared out of her view, and my voice reverberated off the walls creating an echo and effect that seemed to be made by nothing since I'd disappeared. The lady was stunned at this, and the answer she received was, "I . . . am Paradox."